PRAISE FOR TINA SESKIS

For *One Step Too Far*

'A haunting psychological thriller . . . believable yet shocking with a great twist, this is well worth a read.'

The Sun

'A whip-smart thriller that keeps you guessing right up until the final shocking twist.'

Mirror

'Intriguing . . . dreamily tense . . . a really absorbing read.'

USA Today

For *When We Were Friends*

'Clever, intriguing, chilling – and utterly impossible to put down. Tina Seskis is proving herself to be master of the twist.'

Grazia UK

'One of the world's leading experts at pulling the wool over readers' eyes until the very end.'

Sophie Hannah

For *The Honeymoon*

'Everyone's going to be talking about the twists and turns of *The Honeymoon.*'

Good Housekeeping

'Endlessly gripping . . . It's a stomach-flipping humdinger of a thriller.'

Heat

'Will keep you on the edge of your seat.'

Prima

HOME TRUTHS

ALSO BY TINA SESKIS

One Step Too Far

When We Were Friends

The Honeymoon

HOME TRUTHS

TINA SESKIS

This is a work of fiction. Names, characters, organizations, places, events, and incidents are either products of the author's imagination or are used fictitiously. Any resemblance to actual persons, living or dead, or actual events is purely coincidental.

Published by Lake Union Publishing, Seattle

www.apub.com

ISBN-13: 9781542093583
ISBN-10: 1542093589

Cover design by whittakerbookdesign.com

Printed in the United States of America

For my husband and son

Do I start at the beginning or begin at the end? The dichotomy is killing me. I am slowly dying, seeping into the morass that is the middle. Neither here, nor there. Neither this, nor that. What made me do it? Hate, for sure. Love, too, in a way. But whatever my motives, how on earth did I manage it? How did I cope with the lies, and the confusion, and all the goddamn effort? Maybe I just enjoyed it too much. Needed it, even.

And now? Well, now everything is destroyed, of course. Could I have handled it differently? For sure. Am I to blame for everything? I would say not. Not everything. But we shall see. After all, the truth will always out. Eventually.

And so now I will always be something other than what everyone thought I was. Something other than what I wished to be. That is the price I will pay, forever. And so be it.

PART ONE

The Beginning

THE EARLY NINETIES

1

Alex

As soon as she walked through the door, Alex noticed her. Nicely dressed blonde girls rarely made an appearance at the front desk of Finsbury Park police station in 1992. Normally it was a place frequented by errant drivers, begrudgingly bringing in their documents as requested by an overzealous traffic cop; or victims of muggings; or people who'd had their car stolen; or else known criminals being booked in for the umpteenth time, the looks on their faces ones of insouciant arrogance, fully aware they'd most likely get away with it.

This girl was different. She had a softness about her, and yet it wasn't the softness of weakness, Alex could tell that much. It was something much more interesting. He'd been about to leave, as his shift was almost over, but he found he was happy to handle this enquiry. His first impression of her was one of intrigue. He'd never forget the feeling.

'Hello, yes? How can I help?'

The girl looked embarrassed, and he tried to guess what it was she was about to say. She glanced over her shoulder, and a strand of her white-blonde hair slipped across her cheekbone, half-covering her left eye. She pushed it back with a barely conscious gesture, and he noticed there was a circular mark on her left ring finger, although her hands were bare. When she spoke, it was with a low American burr, which surprised him. He imagined she'd have a well-spoken, English accent.

'I want to report something,' she said, 'but it's a little, er, delicate.' She didn't need to look over at the sullen youth, dressed top to toe in sweatshirt material and waiting for his drug-dealing friend, to let Alex know that it was something juicy. He tried to guess how old she was. He reckoned she was early twenties, yet she looked younger.

'OK, do you want to wait there a moment?' Alex said. 'I'll be with you shortly.' When he said the word 'shortly' his mouth felt dry and his voice had a squeak to it that reminded him of when he was a teenager. He turned quickly, so she couldn't see him blush, and went out to the back office, where he told his colleague Gillian that he was taking someone to one of the interview rooms, and could she mind the front desk. Gillian smirked, and he flushed. She wasn't one to talk anyway. She was always flirting with the prisoners or sleeping with her colleagues. Alex found it extraordinary how she could be so brazen about it, but Gillian was one of those characters who just laughed when someone tried to tease her, and so she got away with everything. Alex admired that about her – plus she'd always looked out for him, ever since they'd got caught up in the poll tax riots together. She mothered him, in truth.

When Alex returned to the front counter, he buzzed the young woman through and beckoned her to follow him into the innards of the station. He could smell her perfume now, and it was delicate and summery, discordant with the aromas of grime and crime that were ingrained in the place. As he led her to a spartan interview room, her demeanour was nervy, on edge. He asked her to sit, and she did so, her hands folded in her lap, the right covering her left. It was a domestic, Alex was sure of it. He searched her face for bruises, wondered what kind of a bastard would hit someone like her.

'So, what's your name?' he said.

'Eleanor Jackson.'

'And what can I do for you?'

'Well . . . I . . . I think I'm being stalked.'

'Oh.' He failed to hide his surprise. 'In what way?'

'It's just that I . . . I chatted to him a couple of times, and now . . . well . . .' She stopped, looked about the room, as if bewildered at how she came to be in such a place. She was wearing a blue linen dress and bright white plimsolls, and she looked as though she was worried that even being here was contaminating her. A tiny diamond stud glinted in her nose, which he hadn't noticed before.

'It's OK,' Alex said. 'Take your time.'

'Well . . . I think he may have got the wrong idea, and now he keeps asking me out, even though I keep saying no. And the phone rings during the day, when I'm home alone, and there's never anyone there.' She spoke quickly now. 'Plus he gives me gifts, although I don't want them, and stares at me through my window. And then the other day when I came to use my boss's car, the tyre was flat – for no reason – and he came and helped me change it.'

'What, and you think he may have let the tyre down?'

'Yes. No. I don't know. I know it doesn't sound like much, but he's just making me nervous.' She raked her fingers through her hair, and again he noticed the mark on her ring finger. Was she married, or not?

'OK, what's his name?'

'Gavin Hewitson.' She looked at him straight as she answered, and she seemed so vulnerable, and he felt so protective. Often in this job he found the punters nothing more than a necessary evil, but he found he wanted to help this girl, sweep her up and make sure no one could ever hurt her. And it was such an extraordinary feeling that he had a sudden urge to simply walk back out of the room and call Gillian and get her to deal with it. It was like being at a crossroads, where three of the routes contained mountains with impossible passes, and one led back the way he had come, to safety. Part of him so intensely wanted to backtrack, avoid what he sensed lay ahead of him, yet he managed to stand his ground, and took all the details as dispassionately as he could manage. He found it hard to look at Eleanor Jackson. She had an outer calm that belied the tale she was telling him. Her accent was dulcet and sugar-coated, so Brady-Bunch-perfect in its cadence she almost sounded as if she were putting it on. Her hair was so soft it kept sliding into her eyes. He wanted to lean over and tuck it behind her ear. He wanted to cup her face, kiss her Cupid-bowed mouth. He wanted to—

Oh God. He needed to compose himself. He pretended to look at his watch, playing for time. He had no comprehension of what it said. 'Er, I just need to go and check something,' he said. 'Can you wait here?'

'Sure,' she said, and the way she smiled at him was as if she were reassuring him, and he wondered if it was obvious to her, the effect she was having on him. As he exited the room and marched along the corridor, feeling agitated and unsettled, he realised he'd never felt quite like this before. Up until now girls were to be kept at a distance. They were Trouble. But she, Eleanor, was In Trouble. She needed help. Who knew what this stalker was capable of? The police needed to protect her. *He* needed to protect her. She'd come to him. He was her Knight in Shining Armour.

As Alex arrived at the front desk, he had no idea why he'd gone there. He stared helplessly at Gillian's wide expressive face, her eyebrows raised in amused surprise. But it seemed that Eleanor Jackson had come into his life and thrown a curve ball across it, leaving him behaving like a love-struck teenager. If he wasn't careful, the others might pick up on it too and then he'd never ever live it down.

He'd made it this far. He needed to keep it together.

Alex took a deep breath, picked up a police-issue notebook, gave Gillian what he hoped was a casually nonchalant look, and then marched as confidently as he could along the corridor, back towards the beautiful and intriguing Ms Jackson.

2

Eleanor, several months earlier

After the violence of the door slam the room was too silent, as if emptied of air, of every last vibration. Eleanor remained sitting still on the couch, too stunned to go after him. What on earth had just happened? Had Rufus told her to *leave*? He couldn't have – they were in love. She'd travelled thousands of miles to be with him. He was her very own English boy, with his BBC accent, his floppy hair, his slouchy jeans and posh parents in their rectory in the country. He was a gentleman, who it seemed had turned overnight into an asshole.

Eleanor's state of dazed, torpid denial was long and impossible for her to measure in terms of minutes or hours. It seemed her mind was struggling to make sense of the fact that she was here in her new life in London. Alone. Friendless. Boyfriendless. Her muscles felt sapped of energy, and there was just a low electric kind of buzz in her brain. She needed something to kick-start her back into action – and yet she didn't have any of her old techniques to hand, which was probably just as well. She imagined her mother saying, 'I told you so.' She pictured her father, stately in his expensive-smelling, book-lined office, his job an apparently relentless campaign to help other people, and she knew that if she rang him and begged him to come, he wouldn't.

Eleanor's immobility was only finally interrupted by a peculiarly English habit she'd got into. At long last she stood up, her joints popping. She went into the kitchen, put on the kettle, opened the cupboard directly above it, got out a teabag and a bone-china mug with a picture of a sausage dog that wrapped around its circumference. Her movements were robotic, the habitual nature of them comforting. She switched on the radio and a noisy song by a newish band that Rufus loved and that she couldn't remember the name of came on. The kettle gurgled and spluttered as she poured the water into the mug. At last the DJ's gravelly tones gave her the answer. The Stone Roses, that was the band. That was who Rufus loved. Not her. She opened the fridge and eyeballed its contents as if they were foreign objects. The remains of the take-out pizza they'd shared last night. An almost empty bottle of wine. Three yoghurts: all black cherry, her anathema, his favourite. A punnet of strawberries, their surfaces seething with white fungus, although she'd only bought them yesterday. A thick, squat cucumber. A carton of orange juice, bulging slightly. A dribble of milk. Last night had been normal. Normal meal. Normal time together on the couch watching TV. Normal benign reluctance from him when she'd tried to initiate sex in bed. Nothing out of the ordinary at all. She racked her brains, continued to rake through the minutiae of their last few hours together. After Rufus had resisted her advances, he'd turned over and gone almost instantly to sleep. She'd lain in the dark, listening to his soft, steady breathing, reaching out to touch the warm skin on his back, as if to make sure he was there, that she was here, in London. That she really had done this. Her sleep had been flooded with rainbow-coloured dreams that she'd forgotten the instant she'd awoken, when his alarm had gone off at seven.

This morning Rufus had got up straight away, as usual. He'd gone in the shower first, as usual. He'd eaten a bowl of Weetabix, with banana on top, as usual. And then he'd leant against the sink, with his back to the window, and proceeded to tell her that he was confused, and that he might still be in love with his old girlfriend, and that it was probably best if she, Eleanor, moved out for the time being. And when she'd pointed out, not unreasonably and suitably loudly, that he was an unfathomable bastard, he had turned the anger on her and stormed out.

Eleanor poured the last of the milk into her tea, but her hand was shaking so much she slopped it over the counter, and it looked to her like thin white blood. Perhaps, if she cut herself, her veins would bleed blankly too. She felt in danger of becoming ghostlike, might soon be able to drift through walls. She thought about calling her mom, but how could she admit it to her? She'd been the big girl off on her big adventure, to join the love of her life in London. She and Rufus had met while volunteering at summer camp in upstate New York. They'd spent every second of their spare time together, and even that hadn't been enough time. And when he'd presented her with a 'promise ring' at the airport, just before he'd reluctantly got on the flight back home to England at the end of the summer, she'd known he was The One. And yet still she'd hesitated, for at least a week or two, when he'd called her at her mom's place in Maine and begged her to come to London to be with him. When at last she'd capitulated, she'd waited tables to help pay for her airfare. It had taken an age to sort out the paperwork, but several months later she'd finally arrived, pale and fizzing and nauseously excited, at Heathrow. Had that really only been four weeks ago?

Eleanor took her tea and went over to the window, from where Rufus had delivered his weirdly dispassionate termination notice. The early spring day was pin-bright. The grass in the shared back garden was crisply frost-tinted, the sky a deep religious blue, so opaque it looked as if it might be solid to the touch. She could see daffodils brimming with brightness, the rubber-duck yellow of their newly opened petals arguably the best colour in the entire goddamn world. It was England at its finest, how she'd dreamt the countryside would be, and yet she was here in the city. She had never imagined London would be like this. She'd never even thought of the flowers.

Eleanor had no idea what time Rufus would come home. Should she sit it out, wait for him, ask him what the hell was going on? Or should she pack her stuff and leave, as he'd suggested? She didn't know where she would go.

Eleanor sipped her tea, but it was cold already and tasted sour. At last it began to sink in. *Rufus loved someone else.* His ex-girlfriend. Eleanor wondered when they'd got back together. Before or after she'd got on the plane? How in hell had he kept up the pretence these past four weeks? And, more to the point, why? Had he simply been biding his time, trying to work out who he preferred? That would explain his reluctance for intimacy, and the way everything had felt different in London. She'd put it down to real life getting in the way of the romance of camp – the pseudo-innocent sunset trysts down at the stream, the nights sitting by the campfire, gazing into each other's eyes, the sweet abstinence they'd managed, at first. Love had filled the hole in their souls on those heady summer nights. He'd been her beautiful English boy. She'd been his muse. His salvation.

And now . . . The possibility that Rufus hadn't yet slept with his old girlfriend again was even worse than the prospect that he most probably had. Eleanor didn't like thinking of herself as an impediment, of Rufus gazing into this other girl's eyes instead of hers, her rival returning the look limpidly, the pair of them wishing they could be together, but being honourable, because of *her*. It made Eleanor feel sick. She turned from the window, scraped at her scalp above her ears, yanked at her hair. Her mind whirled and fizzed, and eventually grew hard.

He loved someone else. It was over.

Eleanor made her decision. She'd leave right now, before Rufus got home, although she was fairly certain now that that wasn't quite what he'd meant. He'd got flustered, said cruel things, things he'd surely regret. But at the end of the day he'd said them. They were out there. Perhaps one day he'd pay for them.

Eleanor packed her suitcase, filled it with the items she had removed with such care only recently. She took off the promise ring he had given her – a sparkly Walmart special that had always irritated her finger and had left a circle of flaky skin. A stopgap, he'd said. He'd take her to Hatton Garden one day, he'd said, although she hadn't even known what that was. He'd love her forever, he'd said.

Oh God.

Eleanor slammed her suitcase shut as theatrically as she could manage. She wasn't going to sit around where she wasn't wanted. She went into the kitchen and placed the ring on the pale pine table, along with her keys and a brief note that she scrawled on an envelope. She dragged her suitcase along the corridor and out into the hallway. As she shut the door to the flat and heard the click of the latch behind her, she realised there was no going back now. Yesterday she'd been just another young girl in love . . . and today she was an American alone, lost and heartbroken, in London.

3

Christie

Two hundred miles away, in Manchester, Christie Gallagher was trying her hardest not to giggle. An intimate wedding to a mysterious stranger? An unknown person with an axe to grind? A sinister family secret? What a load of utter claptrap. Her sister Alice might well believe in all this psychic stuff, but everything the fortune teller had said so far was either plain wrong or else so generic it meant nothing. For a start, Christie and her boyfriend Paul were already engaged, so she wasn't actually in the market to marry a handsome stranger, even if there had been one on the horizon. Madame Magdalena hadn't spotted *that* little detail, had she? Christie felt a little disingenuous now that she'd taken off her diamond ring, but she wasn't going to give Madame Magdalena any clues. Surely she shouldn't bloody well need them.

The fortune teller leant forward suddenly and peered at Christie. The huge golden hoops in her ears glinted in the dim light. Her eyes were black as a bird's. Christie was almost certain she was wearing a wig, and she imagined the woman's scalp, bald and moley, errant straggles of wispy hair plastered to it. As Madame Magdalena clasped Christie's hand her skin was dry and papery, and Christie had an almost overwhelming urge to pull her hand away, but she didn't dare. The clairvoyant's voice was a long slow hiss, like a tyre being let down. 'Never trust,' she said. 'Never trust your husband.'

Christie felt a cold feeling at her back, as though someone had opened a door behind her, out into snow. She nodded as amiably as she could, but a shiver had started at her neck and was worming its way into her spine, vertebra by frozen vertebra . . . and then she felt as if someone had punched her in the coccyx. The fortune teller might have got pretty much every factual detail of the reading wrong, but it seemed she had a knack for spotting someone's Achilles heel – and Christie's was most definitely an inability to trust. And no wonder.

Christie pulled herself up. This was *Paul* they were talking about. The woman was clearly spouting nonsense. She glanced anxiously around the room, at the red velvet curtains, the black lace tablecloth, the cobwebby lighting, and wondered how she could make her escape.

'I'm sorry,' Christie said, 'but I have to go now. My sister's waiting for me.'

'Oh, but I haven't finished, my dear,' the crow-woman said. Her voice was like a gurgle through pipes. 'There is so much here that I need to tell you.'

'No, it's OK, I don't want to know. Honestly, it's fine.' Christie yanked her hand away and stood up.

As she backed out of the room, Madame Magdalena started repeating, over and over, in an eerie watery voice that Christie found hard to ever forget, 'Never trust, never trust, never trust,' as if it were a rare and ancient mantra.

4

Eleanor

Although Eleanor might not have had enough money to buy a flight home, thankfully she could afford a hotel for a while. Not a nice hotel, of course – but a roof over her head at least. Someone had once told her that the cheapest places to stay were always around the railroad stations, and so she'd taken the subway from Hampstead and got out at King's Cross, mainly because it was the first place with a railroad symbol that she'd heard of. The hostel she'd found there was the epitome of crummy, and not in even her darkest moments in New York had she ever ended up anywhere that bad. It was set in a tall thin house in a Georgian mews terrace that must have once been elegant, but the net curtains were grey from age and the windows were black with spewed fumes, and the single mattress on her bunk bed had map-of-the-world-shaped stains on it. Her room-mates seemed even more down on their luck than she was, with some of them getting up to things she'd rather not have to witness, whether the lights were out or not. The bathroom across the corridor was almost as bad – the inside of the toilet was brown, the seat was covered in urine. There were several nail clippings and a globule of phlegm in the limescale-encrusted basin, and the shower was cold and clogged up with hair. Two nights here had felt like two lifetimes.

And yet still Eleanor didn't call home. Perhaps she simply couldn't face the humiliation. Despite her mom never having even met Rufus – she had just been shown a couple of photos, including one in black tie and tails from his Oxbridge days – she hadn't trusted him. But, as Eleanor had told herself at the time, that was how her mom felt about the entire male species – and yet now it seemed her mom had been right to be cynical. She and Rufus had gone from starry-eyed lovers to a young cohabiting couple to dumper and dumpee within just eight months, and four of those they'd been apart anyway. Slam dunk.

Eleanor poked her head out of the cracked, scuffed door, looked about at the peeling black-and-red-striped hallway, and made a dash for it. She'd heard yelling from the room next door and didn't want to run into any trouble. The staircase had no carpet, only beige disintegrating underlay, which at least muffled her footsteps. The hallway stank of sweet fetid rubbish mixed in with human smells, and it was a relief to wrench open the heavy black front door and escape.

Out on the street the wind was gusting, and the air felt damp, with a dull toxic quality to it that seemed to have been made worse by the sun. This was not the cutesy London of Hampstead, where until a couple days ago she'd lived with Rufus, the place with the sunny little garden filled with bright happy colours you saw in children's books. This new London, although only five stops away on the Tube, was grey, and unforgiving, and loud and menacing, and full of harried people and dirt and rancour and disappointment. As Eleanor walked, she was amazed at how calm her mind was, and she wondered if it was some kind of natural reaction to extreme adversity, in that she couldn't fall apart right now even if she wanted to, because survival was paramount. Perhaps that was why people enjoyed wars, she thought. Unimaginable tragedy, rather than breaking spirits, seemed to reinforce them. Perhaps peacetime was what brought out the neurosis in people, as there was nothing else to worry about, no one to rail against. And then she told herself to ignore all her father's psychobabble nonsense, as sadly it had never got either of them anywhere.

Eleanor tried to work out her options. She couldn't go home, as she had no money for the flight. And although either of her parents would help her, she couldn't face asking right now. And even if Rufus might yet take her back, she would never actually go back. No way. Not if he was in love with someone else.

As Eleanor stood at the lights to cross a four-lane road that was dense with cars and trucks and vans going nowhere fast, a young woman was waiting alongside her. The woman had a screaming toddler on reins, and a splodge of a baby in a stroller, and a cigarette in her mouth, and she wore track pants and a puffa coat with a fake-fur hood – and although she was overweight anyway Eleanor thought she was almost certainly pregnant. As the girl caught Eleanor looking at her, she turned and said, 'What you starin' at?'

'Nothing,' Eleanor muttered, and walked on as quickly as she could, her cheeks still flaring, relieved when the girl didn't follow her.

Children. Perhaps that was it. Maybe that was her route out of this mess. Eleanor hadn't seen *Mary Poppins* a zillion times for nothing. And she'd done plenty of babysitting for the couple in the next-door apartment when she'd lived with her dad in New York. She loved kids. Maybe she could get a job as a live-in nanny, at least to tide her over. That would solve all her immediate problems in one go.

Eleanor turned on her heel and re-crossed the road, almost running in her desire to get back to the hostel. She clattered up the stairs and asked the skinny, pocked girl on reception if there was a *Yellow Pages* and a pen and paper she could borrow. The directory was four years out of date and dog-eared, but there was a section on childminding services where Eleanor found a few listings to call. She scribbled them down and headed straight out again. A few yards along, on the other side of the road, she found a red phone box that once, as an American, she would have cooed over, but now she was simply thankful it was in working order. The tiny space stank in a way she couldn't even begin to describe, and the receiver was hanging almost in half, but when Eleanor picked it up there was that curious English dialling tone she'd only ever heard on TV before. The first two agencies she called weren't interested, because she didn't have formal nannying qualifications, and the numbers for the next two appeared to be out of service. The fifth number was permanently engaged, but at last Eleanor managed to reach a posh-sounding woman who, although she couldn't help, was at least nice enough to give Eleanor another number to try. This time she got through to a place in somewhere called Bounds Green that sounded more promising. Yes, she was looking for live-in, she said. Yes, she had the correct paperwork to work in the UK. Yes, she was available immediately. Yes, she had experience with children. They asked her when she could come in, and she said she could be there before the end of the afternoon, and so they agreed, and she was.

5

Christie

As Christie fled the fortune teller's room out into the brilliant sunshine, two little children were walking by with their parents, brandishing candy-flosses as big as their heads, and their innocence was so beguiling that Christie almost wanted to run over and kiss them, in an attempt to cleanse herself of the feeling that tainted her now. A man was yelling, 'Roll up, roll up!' not even ironically, trying to persuade passing men to have a go on the 'high striker', and Christie was glad of the brightness of his tattoos, the jollity of his tone, despite his broad Mancunian vowels. People were milling about the green, trying to toss rings over yellow rubber ducks to win goldfish in clear plastic bags, laughing unselfconsciously, and it was good to be out of the dark, lace-lined room and be reminded that real life was light and bright still.

Christie was surprised at how shaken up she'd been by the fortune teller, but it wasn't just what she'd said. It had been the oppressive atmosphere, the vague sense of nefariousness that had permeated the room. Even so, Christie had managed to be suitably nonchalant to her sister, who was waiting outside for her, keen to swap notes, find out what Christie's future held, which was typical Alice, of course. Alice's head had always seemed somewhere in the clouds, wrapped up with the moon and the stars, even when she was little. Even now she seemed genuinely willing to leave her future to destiny and, to give her her due, she'd always seemed pretty happy with the outcome. Christie had been the more driven one, who'd gone off to Cambridge no less, but qualifications and careers had never seemed important to Alice. Christie admired her sister's conviction, even if she did think it was crazy.

'Well, then,' Alice was saying, putting her arm through Christie's. 'What did she say about Paul? How many kids are you going to have?'

'Oh, she didn't say anything about that,' Christie said, crossing her fingers.

'Well, what *did* she say?'

'Nothing much.'

'Are you going to become a top headteacher?'

Christie smiled. 'She didn't say anything about that either.'

'Are you all right, Christie?'

'Yes,' Christie said. 'I just found it all a bit weird . . . creepy, in fact.'

Alice laughed. 'That's what I love about it,' she said. 'The mystique. But, come on – she must have said *something* to you.'

'Not really,' said Christie, walking on past the various stalls towards the exit. 'She just implied that I hadn't met my future husband yet, which she was obviously wrong about, and so after that I pretty much switched off . . . Hey, look, shall we get some doughnuts?'

Christie's diversionary tactic was prompted by the hot-sugar smell now drifting across the air towards them, and it was almost tangible, as if she could reach out her tongue and feel the crunchiness.

'Yuk, they're too greasy,' Alice said, marching past, clearly not prepared to be distracted from grilling Christie that easily. But by the time the sisters had reached the final stall, which was bowed down by slightly grubby-looking oversized cuddly toys that no one ever seemed to win, Christie had still refused to be drawn, and so they left the fairground and parted ways on the corner, Alice grumbling good-naturedly about Christie's evasiveness.

As Christie walked home past the house with boarded-up windows and a haywire hedge, she still felt a little uneasy somehow, which she knew was irrational. She straightened her shoulders as she approached her front door, put the key in the wonky lock and jiggled it expertly. This was *not* going to affect her.

'You're back early,' said Paul, looking over his shoulder as she padded into the kitchen in stripy threadbare socks, having taken off her boots at the door. 'Win any coconuts?' He winked at her.

'Nah, not today.' She went to the cupboard, pulled out a glass, filled it with water at the sink and downed it in one go. There was a smell of warmth and baking, and normally in these circumstances Christie would fold herself into Paul's arms, and he would be covered in flour and his sleeves would be rolled up, and they were still at the stage where they might even end up snogging, which was pretty amazing, seeing as they'd known each other for years. There was something about them being engaged now that had relit the passion – or at least there had been, until this afternoon's events.

'Was it fun?' he persisted.

'Yeah, it was OK.'

'Oh, like that, was it?' She could hear the gentle humour in Paul's voice. 'How was Alice?'

'Fine,' Christie said, as she went over to the kitchen table and sat down.

'Really? You don't sound convinced.'

'No, it's nothing like that. She was on good form.' Christie hesitated. Her trip to the fortune teller would make a pretty funny story . . . but in the end, she decided against it. It wasn't worth stirring things up.

As Paul crouched down at the oven to peer through the window, which even from here Christie could see was steamed up, she shook her head, like a dog. It was no good – it seemed as if she had an earworm now, one that she couldn't get rid of. *Never trust never trust never trust.* For goodness' sake, Christie thought – how could a complete stranger possibly know anything about her situation? And besides, Madame Magdalena had referred to a non-existent *prospective* husband as the untrustworthy one, not Christie's actual real-life fiancé, Paul Ingram. So the fortune teller had been wrong about all of it, and Christie needed to remember that. She needed to remember that just because her university boyfriend had turned out to be a cheating tosser, that didn't mean that she shouldn't trust Paul, who was the most honest, decent bloke ever. He'd never been late for a single date, even when they'd just been friends. He'd taken her to sweaty gigs and grimy comedy clubs, reminded her of the real life that existed beyond the rarefied quads of Cambridge. He'd given her a lifelong love of the Happy Mondays. But most of all he'd made her laugh again. He'd laughed her into loving him.

Paul took his bread out of the oven with a triumphant flourish, and it was a pumped-up plaited stick that was thicker at one end than the other.

'Woo hoo, well done,' said Christie. After Paul had mock-bowed and turned around to thwack it on to the wooden countertop, Christie opened the *Telegraph* and started to do the crossword. She was trying her hardest to seem normal, but she knew she was being too quiet. Usually she would be chatty, going on about who she'd bumped into, or what Alice was up to, or asking for help at what five across might be. Paul didn't seem to mind though, and was doing the washing-up now, uncomplaining at the lack of assistance. He was wearing her pink rubber gloves and was so tall he had to bend over the sink. He'd taken out his contact lenses and his glasses had steamed up, but still he looked handsome to her, and she reminded herself how nice he was, how good they were together.

'You sure you're all right, Christie?' Paul said, at last.

'Hmmm.'

Paul raised an eyebrow. She hesitated, unsure whether to try to explain. She didn't want him to think she didn't trust him, which was ironic when she came to think about it. And yet the atmosphere didn't feel right to tell him somehow. Maybe she just needed to give them both a break.

'Hey,' she said. 'D'you fancy popping to the pub in a bit?'

Paul hesitated. 'Not really, love,' he said at last. 'I've got a heavy day tomorrow, and then a team night out in the evening.'

'I thought that was Thursday?'

A look came over Paul's face that normally she wouldn't even notice, but it was there, and she did. *Was he lying?*

'No, it got moved, Christie,' he said. Was there annoyance in his voice, at being asked? Or unnatural neutrality? She wasn't sure.

Christie went into the living room, picked up her book and stuck her nose into it. Her heart was racing. What was going on? Why was she doubting him over something so trivial? Surely she shouldn't be letting a *medium* affect how she felt about the man she was going to marry in a few weeks.

Christie had read the same page three times by the time Paul came in, and he'd made her a mug of tea, with just the right amount of milk, and he'd brought her two chocolate Hobnobs. And as he leant over and gave her a kiss on the cheek, she decided she was being completely mad, and that it must just be pre-wedding nerves.

6

Eleanor

'So, Eleanor, what brings you to London?'

Eleanor was sitting in a sunny, cluttered living room, full of toddler paraphernalia, which smelled ever so faintly of biscuits. Her interviewer was one of those very smiley women who managed to smile even when she was talking, which Eleanor had always thought was quite a feat. She seemed nice though, and was giving off a very good vibe – and yet it felt so alien to Eleanor for someone to be friendly that it disarmed her. She put her hands to her face and discreetly pressed on her cheeks, as if to push at her tear ducts, stop the drops forming.

Eleanor knew this was her chance. It was her fifth interview for an au pair position, and in the interim she'd been staying in the fleapit hostel in King's Cross, feeling as though she were inching closer and closer to the abyss. The last four interviews she'd attended had ranged from disastrous to fruitless, but she'd learnt from each one, and today definitely felt the most promising yet. The job was based somewhere in North London that wasn't even on the subway and had consequently taken Eleanor an age to get to. Lizzie and Oliver Davenport. A little boy, Barney. His twin sister, Jessica. The father worked for Hewlett-Packard, and might even like Americans in that case, although he wasn't actually here, apparently leaving such decisions to his wife. Hopefully though,

Eleanor would get the job, and Lizzie would give her a nice room at the top of the house, and a weekly allowance, and Eleanor would do a great job for them, and that would be her escape route out of the unfathomable mess she'd landed herself in. This could be her opportunity to prove something to herself, and to everybody else too. She'd been praying that this would be the one. She was down to her last fifty pounds now, so in truth it had to be.

Lizzie coughed gently. 'I said, what brought you to London, Eleanor?'

Eleanor jumped.

'Oh, sorry,' she said, and then hesitated, before deciding on a different tack from the one she'd taken in her previous interviews. An honest one. 'A boy,' she said, at last.

'Oh?' Lizzie replied, her eyebrow raised.

'It didn't work out.'

'Oh . . . OK,' said Lizzie, her smile fading ever so slightly. 'And so why do you want to be an au pair?'

'Well, I love kids,' said Eleanor. 'And I used to babysit lots back in New York for my dad's neighbours.' She swallowed hard, and raised her tone a notch, and as she spoke, she could hear her voice wavering. 'And, anyhow, I don't want to just give up and go home, I want to make a go of it in London – and I think this job would be perfect.' She smiled then, and after a tiny pause Lizzie smiled back, and it was as if there was a bond between the two women somehow, as if Lizzie understood exactly what Eleanor was going through, had maybe experienced something similar.

Eleanor looked about the room and thought how nice it was, with its stripped wooden floors and terracotta linen curtains at the windows, the deep-blue shag rug, the deluge of brightly coloured toys adding to the atmosphere rather than detracting from it. Photos of curly heads danced at her from the mantelpiece, and they looked so healthy and happy. This was a home, Eleanor knew that much. A real family home. It seemed it was what she needed right now.

After a few more enquiries as to where Eleanor was from, and what visa she had, and what she thought of London so far (not much if it was all like King's Cross, Eleanor had said, and Lizzie had laughed), and how it was different from America, Lizzie said OK, that was enough questions. Perhaps it was time for Eleanor to meet the twins.

7

Christie

It was three weeks to the wedding and until a minute or so ago Christie had been feeling pretty much back to normal about her fiancé. She'd been looking forward to a girly weekend with Alice and a couple of her closest friends, as Paul was heading to Blackpool for his stag do, which had been organised by his best man, Martin. There were twelve of them going for two nights, and they were staying in a cheap hotel just off the promenade, and Martin had arranged a stripper.

'He's done *what*?' said Christie when Paul mentioned it, as casually as if Martin had booked the lads into a tea dance at the Tower Ballroom. She and Paul were outside in the minuscule back garden of their two-up two-down cottage, and Paul was conducting a mass pruning session. Christie was potting out some pink cyclamens she'd bought from the garden centre, which she thought would brighten the place up. She'd managed to get potting compost everywhere, and it was mixing with water into a kind of thick black paste, making an awful mess of the patio, but Paul, ever tolerant, hadn't said anything.

'That's appalling,' Christie said at last.

'I know. But it's what blokes do.'

'Not my bloke.'

'Oh, come on, Christie. It doesn't mean anything.'

'What doesn't mean anything? The fact that you're objectifying women? Or how I might feel about it?' Christie picked up the hosepipe, turned the tap on full and started watering dangerously. 'Obviously not.'

Paul moved sharply out of the way. She could see his shears glinting in the sunshine, and it made her feel sad that it was such a beautiful day, and they were gardening in the little house they'd scraped together to buy, and they were about to get married, and they wanted to start a family, and this was the *nineties*, not the dark ages, and he was getting a stripper. Maybe he'd even get off with her, as that's what some men did on those kinds of stag dos. But this was Paul. *Her* Paul. He wouldn't do anything to jeopardise what they had . . . would he?

'Where?' she said now.

'What do you mean, where?'

'Where is this stripper booked for?'

Paul looked a little sheepish. 'In one of the hotel rooms.'

Christie shook her head. 'That is disgusting,' she said. She threw down the hosepipe and water spiralled crazily, indiscriminately. Dark piebald patches appeared on Paul's faded jeans and the concrete path, contrasting with the jewel-like patterns that hung and spun in the sunshine-filled air. The earth-sludge on the patio was transforming into shallow pitchy puddles.

'Hey,' Paul said, but more in surprise than in anger, as Christie stalked into the house and slammed the back door, ignoring his plaintive defence that Martin had booked the stripper without consulting him, and that at least he'd had the decency to tell her.

8

Eleanor

Eleanor adored the Davenport twins, for the most part. They were cute little bundles of mischief, and somehow looking after a pair of rambunctious four-year-olds helped Eleanor largely forget that this wasn't how moving to London was supposed to have panned out. But every cloud has a silver lining, she reminded herself, and perhaps she and the Davenports were meant to have come into each other's lives. And so she'd gotten down to the business of learning how to be an au pair, which as well as getting the twins dressed and breakfasted and ferrying them to and from nursery seemed to involve copious amounts of washing and cooking, and remembering such details as how Barney liked peas but not carrots, and that Jessica would only eat toast if it was cut into triangles, and what time to serve the twins' tea to ensure they would be ready for their mother to get them in the bath as soon as she came home from being a refugee legal advisor, whatever that was. And every single day Lizzie would burst through the door at six o'clock on the dot and scoop the twins into her arms and bury her face into their soft curly heads and tell them over and over that she loved them, and those were the times that Eleanor would feel her own losses the most. Rufus. Her father. Her mother. Even her beloved dog Teddy, who'd had the temerity to die of old age and had looked up at her with sad, soulful eyes, knowing there was nothing either of them could do about it.

Sometimes, Eleanor wondered whether people were destined to always let her down. Perhaps there was even something she did to encourage it. After all, her own mother had never seemed able to love her the way Lizzie did the twins, and that fact was a revelation to Eleanor. She had always needed to strive to be smarter, or thinner, or better at piano or algebra to gain her mother's approbation. The house had had to be kept pin-neat, even when she was little. It had been exhausting – no wonder she'd given up in the end. And now that she was so far away from home, she felt almost disconnected from the past, unable to fathom what the truth was about anything any more. She'd tried so hard to forget about Rufus, but perversely it was only now that she was settled, and safe, that she realised how much she missed him. Sometimes, in the evenings, Eleanor would go up to her cosy room in the attic and lie on the bed, staring up at the ceiling, and wonder how she had got here, living in a part of London she'd never heard of, with a hitherto unknown family, and she'd try to guess what life was due to serve up to her next. Lizzie would almost certainly have been a willing confidante, but Eleanor didn't want to burden her employer – or risk alienating her. And Eleanor rarely spoke to Oliver Davenport at all, of course, and it seemed that there was an unwritten code between young blonde au pairs and the husbands. Eleanor knew there was a line, and she was so grateful to Lizzie for giving her this chance, and she'd grown to love the twins so much, that she was determined never ever to cross it.

It was a few Fridays later, and Eleanor had picked up the twins from nursery, and was busy ferrying them out of the post office, where she had finally gotten around to mailing a letter to her mom, telling her what a cool time she was having, how London was OK now she'd got used to it, how she and Rufus were going great. Well, it was nearly all true. The line in the post office had taken ages, and Eleanor was trying to hurry the twins up, stop them dawdling, as they were running late to get home in time for her to make tea. Jessica was walking along the main drag chirpily as ever, her little hand sticky as it held on to Eleanor's, but Barney was lagging behind them, dressed as Spider-Man, dragging his book bag along the sidewalk, clearly exhausted at the end of another long week.

'Come on, sweetie,' Eleanor cajoled him for the hundredth time, with zero effect, as they turned into their own street at last. In fact, the little boy was trailing further behind than ever now, and she could see the weariness in his entire polyester-clad body. She raised her voice into a jaunty sing-song and tried a trick that had always worked with the kids she'd minded in New York.

'Last one to the door is a big banana!' she said. As predicted, that got Barney running, and Jessica too, and it was almost too adorable to see. Just as the twins reached the gate, neck and neck, twenty yards or so in front of her, the next-door house's front door opened and a young man, about the same age as Eleanor, exited. There was something about his demeanour that she noticed immediately, as if he wished he could fold up inside of himself as soon as he saw her. His face was thin and spotty, and his hair was longish. She was about to nod politely, say hi, but at exactly that moment Barney tripped over and fell flat on his face, thereby losing both the race to the door and his cool.

'Shit,' Eleanor said under her breath, and started running.

'Oh, Barney,' she said as she reached him. 'Are you OK, sweetie?' She was blushing furiously, mortified both that Barney had grazed his knee thanks to her stupid game, and that the neighbour had seen. As she picked Barney up, dusted him down, shushed his screams, her neighbour continued to hover, gawping.

'I think he'll be OK,' she said, setting the little boy down.

'Yes,' said her neighbour, still making no move to leave, as Eleanor grappled in her bag to find her keys.

'Er, I'm Eleanor, by the way,' she said at last, to fill the silence. 'I'm the au pair.'

Still he said nothing. She flashed him her most friendly, reassuring smile.

'Hey, what's your name?'

'Gavin.'

'Good to meet you, Gavin. I guess I'll be seeing you around then!'

'Yes.' Gavin paused, looked as if he might be about to say something else, was maybe trying to think of it . . . but Eleanor needed to get the twins in. As she finally shooed them through the front door, she was both relieved and unable to quite decide whether Gavin was a creep – or just shy.

A quarter of an hour later Eleanor was in the kitchen hurriedly peeling carrots. Normally she would have sorted out tea before the twins came home from nursery, but today she'd felt so incredibly tired she'd gone up to her room and fallen asleep on her bed, where she'd proceeded to have a long, confused, spiralling dream that she'd found hard to recall when she woke up. All she knew was that it had started off innocuously enough, before melding into a full-on nightmare, the details of which, unfortunately, she could remember in full Technicolor glory. Rufus, in a scarlet bandana, placing a massive sparkly ring on a chimpanzee's finger . . . Eleanor attacking the chimpanzee, trying to pull at its fur, get at its hand, grab the ring . . . the fur coming off in one thick dark pelt, unveiling a beautiful naked girl, covered in blood, like a newborn . . . Eleanor's mom, in the guise of a giant black bird, wagging her talon fingers at her, shrieking, 'I told you so!' Eleanor had awoken screaming and sweating and had taken an age to compose herself. In fact, she'd only just made it to nursery pick-up on time.

Eleanor put her hands to her eyes and breathed deeply, tried to shove away the images. She still felt out of sorts somehow and she couldn't wait until she could knock off for the evening and go to bed. She was still so tired but, as her dad used to say, trauma always got to you in the end, and she supposed he should know.

'When will Mummy be home?' Barney said now, as he wandered in from the lounge, a waterproof Band-Aid proudly attached to his grazed knee.

'After tea, darling. Like always.'

'Will you play Lego with me?'

'I can't right now, sweetie. I'm making your tea.'

'Please, Ellie.' He stuck out his bottom lip, did his best to look cute.

'No, Barney. Go find Jessie, baby.'

Barney started to grizzle then, and Eleanor couldn't bear to hear the misery in his voice, and so she put down the peeler, leant over and picked him up. He wrapped his little legs round her middle and started bawling. It was odd how he was so much needier than his sister, and he was so heavy, so she plonked him down on the kitchen counter – on top of the carrot peelings, as it happened – and turned to grab a tissue to wipe his eyes.

The kitchen door opened suddenly, and Oliver entered, home from work a good two hours earlier than usual. He was wearing a smart dark navy suit and shiny brown brogues, and his hair was swept back off his forehead. Eleanor noticed his eyes were green and ever so slightly too close together, which suited his face in a way. He was holding a briefcase, which he immediately set down on the floor, and then reached out for his son.

'Hey, little guy, what on earth are you doing up there?'

'Daddy!' said Barney, trying to squirm off the counter towards his father, in distinct danger of falling. Eleanor rushed to pick him up, just in time, and as she passed the little boy over to his father she felt Oliver's hand brush against her midriff. She stiffened.

'He was only there for a second,' said Eleanor, wincing at the whine of apology in her voice.

'Hmm,' said Oliver, as a long strand of carrot peeling fell from his son on to the wooden floor. There was a prickle of something in the air and Eleanor could feel her face flush. She'd tried not to notice the vibe Oliver gave off sometimes. Maybe she was mistaken.

'What's happened to his knee?' Oliver said now.

'Oh, he just tripped up outside, didn't you, Barney?'

'Ellie made us have a race,' said Barney.

'Hmm,' said Oliver again, still staring at her.

'I'm running a little late with tea today,' she said, biting the inside of her cheek.

'So I can see.' His face was impossible to read.

'Sorry.' She looked away from him, picked up the peeler again. Seemingly taking the hint, Oliver left the room, still carrying Barney, leaving Eleanor feeling confused and anxious about what her boss was thinking, how she was feeling . . . furious with herself for appearing like a useless au pair . . . and attacking her next vegetable victim with a rage that seemed to have come out of nowhere.

9

Paul

It had been a difficult run-up to the wedding, most definitely exacerbated by the best man's ill-conceived stag do (it now being a strictly taboo subject, even though Paul had sworn blind to Christie that he'd cancelled the stripper), but in Paul's opinion it had begun even before that. Christie had always been pretty easy-going with him – and then one day she wasn't. He still thought it was something to do with her sister, as Christie's change of attitude had definitely coincided with the day she and Alice had gone to the fair together. But whatever the reason, suddenly Christie had started asking Paul where he was going, and with whom, and what time he'd be back, and although he knew she'd been betrayed by an old boyfriend before, that was all way back in the past for one, and for another it hadn't sodding well been him. Secretly, it riled Paul that it felt like Christie didn't trust him either now, was almost trying to trip him up. But the wedding itself had passed seamlessly enough, apart from his father's usual cantankerousness. And fortunately the honeymoon in Crete (miraculously organised by him!) had proved such a triumph that Paul had even thought he'd got the old Christie back. Until her bombshell, of course. He still could hardly believe it.

And so now here they were, barely nine months later, and things between them were fragile again. But maybe all women were hard work when they were pregnant, Paul thought. Perhaps it was simply the hormones. He sighed as he reached their street, expertly reversed into a parking space opposite, braced himself for going inside. He never quite knew what he was going to get when he got home, and it made him constantly on red alert for an attack. It might not be anyone's fault, but it was exhausting.

As Paul entered the hallway the air smelled warm and moist and vaguely animalistic. He wondered what on earth she was making for tea, as it didn't smell very appetising. He'd definitely have to pretend to enjoy it, though. He couldn't risk any jokes, the way she was at the moment.

'Hi, love,' he called, determinedly cheerful, as he pushed open the kitchen door.

'You're late,' she said. There was a set to her jaw that Paul didn't like the look of.

'Sorry,' he said airily, kissing the top of her head. 'Traffic.'

Christie didn't answer. It seemed he'd done something to upset her again, although she'd sounded fine when he'd rung her thirty-eight minutes before to say he was just leaving. God knows what it was this time.

And then Christie's eyes lit up and she gave him a flash of that beautiful smile, and it was one of those moments he would always remember. He felt his shoulders relax, for just a second – and then her face clenched again, and a muscle started to pulse in her forehead. A lock of wavy hair had fallen down over one eye, and her face was full and rosy, and it was odd how sexy he still found her at nine months pregnant, especially when she was fired up, like now. It confused him.

Without warning Christie doubled over next to the sink and started keening, her long hair hanging down in heavy skeins, reaching almost to the quarry floor tiles. As her hand gripped the draining board, the veins were leaping out of her skin, as if there were too much life in there, as if something had to give. Her bump looked unfathomably enormous. What the hell, Paul thought. What the fuck was she doing?

At last Christie straightened up. She smiled, completely calm now, and even through his confusion he thought how much he'd always loved the way the left side of her mouth curled up ever so slightly more than the right.

'Paul,' she said, 'my waters have broken. We need to get to the hospital.'

10

Eleanor

Despite Lizzie proving to be the most easy-going boss anyone could hope for, Eleanor remained less certain of what Oliver thought of her. She'd never dared take a nap in the afternoon again, or at least not without setting her alarm first, and she made sure she'd always prepared tea well before picking up the twins. But Oliver made Eleanor nervous now, and she cursed the fact that the one time he'd been home early, her custody of his children had appeared so shambolic.

Fortunately, it seemed that Oliver hadn't felt the need to say anything to his wife, and Lizzie remained as friendly to Eleanor as ever. In fact, the two women had grown close enough for Eleanor to have fallen into the habit of helping Lizzie with the bath and bedtime routine, even if she was officially off duty by then. She didn't mind though, as it was easier with the two of them and, if Oliver was working late, she and Lizzie would sometimes sit down and have a drink together afterwards, and it was a relief for Eleanor to have someone to talk to. To have someone looking out for her.

It seemed like the skies had been grey in London for forever, but this evening was sunny, and mild enough for Lizzie and Eleanor to be sitting outside for once. Lizzie was smoking, which she tried to hide from Oliver, although Eleanor was pretty sure he must know, because she could always spot the smell a mile off herself. A bottle of wine was plonked on a side table next to them, and the garden was in a delirious state of spring growth, with purple tulips having sprung up seemingly overnight, along with the weeds. The sharp straight line between the light and dark green of the grass, where the sun was moving ever closer to being swallowed up by the house, was edging towards them slowly, inevitably. But for now the air still had a warmth to it, and it made Eleanor feel glad that, if she'd had to end up anywhere, she'd ended up here. She'd landed on her feet, that was for sure. She dreaded to think what might have happened if Lizzie hadn't hired her – if she'd run out of cash while still holed up in King's Cross. Even now, the thought made her blanch.

'So, Eleanor,' Lizzie was saying, as she took a large gulp of wine. Her eyes sparked with easy curiosity. 'You never did tell me. What happened with the boy?'

'What boy?'

'You know exactly what boy. The one you said brought you here.'

'Ohhh.' Eleanor paused. It was strange. The question was like a pin being stuck into a giant bubble, popping it, splattering the remains of her new truth in messy, abstract patterns. Reality felt unmanageable suddenly. *She'd loved him.*

Eleanor's eyes smarted as she shifted on the garden bench, which felt mouldy and damp, as if it needed a hot blast of summer sun to fully dry out. How to explain it? Where to start? *How honest to be?*

Eleanor found herself tracking back to her old life in Maine, where she'd once been a typical young girl, allegedly living the white-picket-fenced American Dream. True, her mom had been away working lots and her father had lived in New York for as long as she could remember, but heaps of her friends' parents had gotten divorced too. Even back then though, she'd felt vaguely disconnected from the real world – not an unhappy kid, exactly, just one not yet awake to her emotions . . .

And then *boom*. Puberty had hit, and when those scary, dangerous feelings had finally threatened to surface, Eleanor had found partying and fuzzy-headedness a pretty effective foil to them. Even now, the memories were mortifying.

When Eleanor looked up to see Lizzie watching her expectantly, with her face cocked to one side, like an inquisitive puppy, she felt an involuntary wash of panic. She forced herself to try to relax again. It was OK. Lizzie didn't know about her past – she was just being curious, and it's not as though Eleanor had done anything *that* bad. All she'd done was go a little off the rails for a while, as did lots of teenagers – but seeing as she was minding Lizzie's kids, she didn't like to mention that fact and risk spoiling everything. She felt safe with Lizzie and the twins, perhaps safer than she'd felt with anyone. Even with Rufus, she'd felt too dizzy and overfilled with passion, and then ultimately wholly rejected, to ever have time to feel anything as prosaic as *safe*. She still wasn't sure what to say. She took another sip of her wine.

'The boy?' said Lizzie, gently. 'What was his name?'

'Rufus.'

'Oh.' Lizzie sounded surprised. 'How very English. And how did you meet him?'

Eleanor paused. 'While working at summer camp,' she said. 'We were both camp leaders.'

'Oh, that's so sweet,' said Lizzie. As she smiled, the dimples in her cheeks and the fine tendrils of dark hair falling around her face made her appear younger, almost like a teenager. A winsome, innocent teenager who had grown up safely in the bosom of a proper, non-dysfunctional family. The older woman's apparent lack of worldliness was endearing in a way.

'I would have loved to have gone to summer camp,' Lizzie continued. 'Like Sandy and Danny in *Grease*.'

Eleanor laughed. 'Yeah, something like that,' she said. It still felt painful to remember that time, despite the memories having transmuted now into a sweet, masochistic kind of ache, full of poignancy and lost hope. And at least meeting Rufus and falling in love had led to the opening up of herself in ways she hadn't thought possible, unaware before then that you could feel so breathy and passionate and wild and vivid, just through the very act of being alive. Even in the long agonising months apart from Rufus, she hadn't been tempted to take drugs, as she'd once done to dull pain. Who needed drugs when you could have love? It was a ride wilder than any other. Love would conquer all.

What a joke. Eleanor took a breath of dense London air, which had a quite different noxious tinge to that of New York, and continued her story.

'So Rufus and I fell in love, and he begged me to come to England, and so I did, but when I got here everything felt different somehow . . . and it sort of went from bad to worse . . . and then he told me that he'd made a huge mistake.' Her pace quickened. 'He said that his old girlfriend had been in touch and that, after a few weeks with me, he realised that he didn't love me after all, and that he wanted to be with her. And so I left . . .' Eleanor tailed off. What else was there to say?

'Well, he's a fool,' said Lizzie. Her tone had a note of something unspecified in it, and Eleanor thought it might be regret. 'I'm so sorry.'

'It's OK.' Eleanor laughed. 'Character-building. Isn't that what they call it?'

'So why didn't you just go home?'

Eleanor didn't answer.

'They don't know, do they?'

'What?'

'Your family. They still don't know that you're not with him?'

Eleanor hesitated. It didn't feel right to lie to Lizzie.

'I'm going to tell them,' she said. 'But I wanted to make sure this job worked out first. I want them to feel proud of me . . .'

'Eleanor.' Lizzie reached across and put her hand on Eleanor's arm, and her touch was warm and alive, energising as well as comforting.

'What you've done is amazing. Remember that. And this job has already worked out – you're great with the twins. Of course your family will be proud of you.'

Before Eleanor had time to reply, a loud, elongated wail started tail-twisting its way down the garden, and even from here they could hear it ramping up every second. *Barney*. Lizzie stood up. 'I'll go,' she said. As she looked down at the younger girl, the light was behind her, so Eleanor couldn't quite work out her expression. 'You stay here and finish your drink.'

A few hours later Eleanor was woken up by the sound of Lizzie and Oliver downstairs, arguing. It seemed he'd been late home, again, and Lizzie, in her wine-fuelled state, wasn't happy about it. Eleanor assumed it was normal to witness rows when you lived with a couple full-time, but she didn't know what they should be like, how bad this one was on the overall scale.

Eleanor lay on her back and pulled the blanket over her head. It was odd being here, and it almost felt as if she'd taken a full circle back to her own childhood, to a state of mind akin to mild dissociation. Here, in a place called Crouch End, with its chichi stores and café culture, and endless strollers and playgrounds and bohemian vibe, had seemed a good spot for her to hide out for a while, lick her wounds, get over her heartbreak without losing face. But now Lizzie's questions had rattled her. Was it so wrong to have not told her parents what had happened between her and Rufus? After all, they'd lied to her for years about the state of their relationships, and God knows what else besides, and at least this way they hadn't had to worry about her. She'd just called them up a couple times, and that had seemed to be enough for them. Out of sight and all that.

Eleanor turned over on to her front and sank her head into the pillow, until she could barely breathe. The noise downstairs had quietened now, so presumably the argument was over, and Eleanor was glad. She hoped for Lizzie's sake that Oliver wasn't being an asshole. In Eleanor's opinion he was more than capable of it, although she had no real solid evidence. It was just a feeling. But since the incident with Barney, he'd made her feel uncomfortable, as if he'd sussed her out now and thought she was bad news . . . And yet at other times, he was friendly, perhaps too friendly, especially if he'd been drinking. But maybe she was wrong. It made her feel disloyal to Lizzie to even think like that.

Men, Eleanor thought. Were they destined to confound her? She wasn't sure. But there was no point worrying about it. All she could do for now was hang in there, look after the twins, help Lizzie . . . and do her best to stay out of Oliver's way. Just to be on the safe side.

11

Paul

Paul grimaced as he swallowed the coffee. It was weak and too hot, and it had first burnt his tongue and now was doing a pretty good job of scraping the skin off his throat too. He felt flailed, inside and out.

He was a father! Thirty-odd hours after he'd arrived home from work to find Christie in labour, he finally had a newborn little girl. Not the healthy, pink princess of his imaginings (nor, thankfully, the blue, dead one of his nightmares), but a wrinkled, gnarly little thing, so apathetic she'd barely reacted to being born. Yet perhaps that wasn't too surprising – it had been a horrendous experience for all of them. First Christie had had to endure a long-drawn-out, excruciating labour, throughout which he'd stayed resolutely beside her, despite him being half-frightened out of his wits, despite her repeatedly yelling at him to fuck off and leave her alone to get on with it. On the couple of occasions he had stepped out to use the bathroom her eerily bovine bellows of anguish had leached through the corridors and pounded inside his head, as if there were no escape from them. The midwife had said that all the women were like that, but still Paul hadn't been sure. He'd never seen Christie like that before, and it was a discomfiting sensation, implying that there was a depth and a rage to her that he neither knew nor understood.

Unfortunately, things had only got more abject from there. It had been appalling to discover, after hours and hours of strain and noise and drama and trauma, that Christie's efforts had been a complete waste of time. It seemed the baby had got stuck – neither in nor out – and as the beeps on the machine had become increasingly insistent, the natural birth process had been brought to an abrupt halt, with low mutterings about distress and heartbeats and a load of other stuff that Paul had failed to understand and that had only elevated his level of terror. He'd had no time to even ask any questions before Christie had been wheeled through to the operating room, where the doctors had performed a swift, brutal emergency Caesarean, redolent of some kind of blood-sluiced butchery ritual. Or maybe they were all like that – Paul had no idea. But either way the air had been thick with blood and tension and fear, and afterwards he'd tried to comfort himself that at least both mother and child had survived. That was the important thing – wasn't it?

'You OK, Christie?' Paul said now, as he hovered next to his wife, unsure whether to sit down or not. The baby was asleep in her plastic crate, her nose twitching, looking vaguely inhuman, like a laboratory specimen. The way Christie looked up at him wordlessly, her face pale, her hair fanned against the pillows, made him feel uncomfortable, as if he'd said something really stupid. He remembered his father used to look at him like that, and he felt a throb start, in his little toe, of all places, before he pulled himself up. Now was not the time for bad memories. He had the future to think about.

'Yes,' she said.

'Good,' he replied. There seemed nothing else to say. He'd tried to imagine this part at least being joyful, but it was surreal, sombre almost. It seemed inappropriate to ask what was the matter with her. Hopefully it was just exhaustion. He wondered if he should pick up the baby, offer her to Christie, but he was scared to, and he wasn't sure who he was trying to placate anyway.

'Well, well done, pet,' he said, patting her hand. The words were asinine, appeared to stumble over each other, as though the air was too dense for them.

Christie closed her eyes. 'It wasn't well done at all,' she murmured. He watched as the outer edges of her eyelids began to glisten.

'Oh, Christie,' Paul said. Instinctively he took her hand. 'Of course it was. You're amazing.' And as he leaned over to kiss her, he truly believed it. He truly believed that they were a family now, and that this strange little addition to his and Christie's lives would help bond them back together . . . That they'd got through the worst part, and everything would be OK from now on. It was up to him to make it so.

12

Eleanor

There had been a temporary pause in the dismal weather, yet still Eleanor was undecided whether to risk it. The forecast had been for rain all day – again – but over to the east the sky had opened up suddenly to reveal a serene celestial white, as if the sun were straining to break through and show the clouds who was boss. Barney and Jessica were still not quite over their chickenpox, but they were both missing being at nursery now, and in truth Eleanor was missing them being there too. A whole week at home with a pair of unwell twins had been exhausting, had tested her childcare skills to the brink. She was proud of herself, though, that she'd managed. But this morning all three of them needed to get out of the house – there was a limit to everyone's patience, after all. Plus Oliver was upstairs today, and even though he mainly kept himself to himself whenever he was working from home, it still made her feel uneasy – trying to make sure the twins didn't make too much noise, in case he was on a call, or stressing about being in his way if he came down to make a sandwich, or that she was seen to be looking after his children properly. It was odd how tense the atmosphere felt between them these days. There was an invisible aura that surrounded Oliver, which she could feel when he got too close to her, and sometimes she noticed the glances he gave her, although she was never quite sure what they meant. She remembered the occasion when he'd brushed his hand against her midriff, and still couldn't decide whether it had been deliberate or not. But mostly she assumed that he just didn't like her, still suspected she wasn't suitable to look after his children. Sometimes she'd even wonder whether that was partly what the rows with Lizzie were about, and then she'd tell herself she was being paranoid.

Eleanor took another long look out of the window, watched the clouds fizzing away, as if on time lapse, the blue breaking through. When the sun finally burst out and the whole world sparkled, apparently cleansed of every trace of dirt and deceit and disappointment, she made her decision.

'OK, kids!' she said. 'Who's up for a trip to the park?'

'Me, me, ME!' yelled Barney.

'Meeeeeeee!' said Jessica.

'OK, gumboots on, get your raincoats. Just in case.'

'It's *wellies*, Ellie,' said Jessica, and then she laughed and started yelling, 'Wellies Ellie, wellies Ellie, wellies Ellie!' over and over. Barney got his boots and held one upside down on his head as he ran around, pretending to be a submarine. When Eleanor had finally calmed them down, and sorted out spare clothes and snacks, the skies were already greying over again, but she decided to risk it. After all, it was only rain. So what if they did get a little wet?

'Come on, sweeties,' she said. 'Hats on.' She opened the door and ushered them out through the front garden and on to the street, and she thought they looked like two little fishermen, in their gumboots and yellow raincoats and hats, and it was in that moment she realised that this wasn't just a job any more. It was so much more than that. The twins were adorable, and they loved her, and she loved them, and it was unconditional, utterly genuine – and she would never ever do anything to risk losing that. She was sure of it.

13

Paul

Paul's life had returned to just about as normal as any new father's can be, but Christie still seemed shattered by motherhood. She seemed so closed in somehow, as if the girl he'd known for years didn't exist any more, and it made him doubt himself, doubt how she truly felt about him. After all, he hadn't been her first love. Her first love had been a posh boy from university, not some sales rep from Manchester with a Happy Mondays obsession. Her first love had broken her heart. In fact, he, Paul, had been the one who'd helped pick up the pieces.

Paul sighed as he made himself a coffee in the drab, functional little kitchen attached to the back of his offices, which looked out on to a bin-filled cobbled alleyway. It was risible that he worked for a multi-national company, with shiny head offices in central London and New Jersey, but that their Manchester office was such a dump. Someone had slopped a teabag all over the floor and it annoyed him that other people could be so slovenly. But as he cleaned up, he knew that wasn't really the issue. The issue was Christie. He'd done his best – having managed to combine all his holiday to take four weeks off work to help out, just about managing to balance convincing his boss that it was necessary with not letting on that there was any kind of problem at home. Paul had spent those weeks shopping and cooking, and putting on sack-loads of laundry, and doing everything possible to make life easier for his wife. The one thing he hadn't been able to do, of course, was the actual feeding, but he'd been a committed wingman. And so every single time his infant daughter had finished on the breast, he'd taken her from Christie and walked her around and around the house, rubbing her little back as she wailed in fury, before finally, cathartically, throwing up all over his shoulder by way of a thank you. Next, he'd proceeded to clean Daisy up, change her nappy, before handing her, quiet and happy and sweet-smelling once more, back to Christie – just in time for them to go through the whole saga all over again. It seemed extraordinary, but somehow there had never been a single spare minute in the day, but Paul hadn't minded. In a way he'd revelled in the responsibility, in that he'd started to feel closer to Christie again. That she'd needed him. For a little while he'd even thought that everything would be OK.

Paul took his coffee and headed back to his desk, ignoring his colleague Alan, who was on the phone, talking too loudly as usual. Paul assumed Alan wanted everyone to hear his conversations, as if he believed his wrangling over the price of package deliveries was the most important thing in the world. Sometimes he wished he shared Alan's passion for parcels, or Christie's for her job for that matter, having combined an encyclopaedic knowledge of medieval history with a love of teaching to prove a formidable force for good. Paul was sure his wife could have ended up running a top school in London, and suddenly he wondered if she ever regretted settling back in Manchester. Was Manchester second best for her? Was *he* second best for her? Is that what the real problem was? Nothing to do with their new baby at all?

Paul sat down, half-heartedly opened the weekly marketing pack . . . but despite his attempts to concentrate, his thoughts remained firmly on his and Christie's domestic predicament. Even when Alan finally stopped talking and hung up, there was no respite from the noise inside Paul's head. He could still hear the effects of Daisy's colic, as if the screaming was imprinted in his ears, ready to invade every brief moment of silence. He could still hear Christie crying. Last night had been one of the worst yet, with Daisy inconsolable, and Christie distraught and in obvious agony, not knowing how to keep the baby latched on, and Paul had lain next to his wife, feeling stressed and desperate, fully aware that his normal strategy of using humour to diffuse situations would only make things worse.

The phone on his desk rang, so loudly it almost jumped, chattering, into the air like a Tom-and-Jerry phone.

'Hello, Paul Ingram,' he said.

'Hi, Paul.' Her voice had that raspy quality to it, as if she had a cold. He'd always found it attractive.

'Oh, hello.' He tried to keep the note of surprise out of his tone.

'Look, Paul, I'm sorry.'

He paused. 'What for?'

'For being so stubborn.'

Paul wasn't sure what to say. He wasn't certain what she was talking about, but he felt that it was an opening, and that he shouldn't blow it.

'Christie, love.' He spoke softly. 'You have nothing to apologise for.'

'I have. I'm a lousy mother.'

Even as Paul muttered horrified platitudes, aware that Alan was listening (although doing his best to pretend not to), he acknowledged at last that perhaps there was something seriously wrong. Before this, he'd tried to put her behaviour down to the baby blues, and overtiredness, and Daisy's colic, and the more she seemed to struggle, so did he – but of course he couldn't admit to that. Christie had enough on her plate.

And yet now Paul was worried that things had gone too far. Last night she'd finally snapped, and it had been scary to witness her jumping out of bed and almost chucking the baby at him, telling him that he could fucking deal with it, before storming out of the room. He'd got up instantly and taken his hysterical daughter downstairs to try to placate her. And then once he'd managed to finally settle her enough to put her back in her cot, he'd found Christie locked in the bathroom, crying. He'd knocked quietly and tried to ask her what was wrong, but when she came out she'd just rebuffed him, got into bed and turned her back on him, and he'd lain awake for the rest of the night, wondering what the hell was the matter with her. He just didn't know how to support his wife, and it seemed that his practical, pragmatic approach was making things worse, not better. It didn't help that he was about to leave for a two-day sales conference that he was presenting at and needed to be on form for. It was in a hotel in Cheshire, and although normally he would have hated the thought of leaving her, secretly he was looking forward to at least getting a decent sleep for once.

After Christie rang off, Paul stood up and walked back across the office, past Alan, who was chewing grimly on a cheese baguette now, past the dark ominous stain where Greg from Purchasing had thrown up after last year's Christmas party, past the solitary, leaf-challenged pot plant that no one ever watered. Despite being on his fourth coffee, Paul still felt so wiped out he leant back against the kitchen units, his palms on his forehead. The kettle took forever to boil, allowing him too long with his thoughts. But perhaps leaving Daisy and Christie alone for the night might even be good for them, he told himself optimistically, as the furred-up kettle limped to an apathetic sputter at last. Maybe it would even make him feel better too – enable him to have a few drinks, let his hair down for a bit. Yes, Paul decided, as he slopped some milk into his coffee, surely a break would be good for all of them.

14

Eleanor

'I want to go home, Ellie,' Jessica said. They'd left for the park just half an hour earlier, but now they were hurrying home along the main road, and Jessica's voice was trembling and her little lip was quivering, and Eleanor felt terrible that she'd so badly misjudged the situation. The twins still weren't well – what in hell had she been thinking, taking them out in this weather? No sooner had they reached the park than the clouds had turned from a bright translucence to an ugly dark violet and it had started to rain, the drops huge and splashy and relentless. And then when the lightning had flashed, swiftly followed by tree-snapping cracks of thunder, Barney had become hysterical and it had been impossible to placate him. Now, Eleanor was doing her best to carry him on her hip while walking along holding poor Jessica's hand, and the fact that the little girl was being so brave only made Eleanor feel worse. She needed to get them home.

An old white saloon car, clearly rusting at the edges, slowed down beside her and honked, and the sound was almost comedic in its ineffectiveness. She briefly looked across at the unknown driver, and then shook her head and turned away.

The driver wound down the window. 'D'you want a lift?' he yelled over the machine-gun noise of rain on metal.

'Er, no, we're good, thanks,' said Eleanor, as rivers of water ran through her straggling hair. She knew better than to put herself and the twins into a stranger's car, no matter how horrendous the weather. She put her head down and carried on walking.

The car followed alongside her now, and she began to feel a little alarmed. She tried to speed up, but poor Jessica couldn't go any faster, and of course they wouldn't be able to outrun the car anyway.

'Eleanor, it's OK,' he said. 'It's me.'

Eleanor turned sharply and stared him down. How did he know her name?

Of course. It was the young guy from next door. What was his name? She couldn't remember now. He still had that odd way of looking at her, the peculiar air of gaucheness.

'Oh, jeez, I'm sorry,' she said through the open window. 'I didn't recognise you.'

'It's all right,' he said. 'I'll give you a lift home if you like.'

'Uhh . . . thanks,' said Eleanor, but as she helped the children into the car and strapped them in, she still felt uneasy. There were no child seats for a start, and the twins were so little. When her rescuer moved off, albeit suitably slowly, Eleanor sat between Barney and Jessica, hugging them anxiously to her. Barney was still upset, but the rain pelting the windscreen and the *thud-thud* of the wipers were combining to drown out his sobs. The inside of the car smelled musty and faintly of weed, and the carpet was squelchy underfoot. Eleanor felt trapped now, and anxious, and she was worried about what Lizzie and Oliver would think. Which was worse? Letting the twins get soaked through when they still weren't entirely well, or putting them into an almost-stranger's recreational-drug-fumed car without child seats? Which transgression was she more likely to get fired for?

As the car turned off the main road at a run-down corner house with a crumbling turret, Eleanor didn't recognise the route, and she worried that her would-be saviour was going the wrong way, might even be about to abduct them. Her mouth felt dry, and she longed for the words to come, but she didn't want to risk annoying him. There was something about him that she didn't like. He was wearing a black bomber jacket covered in badges, and she wasn't sure whether it was meant to be fashionable or not. It was hard to tell. The car was picking up speed now, and Eleanor gripped the twins' arms tightly, in case they crashed.

'Ow, Ellie, that *hurts*,' Jessica said, and her little voice was so full of confusion that, as Eleanor apologised, she could hear her own voice cracking. Another bolt of lightning tore across the sky, but even Barney seemed to sense that he should keep quiet now. Eleanor clamped her teeth together, to stop herself from saying anything, and tried to calm the breath hovering in her throat.

Possibly sensing her distress, her neighbour looked over his shoulder then, and his eyes had a strange, ambivalent gleam to them that she hadn't noticed before, and he seemed less shy now. He gave her an odd, pinched little smile.

'Nearly there,' he said.

15

Paul

'Have you got everything you need, Christie?' Paul said the next morning, for the umpteenth time. His overnight case had been packed and zipped up decisively and he was now standing next to it in the hallway, wearing his smartest black suit, swaying from side to side in his shiny leather shoes, hopefully imperceptibly. He felt as if he were walking on burning rubber. The impulse to leave was stronger than his desire to stay, and it was discomfiting. He never used to feel like he couldn't wait to get away from his wife.

'Well, I think we'll just about survive,' Christie said, a placid Daisy in her arms – and then she smiled, presumably to show she was joking, and it was a relief to see. She often seemed so brittle these days, as if humour had deserted her, and he'd even been wondering if he should suggest she go to the doctor's, although he was unsure how she would take it. He heard her voice adopt a self-consciously casual tone. 'Alice said she'd pop by later.'

'Oh, that's good,' Paul said, but it made him feel even more uneasy. If anyone got Christie fired up it was her sister. Alice might be well meaning, but she was mad as a stick in Paul's opinion, although his wife never saw it. Alice was her darling baby sister in Christie's eyes. They might fall out occasionally, but they were as close as siblings could be.

The thought made Paul briefly sad about his own brother, who he hadn't seen for so many years. Maybe he should think about looking him up one day, tell him he was an uncle.

'Well, I'll see you tomorrow night then,' Paul said at last, and went in for a kiss, but at the very last moment Christie turned away, so he was presented with her cool smooth cheek. The rejection stabbed at him. And yet, instead of showing her how he felt, he bent and belly-kissed Daisy, making a loud continuous flatulent sound, causing the baby to coo and wave her arms about, and it was so nice to see her smiling for a change. Once Daisy was sated Paul stood up straight and said, as casually as he could, 'Well, bye then, pet,' and then he walked out of the door, feeling as if Christie couldn't wait for him to go – and, surely worse, that he couldn't wait to leave either.

16

Eleanor

'Look, I'm sorry, but where in hell are you taking us?'

Eleanor gasped and clapped her hand to her mouth. She'd blurted out the question almost involuntarily – just a mere nanosecond before she realised they'd turned into the far end of their street, instead of coming the way she knew.

'Gosh, sorry,' she said. As her neighbour wordlessly parked up outside the house, she was so embarrassed she did her best to recover the situation.

'Well, thanks so much for rescuing us,' she said brightly as she leaned over Barney, opened the car door and almost bundled him and Jessica out of the car. The rain had eased off a little, but the twins were sodden, although hopefully it was nothing a brisk towelling off and a change of clothes couldn't fix. She tried again to atone for her lack of trust in her neighbour and gave him her best smile. 'Thanks again. I knew I shouldn't have risked taking them out in this weather.'

'That's all right,' he said, locking the car and coming round to her side. Instinctively Eleanor pulled up the hood of her jacket, although it wasn't raining at all now and she was soaking wet anyway, and then she bent down and helped Barney, whose left gumboot had half come off. But instead of the boot going back on, the little boy managed to hop straight out of it and into a puddle in just his sock, making him gurgle with laughter. She remained crouching on the sidewalk for longer than she needed to, but when she glanced up again, her neighbour was still standing there, hovering above her, looking weirdly expectant. The Davenports' immaculately trimmed privet hedge rose up behind him, and it reminded her of a green screen from the movies, and she pictured it magically transforming into a majestic ravine, and she had a sudden urge to leap up and shove him, hard, over the edge of it. She gulped, stood up at last, and took Jessica's icy little hand.

'Well, I guess I'd better be getting the twins in . . .' Eleanor paused. 'Gee, sorry, what was your name again?'

'It's Gavin!' said Barney, his spirits fully recovered now, before Gavin had time to reply himself.

'Well, thanks again, Gavin,' Eleanor said. She held out her hand and it was wet and cold, but Gavin's was wetter and colder. Slippery almost. Slack. 'I sure do owe you.' She smiled again, and so did he, and despite her stress she couldn't help but acknowledge that British dentistry was not a patch on America's.

'Would you like to go out for a drink with me?' Gavin said.

Eleanor just about managed to stifle a gasp. 'Gosh, that's real kind, but, you know, I'm not sure when I'm free.'

'Saturday?' Gavin persisted.

'Er . . . can I let you know?'

'Yes, all right. Shall I ring you and check later? My parents have got the Davenports' number.'

'Er, yeah, that'll be cool. See you later.' Eleanor grabbed the twins and walked away from him, up the tiled path towards the front door, just as the skies let rip again – and so she was unsure whether Jessica's balefully proclaimed, 'I don't like him, Ellie,' had been heard by Gavin or not.

17

Alex, a few months later

Alex could tell that Gavin Hewitson thought he was a jerk. Some people seemed to hate the police almost on principle, and it was annoying. This one especially had that air about him, as though he thought Alex was the type of guy who'd only joined the police to get a badge and a uniform so he could feel better about himself – and maybe it was too close to the truth to sit comfortably. People like Gavin Hewitson pissed Alex off – and that was regardless of the fact that this creep was allegedly harassing the delectable Miss (not Mrs, as it had turned out) Jackson. But at least it had made Alex's stint in the station office, normally the lowest-of-the-low gig that only the losers got, nothing if not interesting.

Right now, Gavin was leaning back in his chair, staring insolently at Alex and Gillian. He was a weedy, shifty-looking bloke, and he seemed familiar somehow. Alex tried to work out who he reminded him of, but for the moment it eluded him. It would come to him.

As Alex started his questioning, Gavin seemed to be trying hard to regulate his temper, and there was definitely something odd about his responses. His speech was stilted and staccato, ever so slightly too high-pitched. Yes, he did know Eleanor Jackson. Yes, he did live next door to her, with his parents. Yes, he had asked her out a couple of times, that was true. No, she hadn't ever said yes, that was also true. No, he hadn't made silent phone calls to her; there must have been something wrong with the phone, and she simply hadn't been able to hear him. No, he most certainly had not sent Miss Jackson unwanted gifts; he'd just bought her some flowers once, and what was wrong with that? Yes, he had driven her home one time, and helped her when Mrs Davenport's car had had a flat tyre, but was that a crime? No, he did *not* stare out of his window at her specifically; he just liked looking out of the window, which he was entitled to do. No, he wasn't prepared to divulge whether he smoked marijuana from time to time, saying that that was none of their business. Yes, he was unemployed at the moment. Yes, he did have a tattoo of the sun and the moon on the inside of each of his wrists . . . but Alex hadn't actually asked him about those. Instead Alex had merely stared at Gavin's arms, and tried to remind himself that the markings, along with his assorted-patch-covered jacket and overlong hair, were not necessarily evidence that Gavin Hewitson was a stalker.

At last Alex and Gillian ran out of things to ask, and it seemed the only option was to issue a harassment order and let the suspect leave. Yet still Gavin Hewitson sat there, looking as though he were debating whether to say something further . . . until at last he stood up and started shuffling on the spot for a second, like a little child wondering whether it was safe to come out of their bedroom once the parental banging and shouting had stopped. He was definitely a freak, Alex decided, and clearly suffering from unrequited love, but unfortunately there was nothing more they could do. For a moment the two men stared each other out, and then Gavin shrugged his shoulders insolently, turned his back on Alex, and followed Gillian out of the room. As Alex tailed them down the long corridor towards the exit, there was something about the lope of Gavin's walk that set off an alarm in Alex's brain. It was one of the most annoying things about being in the police – when you had to watch the suspect just walk away, knowing that they had won. The number of times Alex had wanted to take the law into his own hands . . .

Alex checked himself. Women like Eleanor Jackson didn't cross his path very often, and so he couldn't let his emotions get the better of him. In this case especially, he had to make sure he played it right. This wouldn't be the last they'd see of Gavin Hewitson, though, Alex was pretty sure of that. He just had to be patient. He just had to sit tight and wait.

18

Eleanor

The twins were still at nursery, tea was all prepared, Eleanor had put a wash on, tidied up the toys – and now she was holed up in her sweet little bedroom in the loft, curtains drawn even though it was daytime, lying on top of her bed, her mind tumbling, gathering pace. She had tried so hard not to feel sorry for herself, but it seemed like whatever she did, however she fought, life was destined to be one long uphill struggle. *Jesus.* All she'd done was be friendly to the neighbours' son, because he'd rescued her and the twins from a thunderstorm, yet it seemed as though he'd got completely the wrong idea. Fine, he'd asked her out for a drink, which wasn't a crime, but it had so taken her by surprise she hadn't known how to handle it, what to say. And even though she'd politely declined when he'd phoned her to get her answer, the next week he'd asked her out again, and then the week after that, and she'd tried so hard not to be rude about it, but perhaps that had been part of the problem. Maybe she'd somehow encouraged him. Soon after that the silent phone calls had started, in the middle of the day, when he knew she was alone. And then the unwanted gifts – and now her next-door neighbour's presence was like a curse and a threat and an irritant, all rolled into one, and it was weighing her down, scaring her. Even the police didn't seem able to help. What was the point of her even having gone to them if they couldn't actually do anything?

Eleanor turned over, stared at the wall. Half-formed sentences dipped and dived, emotions flitted, her heart squeezed and released, squeezed and released, time passed . . . until at last, at long, long last, she acknowledged what else was bothering her. *She missed Rufus.*

Eleanor let out a long, low groan, and it sounded tortured, otherworldly, as if it were coming from someone else. How could she have imagined she could simply put her lover out of her mind, turn herself into an au pair extraordinaire, and forget what London was supposed to have meant to her? Denial. Denial was her forte, she could see that now. When in doubt, stick your head in the sand. When you've been hurt, stick your head in the sand. The sand was proverbial, of course, and could take all forms. Love, drugs, toddlers. She'd turned to them all.

As Eleanor lay there, a picture entered her head, and it was vivid and photographically remembered. A camp in the middle of the woods, where the lodges were nestled into the trees, and the water in the stream ran fast and cold, and the moon hung in the air like a promise. Rufus himself had been floppy-haired and complicated and British, and her heart had opened up to the most enticing of possibilities, and she had felt as pure and loved and complete as she ever had. And now he was lost to her, and she wanted to know why things had to change. Why nothing could ever stand still in time, just when it was all so wonderful . . . And that was what destroyed her now, realising that that was just the way life was, and would always be. That things never ever stay the same, not even when you have it all, there in your hand – it's always destined to change. Get better. Get worse. But never remain. Never stay perfect. After all, timeless perfection was what paintings were for.

Eleanor jumped up from the bed, paced the room, clenching her fists together, clamping her jaw. Where *was* Rufus? What was he doing? Having tried to deny his existence all these past months, she longed to go out *right now*, head over to Hampstead and knock on his door, tell him he'd broken her fucking heart and that she'd *trusted* him, and she was so very tempted she even put on her coat, started doing up her sneakers. But when the phone rang again, its baleful rhythmic trill cut through her madness and stopped her in her tracks . . . which was almost certainly just as well.

She had to answer it, of course, just in case it was the nursery, or Lizzie or Oliver, and he knew it. She awaited the not-quite-heavy breathing that often followed her brusquely aggressive 'hello' and which she'd become used to, but thankfully today she was spared.

'Miss Jackson? Hello, this is PC Alex Moffatt from the Metropolitan Police.'

'Oh. Hi.' She wasn't sure whether she was pleased to hear from him or dreading what he had to say. Eleanor could feel that her own breathing was heavy now, rising and falling, reverberating against the phone's mouthpiece, and she prayed PC Moffatt couldn't hear it. She tried to stay calm, but it was as if her energy were throbbing through the phone lines, sparking against his. She gazed out of the living room window and saw a silver plane flying low in the sky, and the way the sun glinted off it reminded her of a freshly caught fish, like the ones her uncle had sometimes brought her mom. She vaguely wondered where the plane was going, whether it was headed for America. For home.

'I was calling to let you know that we've spoken to Mr Hewitson,' the nice young policeman was continuing, 'and we've issued him with a harassment warning, which means he shouldn't approach you any further, or attempt to talk to you.'

'Oh.' Eleanor paused, rubbed mindlessly at her ring finger. 'So he's definitely not allowed to phone me any more?' she added.

'Yes, that's right.'

'Or talk to me?'

'No, he mustn't approach you.'

'But what if he carries on spying on me out of his window for hours on end?'

Eleanor heard PC Moffatt pause. 'I'm afraid there's nothing we can do about that, Miss Jackson, as unfortunately he does live next door to you. You'll just have to continue to keep the curtains drawn. The only real option, if you wanted to have no further contact at all with Mr Hewitson, would be for you to move out.'

The plane had disappeared into the ether now, and for a moment Eleanor wished she were on it, could give up, go home. Instead she turned her attention to the acer tree directly outside the window, watched its leaves rustle and shimmy, occasionally detach themselves, and they were so brilliantly scarlet they reminded her of Maine too. Did America beckon? She wasn't sure. But in this moment her situation felt hopeless, as if wherever she went she would always feel the need to move on, for the most unpredictable of reasons, and suddenly all she wanted was for someone to rescue her, protect her from feckless faithless lovers and stalkerish next-door neighbours.

'Are you still there, Miss Jackson?' PC Moffatt asked now.

'Oh. Yeah, sorry.' Eleanor held the phone between her chin and her shoulder, scraped her silky hair on to the top of her head, tied a slippery knot in it, and attempted to unravel her thoughts.

'Listen, I know it must be hard for you,' PC Moffatt continued, and he sounded kinder now, more understanding. 'But if you have any more bother at all, please feel free to come back in, or you can call and ask for me directly.'

'Thank you.' She recalled now how nice PC Moffatt had looked in his uniform, how blue his eyes had been. At least she had him on her side. That was one thing in her favour. She thanked him for the call, said a polite goodbye and put down the phone.

19

Paul

The evening was in full swing, but Paul's thoughts were elsewhere. As he grimly tackled the taste-free lemon tart that constituted dessert, he found himself remembering word for word the conversation that had changed everything. It was as though it were stuck on an interminable internal loop that was taking hold of a part of his brain and constricting it. He'd come home from work one evening, and she'd run to meet him at the door, her eyes fizzing with happiness, and she'd thrown her arms around him, and he could still feel the shape of the words now, as she'd kissed him and told him simultaneously. He'd pulled back, his tie akimbo, his mouth smeared with her lipstick, and stared at her.

'You're *what*?' he'd said.

'I'm *pregnant*!' And then she'd started covering him in kisses again, but he hadn't wanted to kiss her any more. He'd wanted to run out of the room, flee the house, tear down the street and get as far away from her as possible, until he could get his head around it. But he hadn't, of course, and maybe in hindsight that was where the real problems had started.

'Christie, it's too soon, darling. I'm not ready to be a father. In fact, the truth is, I don't know if I'll ever be ready.'

Paul cursed himself now, that he'd never said that. That he'd never said anything. Maybe just saying it, voicing his fears, would have been enough to get beyond them. He'd been worried about upsetting her, though – of arousing her newly acquired insecurities, of making her think he was suggesting an abortion, which he wasn't, not necessarily. He hadn't known what he'd been suggesting. All he'd known was that he'd been terrified for her, for him, for the baby. He'd dreaded what kind of a father he could possibly hope to be.

And so instead of being truthful Paul had gently extricated himself from his wife and disappeared into the bathroom, and by the time he'd come out he'd rearranged his face into the one he thought she wanted to see. The one he'd done his utmost to keep up for the best part of a year. It had been a corrosive and wearying secret to keep. It seemed he'd been tired ever since.

Paul felt a pressure thrumming in his temple. The room was too warm and Steve Channing, the Financial Controller, was sitting next to him, droning on about EBITDA, which Paul wasn't remotely interested in, especially not over dinner. As Paul nodded politely, he was thinking about how much he hated these events. His presentation that morning had gone OK, but he hadn't felt a hundred per cent sure of the figures, and it was as if his brain hadn't been working properly, and he knew his boss had noticed. The afternoon had been quite fun, taken up as it was with the obligatory naff team-building exercise, but constructing a raft had all felt so pointless to Paul that by the end he'd felt like resigning on the spot and walking out.

And now it was much later, and Paul still didn't want to be here, but for a different reason. With the benefit of distance, he realised how much he missed Christie, missed how they used to be together. Baby or not, they *loved* each other . . .

And he loved Daisy too.

What the hell. *Of course* he did. He'd been being a fool. In fact, Paul felt such a sudden strong need to see his little family, sort everything out, make amends for his hitherto secret aversion to fatherhood, that he longed to drive home right now and beg for them to start over, but he couldn't. He was drunk.

Paul took another slug of wine and gazed helplessly around him. The hotel was modern and cavernous, and architecturally so bereft the word 'bland' was a compliment. White cloths had been thrown over the round tables, and a five-by-five-metre square of melamine floor had been taped to the carpet, creating a dance floor where a DJ played cheesy pop songs, complete with flashing lights. Paul stifled a yawn. A couple of rounds in the pub would have created a far greater camaraderie than this dismal event, he thought, and would have been way cheaper, to boot. Maybe he should offer to organise the next one.

Just as the waiters (black-suited, bored-looking) were bringing pots of coffee and bomb-shaped petits fours, a sure marker that Paul would be able to sneak off to bed without attracting comment, the Sales Director arrived to grace them with his presence.

'Now, then,' he boomed, as he sat down beside Paul. 'Let's get this party started.' He clicked his hairy fingers, and soon a tray-load of shots was delivered to the table, in celebration of the company's best first quarter since 1988, to be consumed in a communal display of enforced, chest-beating bonhomie. As the liquid burned and danced its way down Paul's throat it made his head swim a little. Almost immediately afterwards another round was ordered, and a cheer went up. Paul smiled dutifully, longing for the Sales Director to bugger off and accost the next table, so he could go up to his room and call Christie, try to explain his epiphany.

When Paul eventually got his opportunity to escape, 'It's Raining Men' had started playing. As he stood up, his head felt light. Carol from HR was just walking past on her way to the dance floor, and so she dragged him with her, and despite his protestations he was given no choice, and it *was* a catchy song, and it felt so good to finally accept that he was happy to be a father, on top of all the vodka, he was almost euphoric. And then after that 'Step On' came on and the Happy Mondays were his favourite ever band, and then Trevor from Purchasing handed him yet another shot, and soon they were all on the floor doing 'Oops Upside Your Head', and Sonya from Accounts was sitting on the floor in front of him, between his legs, and it felt so great to be carefree, laughing again . . .

When the song finished Sonya giggled as she pulled him up, and he staggered a little, and everything went hazy, and there were bright disco lights spinning, as if inside his eyeballs, and the music was booming, and he had a vague memory of more shots, and more laughter, and more dancing . . . and then the next thing he was aware of was a tongue stuck to the roof of his mouth when he awoke, confused and feeling like he'd had his head bashed in, at some time in the early hours of the morning.

20

Eleanor

Finsbury Park felt marginally less threatening the second time Eleanor visited it, and it occurred to her that familiarity was a powerful weapon in dealing with life. At least she knew exactly where she was going this time, plus she found she was almost looking forward to seeing that handsome young policeman again. There had been something about him, and maybe it was his uniform, or the fact he'd been so kind to her on the phone, which had made her feel marginally less terrified, knowing she had him on her side. And even though the silent phone calls had continued, as had the packages through the post, at least Gavin Hewitson had stopped physically approaching her now.

Eleanor pulled open the station's heavy black door and entered the strip-lit anteroom, moving out of the way of the obese, football-shirted man coming out. She approached the glassed-off front desk purposefully. She was wearing a plain white shirt and tight dark jeans, and her shiny hair cascaded over her shoulders. She looked wholesome and clean, out of odds with her surroundings.

'Hi,' she said to the officer on duty. She tried to rein in her East Coast drawl. 'I'm here to see PC Moffatt.' The policeman, who was large-faced and pasty, immediately stopped smiling and appeared mildly annoyed for some reason.

'Who shall I say wants to see him?'

'Er, my name's Eleanor Jackson. He'll know what it's regarding.'

The policeman lumbered off, and the way he walked it was as if he had one leg shorter than the other. Perhaps he'd been shot, Eleanor thought, and then she remembered that this was England, and the police never got shot here, not even in the roughest parts of the capital. They didn't even have guns, just truncheons, which was laughable really. It must be an odd feeling, she thought, on the one hand to feel so safe that guns were not deemed necessary, and yet on the other to be left so vulnerable. As she sat down on one of the plastic chairs in the waiting room, she noticed a trace of body odour and lavender in the air, and although it was musty it wasn't wholly unpleasant.

After a few minutes the limping police officer returned and sulkily beckoned Eleanor through to the rear of the station, where the policewoman she'd seen on her first visit was waiting for her. Her name was Gillian something, Eleanor remembered – the same as her auntie – and she felt a sudden pang of homesickness again. She swallowed, hard.

'Oh, I thought I was seeing PC Moffatt,' she said as she was ushered down a pale-green corridor that had scuff marks all along it at waist height, as if a bike had been ridden down it.

Gillian looked amused. 'He'll be along in a minute, love.' Did she just raise her eyebrows at her, Eleanor wondered. Was she laughing at her? That wasn't cool. Being stalked wasn't funny.

'OK, now let's see,' said Gillian. 'You received this package when?'

'Yesterday.'

'By post?'

'Yes.'

'Have you opened it?'

Eleanor looked at the policewoman. Was she deliberately being obtuse? She nearly said, 'What does it look like?' but refrained.

'No.' They stared at each other, and the atmosphere was fraught for a second.

Henley. That was it. WPC Gillian Henley. 'Shall we open it now?' WPC Henley said encouragingly, and Eleanor realised that she wasn't being mean at all – it was just that her natural tone was ironic and a smirk was never far from her lips. It seemed to be an English thing. It was disconcerting.

'OK,' Eleanor said. As she stared at the package, she was filled with an odd sensation. It wasn't hatred as such – it was far more complex than that. There was pity there, definitely, for the trouble that Gavin Hewitson had gotten himself into. And there was sadness too – that it seemed Gavin wanted to be loved by her, and she wanted to be loved by Rufus, and Rufus had run back to some unknown other girl, and the world was full of unrequited love and loneliness and fucked-up heads that even the most expensive shrinks in the world couldn't fix, because of course they were fucked up too. She pictured her father in his Upper East Side consulting room, with his high-end clients and his ever-expanding wealth and his estrangement from his second wife and now seemingly his daughter too, and she wondered what it would take, whether it would ever be possible, to make the world roll on by, everyone giving and receiving love in perfect proportions. There being enough love in the world for everyone.

As Eleanor watched WPC Henley pull on a pair of blue surgical gloves it almost felt as if they were about to embark on a weird mash-up of Russian roulette and pass the parcel. The Formica top of the table was scratched, and she could make out the word 'wank' engraved in it. The parcel was wrapped in brown paper. The label was typed. The post code was Camden. WPC Henley tried to pull at the packing tape, but because of the gloves she couldn't find an edge and Eleanor felt tempted to lean over and help her. Next, the policewoman tried with a pair of scissors that she appeared to retrieve from her cleavage, like a magic trick. They both held their breath.

WPC Henley pulled out the items by her fingertips and dropped them on to the plastic sheet on the table between them.

'Oh,' said Eleanor. The panties – black, crotchless, cheap – lay there with all the appeal of roadkill. A novel entitled *Revenge of the Wronged* with a bare-chested man on the cover was its accomplice. The final item was a bullet. WPC Henley was definitely not smiling now.

'Oh, Lord,' she said, as the bullet bounced and clattered, before finally coming to a standstill next to the underwear.

'Yeah, and to think it all started with a ride home from the park,' Eleanor said, and she gave a high little laugh. She could feel her fingers shaking and so she clasped them together, gripped her knuckles, held them in front of her mouth. She gnawed at her left forefinger. The pain seemed to ground her somehow.

'Well, thanks for bringing the package in,' WPC Henley said. 'I'll, er, book the items in.'

'What should I do now?' Eleanor asked.

'What d'you mean?'

'Well, is that a threat on my life? The bullet, I mean.'

WPC Henley looked uncomfortable, and Eleanor could tell that she didn't know what to say. Suddenly Eleanor needed something. Someone. She wasn't sure where things were meant to go from here. She pictured herself walking out on to the litter-strewn street, pushing past harried mothers and loping sullen-faced men who would eye her up, as if she were a foreign object, or a possible target. She visualised negotiating the road junctions, making sure she remembered to look the other way. She imagined Gavin jumping out at her, grabbing her from behind, smothering her screams. She pictured Rufus, naked, entwined in someone else's limbs. She thought of her family, thousands of miles away. She remembered the policeman who had first taken the report, the cute one with the sandy hair and bright blue eyes. Everything felt too much.

'I thought you said PC Moffatt was coming,' she said, staring beseechingly at the older woman. 'Is it possible for you to go get him?'

21

Alex

Alex sat opposite his sergeant, a sparky second-generation Indian woman who, despite barely reaching his shoulder, was as tough as they came. He and Manisha had gone down to the canteen together for once, and Manisha was just finishing up her fish and chips, which had been as disgustingly greasy as the rest of the chef's offerings. Alex had made do with a coffee, as he felt too nervous to eat. He made his request just as Manisha put down her knife and fork, and then he sat back on the black plastic bucket chair, dabbing at his mouth with his fingers, waiting for his boss's response.

'But you took the original report,' Manisha was saying now in her flat Leeds accent. Her eyes slanted upwards, and she had dimples in her cheeks and lustrous skin, and he was curious whether she wore traditional or Western clothes when she wasn't in uniform. Even though they got on well at work – in fact she was the best skipper he'd had – he'd never liked to ask.

'And seeing as you've now interviewed the suspect too,' Manisha continued, 'it makes sense for you to carry the case through. What's the problem?'

'It's just that . . .' Alex didn't know how to broach it. It sounded ludicrous. He could feel himself blushing, but this felt too important to risk screwing up. His future snaked away ahead of him, with a strawberry-blonde vision of loveliness at the heart of it.

'I've got feelings for the victim,' he said now.

'You what?' Manisha looked like she might laugh, and then she didn't. 'For God's sake, Alex, this isn't an episode of *The Bill*, you know.'

'I know, but I didn't want to risk compromising myself. I thought it was better to be honest.' Alex decided not to mention that he was actually planning on asking the victim out, just as soon as he found an opportune moment. It was as if the American girl had cast a spell on him, and he wasn't going to let her go without a fight. It made life feel more exciting somehow. More vivid. It made him feel more alive than he ever had. It seemed she saw him as some kind of saviour now, which was a start, but he had no idea whether she would be romantically interested in him. It didn't help that she already had a stalker, of course, and perhaps an ex-husband, so it was clear that she had quite enough on her plate for the moment. He would certainly have to play it carefully. But it would be worth it. *She* would be worth it. An unfamiliar feeling made its way into Alex's psyche as he sat and watched Manisha take a slurp of her coffee and shake her head at him fondly, as if he were an errant little boy. He wasn't sure exactly what this new emotion was, but when Manisha finally said that, all right then, Gillian could deal with it, he felt his heart jump, and he gave his boss his most impishly twinkling grin of thanks.

22

Christie

Something bad had happened, Christie could tell. It was early Friday evening and the signs could no longer be ignored. When Paul had first come home, she'd felt so guilty about how miserable and moody she'd been since having Daisy, and the effect it must have had on her husband, she'd decided to ignore the fact he hadn't called her the previous night, as he'd said he would. But now she wondered . . .

'So . . . you never actually told me how the conference was,' she said. She was lying along the length of the couch, propped up against the pillows, Daisy in her arms in a state of post-feed milky bliss, the fading slanting sunbeams having rendered her daughter's mood unusually woozy and content. It had been good having Daisy to herself last night, and it had surprised Christie – and although she hated admitting it, somehow it had felt easier without Paul there. Daisy hadn't been nearly so colicky. She hadn't felt quite so useless.

Yet Paul's demeanour now was sending Christie's stress levels rising again. It was almost as if there had been a 'before', when she'd still had trust issues, for sure, but deep down she'd known that Paul was rock solid. (After all, wasn't that partly why she'd married him? Good old steady Paul, who would never ever betray her. And wasn't having been betrayed partly why she'd come back to Manchester in the first place?)

And now this was the 'after', where she had no fucking idea what was going on.

Christie didn't know why she was acting so calmly, but perhaps she was simply buying herself time. She wondered just what had happened at Paul's work do, and whether it might even be her fault. Maybe, ever since she'd seen that ridiculous gypsy woman, she'd unintentionally been transmitting her doubts on to him, and so he'd decided he might as well go ahead and transgress if that was how little she thought of him. Or perhaps she simply hadn't tried hard enough to keep him. She'd spent the last two months dressed in slack-kneed leggings and sloppy sick-encrusted sweaters. She'd had leaking breasts and a screaming baby she hadn't been able to manage. She'd let her hair grow wild. Before this week she hadn't put on make-up in ages. The irony. At last she'd made an effort, and maybe it was too late.

Christie pulled herself up. This wasn't *her* fault. She was a new mother. She was struggling. That was quite normal. It didn't give her husband carte blanche to go off and do whatever. But what *was* 'whatever' in Paul's case? Weirdly, Christie decided she didn't want to know at the moment. What she didn't know wouldn't hurt her. Denial was the key to this right now, she was sure of it. And besides, it was probably nothing. Maybe she just needed to give the poor bloke a break.

Paul still hadn't answered her, and so she ignored him. Daisy started cooing and gurgling, and Christie gazed into her daughter's eyes with a love she wasn't sure she'd felt before. This love was unconditional, and it felt more manageable somehow. After all, she knew she would always love her daughter, whatever happened, whatever she did. It was in the blood. Romantic love could never be that. Not even the most devoted of partners could *guarantee* undying love, no matter how much they believed in it. There were too many opportunities to screw it up. In fact, if anyone did ever manage lifelong devotion, it was seen as almost a miracle. Sixty years of marriage was lauded as an achievement, in the same vein as climbing a mountain or something. She was surprised she hadn't thought of it like that before.

'Christie, I've got something I need to talk to you about,' her husband said at last. He was sitting on the leather chair by the fireplace, although normally he would sit at the end of the couch, her feet pressing against his legs.

Christie carried on gazing at her baby, noticed the little crinkle between her eyes, the exact one Paul had. She noticed the way her skin was blue-tinged at the temples, how her ears were so perfect and pointy, her eyelashes like a dolly's, and she realised she'd never stared at Daisy before. Not like this. Before she'd only ever looked at her daughter with despair that she wouldn't stop crying, or disbelief that she really was here, that she belonged to her, and that Christie was responsible for her – for her very survival. It had been terrifying. Or else she'd peered from the doorway of Daisy's bedroom, to check if she truly was asleep, and then once satisfied would make a swift relieved exit, so as not to wake her.

'Christie!'

The baby jumped at her father's tone, her plump arms and legs startling into a comedy star shape, her little dark eyes widening with fear. It was possibly the first time she'd ever heard a man's voice raised.

'I said, I've got something I need to talk to you about.'

Eventually Christie turned to her husband, and she felt pity for him then, for what he was about to do to their little family.

Never trust never trust never trust.

She felt dangerously calm now, as if the pin had been pulled out of a grenade, and the whole world was waiting for it to detonate.

'What?' she said.

'I . . . I got really drunk last night.'

'I know.'

'How do you know?'

'You look like shit. Your breath still stinks of booze.'

'But it's not just that.'

'I know.'

Paul looked stunned. 'You know what?'

'I know that you slept with someone.' She couldn't believe that she was being so unemotional about it. Is this what betrayal felt like, when it was the second time around? Just a dull sense of inevitability? Proof that you'd been right all along?

'You *WHAT*?' If little Daisy had been disgruntled about her father's tone of voice before, she most certainly objected to it now. The baby erupted into a tirade of howling that belied her size. Paul's fists were clenched, and his brow was lowered, making him look almost Neanderthal. 'What did you say?'

Christie got up from the couch and turned away from Paul, took Daisy over to the window and gently shushed her, tried to rock away her tears. Miraculously, Daisy responded almost instantly. A car passed by on the street, slowly, and it was an old midnight-blue Rover, like her father used to have. She felt blank, on the edge of hysteria perhaps. 'You heard,' she said.

'No, Christie, please.' Paul stood up then, and when she turned from the window at last, he was standing in the middle of the room looking as if he were about to cry. 'You've got it all wrong. Look, yes, I was drunk, and overwrought, and knackered, and worried about you. And then the boss kept ordering shots, and I decided to go to bed, and then this girl from HR persuaded me to have a dance . . .'

'Paul, I don't need to hear this. What is *wrong* with you?'

'But you do need to hear it. I can't live with myself without telling you.' Paul really did have tears in his eyes now. 'And I let my hair down and got gloriously, horribly trashed. And it was because I realised that I *do* want to be a father, and I *do* love Daisy, and . . . ' Paul's voice faded to nothing. Even he didn't seem to know how to take the conversation from there.

Christie found her thoughts drifting, somewhere on the edge of her consciousness. Thin foggy images floated past. Flowing hair, billowing sheets, another girl in *her* student bed. Disbelief. Rage. Madness. The old clairvoyant with her beady eyes and golden hoop earrings, her gleeful proclamations. Her sister, Alice, smiling serenely. Her baby, Daisy, bellowing lustily, her face scrunched up like a popped balloon. And now her husband, Paul – until today the most buttoned-up man in the history of the universe – *weeping*. She couldn't make sense of what was going on. All she knew was that she lived in Whalley Range, and she was married, and a mother, on maternity leave from her job as a history teacher, and she'd had her heart smashed to pieces once already, and now her supposedly doting husband had just told her he'd only just decided he liked being a father. Only just decided he loved their daughter! My God, no wonder they'd all been struggling.

'Fuck off, Paul,' Christie said, and then she walked steadily out of the room and shut the door, the baby in her arms quiet still, but dangerously so, almost certainly on the cusp of apoplexy.

Is it any excuse that this all started because I was treated so badly? It's comforting to think that in a way. I don't want to have to ponder it, but I need to do something, here in the empty air of my prison cell. I spend twenty-odd hours a day in here, and there's only so much TV I can watch, only so long I can stare at the cracks in the walls. I have to live inside my head at least some of the time. I so longed and wanted and needed to be loved. I was so determined to make the best of what life had thrown my way. I made things happen – for my betterment, yes, but for others' too. My kids, for a start. I wanted to be the very best version of myself that I could possibly be. And it worked. For a while.

But now everything is ruined, and I only have myself to blame. The crimes that have been committed are mine. The world has shrunk, and the future feels oppressive, the vacant seconds and minutes weighing down on me, unnerving me. It's ironic that before this there was never enough time. It was life crammed full to the gunnels; busyness writ large. And now there's nothing but time, stretching out and away, to infinity and beyond. I've never thought of it before, but that must be why they call it 'doing time'. I'm doing time, here in this dark empty room, because there is simply nothing else to do.

PART TWO

The middle

2001

23

Alex

He spotted her across the fug of the canteen, and he realised he hadn't seen her in years. He'd just endured yet another gruelling shift, where he'd been told to go fuck himself by a pair of youths on a moped, and then had found an old woman dead in her chair in the freezing cold, and it had made him sad that no one had visited her, or known, and that it had taken the smell emanating from under her door to finally make someone raise the alarm, but that was just how things were at the dawn of the twenty-first century. He was so dead on his feet he'd come in to grab a coffee before heading home. Seeing his old boss perked him up, though.

'Well, hello stranger,' Alex said, tapping her on the shoulder.

Manisha turned and flashed those extraordinary brown eyes at him. Her skin had lost the deep gleam of youth, but she was still slim, still looked younger than her years. She was wearing black bootleg jeans and a neat red cardigan, and there was his answer to what she looked like out of uniform. She seemed taller now, but he realised she must be wearing heels. It seemed she hadn't lost her appetite for police canteen food, though, as a huge slimy-looking portion of shepherd's pie was plonked on her plate, alongside some yellowing peas. Hollow legs, she'd always used to joke when people asked her where she put it.

'Well, I never! Alex Moffatt!' she said, her Leeds accent as strong as ever. 'The only copper I know who married his crime victim.'

'Ha, that's one way of putting it,' he said.

'How are you? Still with the blonde goddess?'

'Yes,' he said. 'In fact, we've got two kids now. You?'

'Nah, no kids,' she said. 'But I finally caved in and got married.'

Alex was uncertain how to respond. 'It's OK, pet,' Manisha said. 'I love him now.' She winked.

'So, what are you up to?' he said.

'I'm in SO15. You?'

Alex felt deflated suddenly. How come Manisha had done so well, made it into such a great unit, and he was still stuck in Response? Why did Manisha have what it took, and yet he didn't? He might have managed to snare Eleanor, but his domestic happiness didn't seem to have helped his career any. Where was he going wrong?

'Well, I'm still working on team at the moment,' he managed, at last. 'Looking for openings . . .' He felt his eyes prick alarmingly, and he coughed, wiped his nose, reminded himself that he was pleased for Manisha. She'd been a good boss, as well as a good laugh, unlike some of the other tossers who'd moved ahead of him. She'd held her own in a culture that had threatened prejudice against her in nearly every way. She'd supported him when he'd asked her to, and in fact was almost certainly partly responsible for the fact that Eleanor was now his wife. Good for her.

'Look,' Manisha was saying now, as she picked up a muffin and added it to her tray. 'We might be looking for new people. I can't promise, pet, but seeing as a) you caught that little stalker bastard and b) you're the subject of one of my very favourite dinner-party stories, why don't you give me a call in a few days?'

Alex nodded, took down Manisha's number, said goodbye . . . and as he left the canteen, he turned and watched her move along the line, tiny and Asian and female, and reminded himself that if she could do it, well, then, sure as hell so could he.

24

Paul

Even though the evening sun was divine, and the air was wondrously hot still, and there was a low babble of kids laughing, and the sound of ball against willow, and one of the fellow dads was telling a pretty entertaining joke, none of it could distract Paul from his perpetual trepidation. Even as he watched his seven-year-old son tearing across the grass grinning, waving a bat, he was waiting for the next transgression. 'Mischievous, my arse,' he'd said to Christie, when they'd last discussed it. 'He's a little fucker,' and he'd only been half-joking. Christie had pretended to be outraged, but in truth she could barely control their youngest child either.

Paul sighed, took a sip from his bottle of beer and wondered why fatherhood was so sodding hard. He and Christie had come a long way from those very early days with Daisy, when Christie had post-natal depression (as it had turned out), and he'd secretly been so terrified of the whole concept of parenthood he'd acted like a bloody robot. Fortunately Christie's meltdown, when she'd assumed that just because he'd got trashed at a work do and failed to call her meant that of course he must have slept with someone, had been the catalyst for them to finally be honest with each other, albeit loudly enough for the neighbours to hear. He couldn't believe it when she'd told him she didn't trust him because of what some mad old psychic had said. He'd expected such lunacy from Alice, of course, but he'd had no idea that *Christie* would pay any attention to that stuff. And the irony was that the reason he'd got so utterly, spectacularly shitfaced was because he'd been so euphoric about realising he loved his daughter. Apparently his rendition of 'YMCA' had been awesome. The Sales Director had never been so impressed with him. It had helped his career no end. Even helped him get a relocation to London.

Paul snorted at the joke's final punchline and turned away from the pitch, just in time to pretend that he hadn't seen Jake jostle another little boy to the ground. He knew if Christie were here she would have gone over and helped the other boy up, but he felt too embarrassed. Unfortunately though, Christie hadn't come with him to the cricket club, even though he'd asked her, even though plenty of the other mothers came and sat on the terrace drinking wine. Paul wasn't daft. He knew Christie had stayed home because she was trying to facilitate his and Jake's bonding, and although he appreciated her efforts, it didn't seem to be working. Good God, he thought wryly, she'd need to try harder than that. Father-and-son trip to the moon, perhaps?

Paul wiped his forehead with the back of his hand, and when he brought it down and looked at it, the skin was slick and sweat-smeared. He was still surprised at how much hotter it felt down south. He glanced over at Jake, who seemed more interested in picking up the stumps and running around with them on his head than even attempting to field, and Paul could sense the other parents' disapprobation. He himself had been so sporty at that age, and yet Jake seemed to have no real interest in any sports – and had two left feet, to boot. Christie would chide Paul for being so hard on Jake, saying he was still only seven and that everyone was different anyway. Paul knew she was right, but still, it didn't make it any easier to witness.

Paul excused himself and walked a little way around the pitch, parallel to the boundary rope, and sat on his own, away from the other parents. His bottle of beer was nearly empty now, disgustingly warm and glycerine-thick. The evening sun was tilting dangerously, and Paul was sitting in the full glare of it, and the grass appeared to be on the cusp of turning from the lush emerald green that only lawns in England seemed to manage, to the scorched hot earth of the African savannah, almost in front of his eyes. He debated whether he should simply take Jake home, as it was apparent that he wasn't having any fun either now, perhaps because the coach was finding it hard to hide his annoyance at Jake's almost-constant misdemeanours. Paul watched tight-mouthed as Jake deliberately threw the ball in completely the wrong direction, so it careered across the grass towards Paul, rather than towards Jake's partner. As the coach yelled at the little boy, Paul's heart went out to Jake, despite himself. How did some men manage such effortless father-son bonding? Where was he going wrong? Or was it inevitable, considering his own upbringing? Or was it simply Jake's character, the type of person he was destined to be?

When the ball came skidding his way yet again Paul suppressed a sigh. He stood up and retrieved it, tossed it gently back towards Jake, who ran over and gamely picked it up, thank goodness, and sprinted obediently towards the coach. And then Jake stopped, looked over his shoulder to give Paul his most insolent grin, before throwing the ball, as hard as he could and uncharacteristically accurately, at the coach's groin.

25

Eleanor

It was funny how people hardly ever spotted that Eleanor was American any more. She had lived in London for so many years that she no longer said 'gas station', or 'garbage', or 'gumboots', and her accent was so soft now that people often missed it. She'd lost her archetypal cheerleader look too. The passing of time, coupled with motherhood, had changed her shape, and her hair had darkened to a dirty blonde which she wore in a simple shoulder-length bob. She knew she wasn't quite the beauty she once had been, but she was happy with how she looked. And so when Alex wound her up at times, hinting that she should lose some weight, she'd just tell him to bog off (now there was a phrase she'd never heard before London!) and mind his own business. Sometimes she suspected that he'd always thought of her as some kind of trophy, and maybe that was part of why she didn't make more effort. It annoyed her. After all, she accepted him exactly as he was, and he should do the same with her too. Plus she'd given him two beautiful children, so he should be grateful!

As Eleanor came downstairs to make breakfast she reminded herself that she loved Alex, even if she didn't get to see him as much these days. He was happier at work again at last, having just got a new job in intelligence, and she was pleased for him – even if he did need to work longer and more irregular shifts than he used to. Before, the pattern had been a clockwork combination of early, late and night shifts that she'd written into her diary months in advance – but in this new job Alex never knew when he'd be called in. She'd got used to it now, though, and it was fine. He'd been passed over for promotion a few times over the years, and she knew it had got to him, although he'd tried to hide it from her. It was funny how he was quite secretive like that, as though he couldn't stand for his pride to be hurt, and she knew underneath the bravado his ego was as fragile as hers had once been. But she guessed it was hardly surprising, after his upbringing, and she thought again how devastating it must have been for him to have been put into care by his own father. She didn't really know how Alex felt about any of it though, as he never talked about it. In fact he seemed to regret ever having told her – as if, through her knowing, his mask had slipped somehow. She'd felt so sad for him.

And so now Eleanor was thrilled for Alex that he'd got this new job, even if he couldn't tell her anything about it. She used to love hearing the tales from when he still worked in the response team, answering an unsavoury smorgasbord of 999 calls throughout the estates of Camden or Kentish Town, or occasionally from one of the enormous homes in Hampstead. There had been extraordinary stories of her husband barging into dark houses, not knowing who was in there or what weapons they had; or talking down suicidal people from the local bridge; or being handcuffed to a ranting stab victim in hospital who'd been arrested for GBH himself. But the tales she'd found hardest to hear were the ones of domestics amongst couples who lived in the most appalling of circumstances, of babies covered in their own faeces crawling on the floor, having just witnessed their mother's head being smashed against the wall by her boyfriend. Eleanor had longed to be able to go round and sweep those infants up and rescue them. Even having had babies of her own hadn't ever taken away that feeling. It was the powerlessness that got to her, and deep regret that this was these children's lot in life – and so perhaps Alex was right when he said that it was better he couldn't tell her anything at all these days, as there were stories far worse than that in his new unit. Eleanor couldn't bear to even imagine.

Eleanor checked in the fridge and realised that there was no milk. Bloody Alex, she thought. He was always coming in at odd hours and demolishing the contents of the fridge.

'Mummy,' came a voice from upstairs. Brianna. 'Mummmmy!'

'I can't hear you, sweetie,' Eleanor yelled back, and turned the radio up a notch. Soon she heard the *thud-thud* of little feet on the staircase.

'I *said*, where are my ballet shoes?' Her seven-year-old spoke with an English accent that verged on plummy, especially when she was cross, like now. Alex spoke with a neutral accent, one of those where you don't even know where someone is from, so Christ knows where Brianna had learned to speak like that. She was such a confident little madam, a star in the making perhaps, whereas Eleanor had been so timid at that age. When she visualised herself walking into that police station all those years ago it almost felt as if she were seeing a different girl, in an entirely other world, and it was hard to connect the two. It was one of those extraordinary stories, where the likelihood of meeting her husband had been so remote, it still felt incredible that she had. She tried to trace the story back to the source, to the moment that changed everything, and decided it had started with her father. If he hadn't forcibly sent her to summer camp, for her increasingly wild-child behaviour in New York, she would never have graduated through to become a team leader years later. She would never have met Rufus. She would never have ended up alone and heartbroken in London. And she would certainly never have got a job as a live-in au pair with the Davenports, nor met their sicko neighbour, who entirely by accident had led her to her future husband.

As Eleanor made herself peanut butter and jelly on toast, she smiled at how some old habits die hard. She sat down at the breakfast bar, where the sun poured through the glass rooflight above her, and it was such a relief to see blue sky for a change. Her mind was drifting today, maybe because her father had called last night to tell her that her grandfather had died, peacefully, in a nursing home in Connecticut – and it seemed to Eleanor now that life carried on, and the passing of time was inexorable and inevitable, until death claimed us all. And although she was sad for her grandpa, the natural deaths of relatives felt like yardsticks in the snow, of where along the line your own life had got to, how much further you still had to travel.

Eleanor took a sip of the black tea she'd made herself and almost spat it out. It was no good. She'd have to go out to get milk. She couldn't survive without a morning cup of tea these days, and that made her truly British in her book. But at least the rain had stopped now. The kids would be fine for five minutes.

As Eleanor came out of the house and walked the fifty yards up the street to the local shop, the air felt clean and fresh, and the springtime sunshine was warm on her back. *That feeling.* The first time the sun has any heat to it. The promise of what is to come over the next several months, despite the inability to ever take the weather for granted in this most unreliable of climates. There was something irresistible about it, about never knowing what each day, or even hour, would bring, meteorologically at least. She entered the shop and picked up a large plastic bottle of semi-skimmed milk. Her heart was still buzzing as she put it down to pay.

'Morning, Eleanor,' said the shopkeeper, looking up from the Turkish newspaper he was reading. 'How are you today?'

'Oh, I'm good, thanks, Hassan.' Eleanor loved the fact that he knew her name, and she knew his, that even though she lived in inner London there was a community here, one she and Alex and the kids were firmly a part of. It reminded her of how her own upbringing might have been, if it hadn't been sawn in two. After the divorce she'd become a mere chattel, ferried back and forth between the rural idyll of Maine and the manic streets of Manhattan. She had become two girls, in two lives, like those twins in *The Parent Trap*. She was amazed she was still sane. She was doing her best to give her own kids the stability she'd missed out on, and even if Alex's erratic shift pattern meant that Brianna and Mason never knew when he would be at home, at least they had both their parents together still. Yes, Eleanor thought, as she turned into her street of Victorian terraces in various states of renovation or dilapidation, England had worked out well for her. It was ho—

Eleanor halted both her thoughts and her body as she saw him – there, right there, directly across the street from her – for the first time in nearly a decade. And although at first she thought she might have been mistaken, she knew that she wasn't, and she felt her heart turn itself to fire, and then to ice, as the sun went in.

26

Paul

On the way back from the cricket club Jake was unrepentant, and that was the thing with him, that he could never be told. Paul had been spilling with fury that Jake was capable of such spitefulness. Sometimes he wished he didn't have to deal with it, and the car was too hot, and his nerves were frazzled. As if on cue to aggravate him further, Jake began to wail.

'Just shut up, Jake,' he said.

Jake stopped. 'I'm going to tell Mummy you said that,' he sniffed, and then he continued crying again, even harder.

'Feel free, Jakey,' Paul said. 'Feel free.' He turned into their road and pulled up outside their house, too fast, scraping the wheels of his beloved BMW against the pavement as he parked. He cursed, then jumped out of the car and yanked open the rear door. He unfastened Jake's seatbelt and hauled him out of his child seat.

'Owww,' said Jake.

'Owww nothing,' said Paul. 'I didn't even touch you.'

'I hate you,' said Jake.

'No, you don't,' said Paul. He screwed up every last bit of his resolve. 'You love me, and I love you. I just won't tolerate this behaviour.'

'I don't love you. I hate you,' Jake persisted.

'What's going on?' said Christie, appearing at the door. She'd obviously just got out of the shower, and her hair was wet, sleeked back from her smooth, even forehead. She was wearing a short brown-and-white-striped T-shirt dress, and she looked great. She would look good in anything, Paul thought. It was something about her body's bone structure, the way she carried herself. Her feet were bare, brown, divine.

'Daddy told me to shut up,' said Jake.

'Only under extreme provocation,' Paul said. He raised his left eyebrow, but Christie looked unimpressed. Daisy appeared at the doorway now, an angelic look on her almost-ten-year-old face.

'Well, that's not on,' Christie said.

'Oh, come on, Christie.' He lowered his voice. 'He annoyed the coaches, then threw the ball at Rashid's nuts, and then he wouldn't stop bawling in the car. He needs to be told.'

Christie didn't look convinced. She took her son's hand proprietorially, which didn't help anything, especially as she was always going on to Paul about presenting a united front.

'Come on, Jakey,' she said, and Paul was convinced the little sod was full-on smirking at him now. 'Let's get you in that bath.'

27

Christie

The bathroom floor was drenched after some over-vigorous wave-making on Jake's part, and right now he was biting bits off the sponge and spitting them out into the bath, no matter how many times Christie told him not to, and he had never been anything different – if Daisy had been a difficult baby, then Jake must have qualified as a bona fide monster. But at least Christie hadn't suffered from post-natal depression the second time around, and now that Jake was older he wasn't quite as much hard work as he once was, and he could be adorable when it suited him. And Daisy herself had grown into a delightful little girl and so, apart from Paul's occasional blow-up with Jake, Ingram family relations were generally OK. Christie even got on quite well with Paul's father these days, the only person in the world who appeared to. He was a curmudgeonly old man, but he was the kids' grandpa and, as she'd said to Paul, he hadn't had the easiest of lives either.

Christie was proud that she and Paul had managed to work through their issues, and their marriage was proof that people can get through the most difficult of times if they try hard enough. She'd long ago got over her insecurities about her husband and trusted him implicitly now, especially as he insisted on always calling her at the end of a work night away now, no matter how drunk he was. They were a team. Even the threat of redundancy and relocating the entire family down south hadn't broken them. When Paul's company had first announced they were shutting the Manchester office, but that he was being offered a job in London, she'd been against it. After all, Paul hadn't much liked the job anyway and, as she'd told him, no money in the world was compensation for doing something you hated. Plus, she hadn't wanted to disrupt the children, and she'd been sure that Paul would find another job locally, if he was patient enough – but Paul had insisted that decent jobs were hard to come by, and that he'd been offered a very generous relocation package, and that it would be insane to turn that down. And so he had quite uncharacteristically thrown himself into the idea of the move and had worked out they'd be able to afford to buy a house if they lived a little way out of London, and he'd even sussed out where the decent schools were, and so at last Christie had agreed. As long as he was sure that that was what he wanted, she'd said, and he'd insisted that it was, and so they'd ended up finding a house in somewhere called Ware.

'Where?' Alice had said, over and over again, when they'd told her, and although Paul had rolled his eyes, Christie had insisted afterwards that her sister was only trying to be funny.

'Well, she's trying, I'll give you that,' Paul had said in response, which Christie thought was a touch harsh, although he might have been joking. She knew Alice could be a bit eccentric at times, especially with her love of all things astrological, which Paul had always thought was completely ridiculous – and, as he pointed out frequently, potentially marriage-wrecking. But Christie had always insisted that their previous relationship problems hadn't been *Alice's* fault.

Jake lay down in the bath and put his head under the water for so long Christie thought he would never come up. She tried to remain patient, knowing that he was looking for a reaction, and so it was only when he looked properly dead that she swept in, scooped him out and told him to stop being so bloody silly – but Jake just laughed and spat a mouthful of water at her. Perhaps, she thought, it was simply that he was still unsettled by the move and was missing his old friends in Manchester. After all, it was hard to tell with kids sometimes. Christie herself was happy down south. She'd met two or three nice friends at the school gates and had found a good job in a boys' comprehensive that she enjoyed, despite southern teenagers seeming as impervious to the rollercoaster life of Henry the Eighth as were their Mancunian counterparts. Her only real worry these days was Paul and Jake's relationship – but what could she do? She couldn't make them get on. She did her best to give them father-and-son time, sent them off to the cricket club together, but it clearly wasn't working. Paul had been fuming earlier about the cricket ball incident, which in truth Christie had found funny, even though she knew that she shouldn't. But when she'd taken Jake off for a bath, purely to give Paul a break, it had only seemed to annoy her husband even more.

As Christie bent down to mop up the ever-expanding puddle on the floor with Jake's towel, she thought that maybe she'd get her mother to have a word with Paul about Jake, as, contrary to the usual stereotypes, Paul thought the world of his mother-in-law, and was more likely to listen to her than he was to his wife. It still made Christie sad that Paul's own mother had died when he was so young, and in such circumstances. Christ, he might pretend to be fine about it, she thought, but no wonder he'd wanted to adopt hers.

There was a creak on the landing. 'Paul!' Christie called. '*Paul!*'

She heard the clatter of shoes on bare stairs, and then Paul stuck his head around the bathroom door. The house was nowhere near as big as they could have afforded in Manchester, and Paul seemed huge as he loomed above her. His glasses immediately steamed up and he peered over the top of them.

'Eee-oop,' he said, in a comedy voice, perhaps to atone for his earlier grouchiness.

'Go away!' yelled Jake, and Christie felt for Paul as his face dropped.

'Be quiet, Jake!' she said. 'Sorry, Paul, I thought you were upstairs. Would you mind getting me a clean towel? I don't trust Jake not to flood the bathroom even further if I leave him.' She glared at her son, who merely looked triumphant.

Paul nodded and disappeared off, before coming back with a frayed pink towel.

'Go away!' Jake shouted again.

'With pleasure,' Paul said, turning on his heel and stomping back down the stairs. Again Christie wondered what she could do about the tension between her husband and her son – until she was distracted by Jake pulling reams of paper off the toilet roll and stuffing it in the basin.

'Just stop that, Jake!' Christie yelled at her recalcitrant seven-year-old. 'And don't be so bloody rude to your father.'

28

Eleanor

Gavin Hewitson, to be fair, looked almost as appalled to see Eleanor as she was to see him. He had cut his hair and his face had filled out, but he retained the same peculiar air of gaucheness, as though he were trying to make himself invisible, and even all these years later it was still unmistakeably him. Eleanor was so flabbergasted she dropped the milk, but the carton was plastic, and it bounced, and she picked it up quickly and carried on walking, praying he wouldn't follow her. Without even having time to think about why she was doing it, she found herself carrying on straight past her house and into the next street, trying her best to look confident, as though that was where she was meant to be going. After a minute or so of head-down, heart-thumping, breath-sapping walking, focused only on her white trainers and the cracks in the pavement, she finally risked a backward glance, but Gavin was gone.

Eleanor was trembling, and somehow she felt even more unsafe now than she had back then. Now she didn't have the choice to just up and flee back home to America – or anywhere else for that matter. This was her permanent home. She had a mortgage, a job, kids in the local schools. But Gavin Hewitson had *been* on her street, possibly knew exactly where she and her kids lived. The very same man who had sent her death threats in the past, veiled or otherwise. As she leant against a low garden wall, she pulled out her mobile and found that her hands were shaking so much she could barely punch in the unlock code. Fortunately Alex was her top number, and as she heard the odd *thrum-thrum* of connection she felt as relieved as she ever had.

The phone cut out after two rings, and so she immediately called back, but this time her husband's phone didn't even connect, and it seemed he'd turned it off now.

'Alex!' she almost howled, stamping her foot in frustration. And that was when it first occurred to her that his new job *seriously* pissed her off. It simply wasn't good enough for the police to always come first and for her and the kids to come second. She'd married a policeman partly because he had saved her all those years ago, had protected her, but now he was no longer around to save her when it actually mattered.

The next number Eleanor tried was also dialled without thinking, and yet this one was picked up straight away, which irrationally only made Eleanor more enraged at her husband, even if he was busy saving the nation.

'Hi, Ellie, how's things?'

'Lizzie,' Eleanor said, 'it's Gavin. I've just seen him on my street.'

'*What?* Oh, you poor love. Are you OK? Did he try to talk to you?'

'No.'

'Well, are you sure it was him? Or that it wasn't just a coincidence?'

'I don't know.' Eleanor gulped a mouthful of air, held it, felt it reverberate in her chest, which was fluttering. 'Lizzie, I'm scared.'

'Where are you? At home?'

'No, I didn't want him to see where I live. I'm in Langley Avenue.'

Lizzie didn't miss a beat. 'Look, just stay where you are,' she said. 'I'll hop in the car and be there in five minutes.'

The food is disgusting here. And yet still I look forward to it, if only to break up the monotony of the solitude. Sometimes I take a look into the inner world that I once knew, and it feels hot, too hot, as if I am burning into the ground, disappearing into a stump of a person. I knew life was getting too dangerous, and that I needed to do something about it. But I'm pretty sure I hadn't meant to do that. And yet what else could I have done? I'd backed myself into a corner, and so perhaps it's inevitable that it's come to this. That I'm officially a criminal.

I attempt some low, breathy intakes of air, try to cool down my thoughts, and I sound like a forties film star, and I see snippets from my early childhood, remember a woman with a fur coat and a cigarette holder, like Joan Crawford. I picture the myriad green of the trees as we crossed the road by the bus stop, remember having to reach up to hold her hand as she steered us towards the park and the swings, my absolute favourite. ***That feeling.*** *I see in my mind's eye a black cat bounding across the path and up the nearest tree, its tail flicking, my giggle of pure delight. I hadn't known what it meant then. That it was a foreboding.*

I was happy back then, I'm sure I was. ***And then I found out.*** *The world feels so much simpler when you don't know, and maybe that was the problem. It's hard to know you've killed somebody. You need to be engulfed in love, wrapped up like a precious doll. And yet instead I was kicked* *around, like a dirty rag doll. And so I railed and I raged and I fucking hated everybody. But not as much as I hated myself. And eventually the hate grew solid and shiny, like armour. I became a glossy, polished version of myself, and I was, to all intents and purposes, happy. For a while.*

PART THREE

The middle, continued

2012 to 2016

29

Eleanor

The rain was spattering on Eleanor's face, and it was freezing, almost literally, and the drops were thin and spitty, and the harder she ran the easier it felt to pretend that all the horrible things in the world weren't happening. These days there seemed to be terror threats everywhere, and she could hardly believe that just this morning a policeman had died and several others had been injured after a so-called jihadist had rampaged through a central London street with a machete. Alex had been on shift, and she'd had to wait forty-five agonising minutes before he'd been able to contact her, and the relief in hearing his voice had made her cry, and it was only then that she'd realised Alex's job was no longer merely conceptually dangerous. Now the threat of attack felt real and ever-present.

Eleanor and the dog turned off the road and pounded up some steps, on to a path that in the summer ran, narrow and straight, through a wide green tunnel of leaves. At those times it felt like the trees were encircling her, as if nature were following her, swaddling her, protecting her from the city, as she passed by the gentrified back gardens that ran down to this old disused railway line. But today the trees were bare and bowed, and it felt as if her nerves were shrieking through her bones, and at first she couldn't work out whether it was the general sense of terror permeating every crevice of the city today, or the latent fear that still lived inside of her, from past traumas.

But no. Today most definitely did feel different. There was something about the grotesqueness of what had happened in town that made her feel the need to move. It was as if running away from herself, from the possibility of the city's new reality, would enable her to escape it. She let Peanut off the lead and upped her pace, her heart roaring and clanging its protest, so much so that she hardly heard the low trill of her phone. She didn't miss a step as she pulled out the phone to answer it.

'Hey, Mum, how's it going?' Brianna spoke loudly, the smooth, confident tones of Eleanor's eighteen-year-old daughter almost gliding through the ether, into her ears. It felt intrusive somehow.

'I'm fine, love,' she said. She stopped running, slowed to a walk. The sky was darkening, preparing for a winter sunset that no one in North London would see today. A single raindrop rolled down the centre of her nose and dangled, about to drip, from its tip. She let it.

'What's up? How's Dad?'

'He's fine, sweetie. Didn't he text you?'

'Yes, he did, but . . . look, was he involved today?'

Eleanor's natural tendency was to lie, to protect her daughter. The fact that she stopped herself, because it seemed too risky, made her feel worse.

'I'm not sure.'

'Oh.' The tone of the single word was noteworthy for its lack of confidence. Eleanor didn't reply, and the silence was a nervy, jangling vibration between them.

'Well, tell him I said hi and to stay safe,' Brianna said, at last.

'I will, sweetie. Don't worry, Bree, it's all fine.'

'This time,' said Brianna, and Eleanor had no answer to that.

As Eleanor hung up, she felt a shiver, so extreme it was like something cold seeping through her head, down into her neck, her shoulder-blades, as if her blood had been frozen and now was slowly melting.

She twisted her neck to look behind her, but there was no one there. And yet, when she turned her head to face forwards again, she saw a solitary man in a thick green anorak walking towards her, head down, and she had no idea where he'd appeared from, and it made her even more nervous. For the first time in years she thought of her stalker, and she felt a dull hum of disquietude. Was it him? *Gavin Hewitson.* He'd come back once before. Was he back again?

Eleanor wasn't in the mood to take a chance today. She turned on her heel and started to sprint in the other direction, away from the man. The rain had done its work and the ground was wet, and cold painful grit was throwing itself up at her bare calves. She turned and looked behind her, and the man was way behind her now. *Of course* it wouldn't have been Gavin Hewitson. The one time she had seen him, over a decade ago, had surely been a coincidence. He'd looked as horrified as she had, perhaps regretting all the trouble he'd got himself into in his love-struck youth, not wanting to risk being arrested again. And afterwards, even though it was totally against the rules, Alex had found out that Gavin had moved to Norwich, and a grateful Eleanor had known better than to tell anyone that she knew.

Eleanor upped her pace as she passed the graffiti-covered bridge and then, after a few more hundred yards, she stopped, panting, out of breath. She raked her hair off her forehead, pointed her face skywards and let the rain come at her. Trailing tangles of creepers were snaking their way through the bare branches above her. As she stared upwards it was almost as if she could see them sprouting and growing, moving towards her, in real time. Everything seemed freakish. She didn't feel like a middle-aged policeman's wife now. She felt like a scared young girl whose boyfriend has abandoned her. A need grew in her, burgeoning like the suckers above her, and it was one she hadn't experienced in such an overtly intrusive way in years. A need for oblivion. Blank, unthinking, unfeeling oblivion. She was finding Alex's job too stressful these days, even when she knew for sure where he was, that he was safe. It was something about the empty impotence. Watching the news and seeing flung body parts, and weeping, collapsing mothers whose daughters were missing, and, a day or two later, the bright hopeful faces of the slaughtered. It was too much at the best of times, but fear for Alex and her children was making her veins crawl and fester, and it was as if she were itching inside, and she couldn't get at herself to scratch it. Her feelings were too trite, the words she knew the newscasters would conjure up equally so – *unutterably sad . . . the loss of innocent lives . . . the malevolence of the attack.* It was hard to know how to respond to it. It was the fact that people could be so full of hate that got to her. That's why she couldn't help but be proud of Alex, that he was a force for good amongst this horrific, ever-present threat that the world endured now. But it didn't stop her wishing he did a different job.

She just wanted him to stay safe.

Eleanor remained stationary. The dog hovered, starting to whimper. The crackling of soft matter underfoot was so subtle as to be barely audible through the downpour still sieving its way through the trees. Her face was wet with cold rain and hot tears. She kept her head thrown back, to the elements, despite the danger she felt, closer now. She was a still-attractive woman in all-black Lycra, provocatively curvy, ripe for picking. It would be easy, so very easy, for someone to take her by the throat and twist her to the ground. So she wasn't really surprised when she felt his mouth close to her ear, and smelled the damp staleness of cigarettes. His voice was shocking in its bald desire.

'Hello, Eleanor,' he said.

30

Paul

Paul had had a bad stomach for ages, but he'd ignored it. Finally though, he'd capitulated to Christie's entreaties and gone to the GP, and they'd done all the tests, and when Paul had gone back for his follow-up appointment, the doctor had confronted him, not aggressively exactly, but certainly without any frills. Dr Singh must have been in his sixties, with a short, neat white beard and side-parted hair, and it was clear that he had seen it all in this practice, and besides he only had ten minutes per patient, so 'anxiety and depression' it was then, and there was no time for small talk.

And so now Paul was walking home from the surgery through the housing estate, with a prescription for happy pills in his pocket, and it was like a shameful secret, and he wondered how it had come to this. He wouldn't take them, of course. The doctor didn't have a clue what was going on in Paul's head: he barely knew him. In over a decade of living in Ware, Paul had only been to the surgery once before this. Paul rarely got ill. He certainly didn't suffer from depression – Dr Singh didn't know what he was talking about. Paul wondered what he should say to Christie. He knew she was worried about him, kept saying he was working too hard, but Paul knew it wasn't that. His gastric problems had first started a few months ago, after his mother-in-law had suffered a severe stroke, which had overnight rendered her crooked-mouthed and helpless. It had been harrowing to witness – plus Paul and Christie had been exhausted by the sudden change in their schedules, by having to travel up to Worcestershire at least weekly for months, until poor Jean had finally died, which had devastated Paul almost as much as it had his wife. Christie was being so stoic though, mainly because there was still no let-up, as now she had her father to think of too. And although Paul normally went with her to visit him, Christie had insisted on going alone today, saying that she and Alice would be busy helping her father go through their mother's things, and that Paul had his doctor's appointment anyway. Paul hadn't liked to argue. Christie had been in one of those moods.

As Paul crossed the road outside the pub where he and Christie had sometimes used to go, before events had overtaken them, he found himself admitting that perhaps the doctor had been right that his mental state wasn't the best. It seemed it had been creeping up on him for years, undetected until it was almost too late. But there was something about time passing, and his mother-in-law dying, and the children growing, and his difficult relationship with his father and his son, that had made Paul start to seriously doubt himself again, wonder where he was going wrong. Maybe he'd been right all those years ago that fatherhood wasn't for him. He loved his kids, of course he did, but Jake was something else these days. Paul didn't know what the hell to do with him, but he was eighteen now and at university, had no obligation to listen to his father, or show him a modicum of respect.

It was a dismal winter's day, one where the clouds seemed to meld with the rooftops, making everything dreary. Paul's eyes were watering – from the cold, surely. An older woman with long silver hair, wearing a shiny blue coat and flip-flops, was bending down to clean up after her dog, a white yappy creature that Paul had seen a thousand times but had never paid attention to before. The dog walked stiffly and was obviously ancient, and he wondered how long the poor creature had left. He wondered why the woman was wearing flip-flops, in this weather. She caught him staring at her, but instead of smiling she looked alarmed, as though she thought he was a weirdo. And maybe he was.

Paul nodded awkwardly and turned away, walking quickly down the hill to diminish the threat the woman had appeared to feel. He decided he wasn't going to tell Christie what the doctor had diagnosed. She was grieving, had enough on her plate as it was right now. And besides, Paul had always been taught it was better to be circumspect, to not confess to weakness – so surely in the current circumstances staying quiet was the best course for everyone.

31

Eleanor

It was a shock to see him. Afterwards she wasn't sure whether it had simply been the fear that had made her heart go crazy, as initially she hadn't even recognised him. Back when she'd fallen in love with him, at an idyllically located summer camp in the States, he'd been wiry, with high cheekbones and a wide, flaring mouth. Now, his face was rounder, and older, and his hair was no longer floppy, but instead neatly trimmed, and his Barbour jacket was befitting a man of his age – and yet the flicker of anguish in his eyes was still sexy somehow. Seeing him here was traumatic, on so many levels.

'Oh, my gosh . . . Rufus?' For a moment she was lost for words. 'What in hell do you think you're *doing*? You . . . you frightened me.'

'I'm sorry,' said Rufus. 'I didn't mean to. I only realised it was you when I got close enough, and then I just wanted to say hello.'

Eleanor tried to catch her breath, calm the thrumming that was working its way up and down from her stomach to her throat, as if he'd physically punched her in the gut. Yet to be fair to him, he wasn't to know that she was an overly nervous survivor of stalking. She stared at her ex-boyfriend, and he seemed to have been distorted. It was as if she were looking at him in one of those fairground mirrors. Shorter. Stockier. *Older*.

'Well, you shouldn't go round creeping up on people like that,' she said at last. She could hear that her tone was hostile, although she hadn't necessarily meant it to be. It must have been the fear, mixed with the relief, and the utter mind-fuckedness of his appearing back in her life, after twenty-odd years. The boy who had broken her heart. Here, on her patch. It was too much.

'How are you, Eleanor?'

'I'm fine. You?'

'Not too bad,' Rufus said. 'I live around here now.'

'Oh.' She didn't volunteer that she did too, and she wasn't sure why. She didn't know what it was about Rufus. He was getting to her all over again. Her emotions were heightened by the unexpectedness of seeing him, certainly, but it was something else too. Even his appearance confused her. It was as if he'd aged overnight but now, while she gazed at him, was miraculously growing younger and younger again, like in *The Curious Case of Benjamin Button*. She wondered if that was how it felt to Rufus too, seeing her for the first time in over two decades. Her wrinkles, magically dissolving, like ripples on a lake. Her shorter, primmer hair growing long and luscious again. Her softer, saggier shape firming up, as if pneumatically.

'Well, look, it's great to see you,' she said. 'But . . . but I need to get going.'

'I'll walk with you,' he said. 'If you don't mind?'

Eleanor didn't have a clue whether she minded or not. Her entire body felt as if it were crawling with too many nerves, too much emotion. Part of her wanted to throw herself into his arms and beg her to hold him, and another part wanted to launch herself at him with a hammer. But mostly she felt shocked. Traumatised even. She wondered where he was going, what he was up to. As she walked alongside him, even in the rain there was a buzz of magnetism between them, but as well as attraction there was repulsion now too, in the very base sense of the word. She wanted him to stay here, but she also wanted him to go, not intrude on her memories of the beautiful complicated boy who had loved her once. She wanted the heartache to remain pure and untainted, fossilised into something solid, something that grounded her in her marriage to Alex. Rufus's reappearance was disruptive. It was disrupting her truth, her life, the history of her love.

'So, what are you up to these days?' she asked, as politely as if he were a distant relative at a funeral.

'Oh, this and that,' he said, as he ambled along beside her. It was his clothes that unsettled her the most. She could forgive the fact that he'd grown older. She could even forgive that he'd cut his hair. But Rufus had always been delicate, and rakishly bohemian – and now his dress sense was so . . . sensible. It was discomfiting. The silence between them was mile-wide now, the rain-filled air jangling, and it was almost a relief when they reached the bridge by the school. It wasn't the exit from the path that she normally used, but she felt the need to get away, give herself some time to work out what in hell was going on.

'So, this is me,' she said, as brightly as she could manage, but her tone gave her away. She called Peanut, to put him on the lead.

'Eleanor, will you have coffee with me?' Rufus said, suddenly. 'It's nothing inappropriate, I promise. I just want to have the chance to explain myself.' His eyes were glassy, and she assumed it was the cold wind. 'I've always felt bad about what happened between us.'

'Rufus, it's all in the past.'

'Nelly, please,' he said, and the nickname made them both start. His tone was softly deep, and it sent a sliver of memory through a tiny hole in her heart. 'Look, I know you're married,' he continued. 'It's nothing untoward, I promise.'

As Eleanor stared at Rufus, she was so confused she didn't know what to think. But now there was that look there again, deep in his eyes, and it made her respond to him, made her want to understand. Maybe a post-mortem would help both of them.

Who was she kidding? Eleanor knew the risks of seeing an ex-lover again, especially one who had dumped her in such cruel circumstances. She also knew that Rufus had been her very first love, and that you never truly got over those. Alex might have rescued her from an unhinged stalker, but Rufus had been the one who had woken her up to what love even was. Surely it was an insane idea to agree to meet up with him . . . and she found herself wanting to ask Alex what his view was, but he was working, and she didn't know when she'd next get to speak to him . . . She tried to resist the thought, but it was there. Why should she consult with her husband anyway, when she could never bloody get hold of him?

'OK,' she said.

32

Paul

In a fit of sudden and unheralded energy, Paul loped up the beige-carpeted stairs of their new, bigger house, doubled back along the landing, yanked open the cupboard door and took out the long metal pole that was propped up in the corner, where he knew it would be. He was filled with an enthusiasm he hadn't felt for a while, and it was a relief. At least this was something concrete he could do to try to cheer up his wife. It was clear the thought of Christmas this year was hard for Christie, although she would never say it. Even the prospect of the kids coming home from university hadn't seemed to lift her, and it was as if she felt torn as to what was the best thing to do. To decorate or not to decorate. To strive to be festive, or not bother pretending. Daisy and Jake were far too old to get all excited about Christmas anyway, she'd said, and so they'd agreed to skip doing the tree this year. Paul thought it was partly a guilt thing, so soon after her mother's funeral – but what was the point, Christie had said, seeing as they were going up to Worcestershire to spend Christmas at her dad's? They wouldn't even be there.

Paul wasn't into grand romantic gestures. His and Christie's relationship had never been a wine-and-roses sort of affair. He wasn't that kind of a man. The right words had always eluded him when Christie was upset, and he wasn't a neck-rubber or a foot-massager either. There was caring and then there was wet, he always said to Christie when she tried to persuade him. But this was a good idea, he was sure of it.

Paul hoisted up the pole and used its hooked end to unlock the hatch and pull down the ladder. The metallic click as it finally slotted into its locked position was curiously satisfying. As he climbed the rungs, he realised he hadn't been up here since he'd put away the decorations from last year, all the way back in January. They hadn't needed their suitcases or camping stuff this year, which were pretty much the only other reasons he ever went up in the loft. There'd been no time for holidays in between work and dashes up to Worcestershire. Paul wondered why Christie had been so insistent she went alone today. Perhaps she just hadn't wanted to risk there being any friction between him and Alice, potentially upsetting her father. Paul knew he needed to be more tolerant of Christie's sister, especially now Jean had died. He still couldn't work out what it was about Alice that got to him so. It wasn't only her ludicrous obsession with Tarot cards and crystals and what the stars supposedly ordained. Sometimes, in his more enlightened moments, Paul thought he might even be jealous of Christie's closeness to Alice. After all, he had no relationship with his own sibling, didn't even know where he was these days.

As Paul hauled himself through the hatch opening, he began to have misgivings about his mission, as though this might be a Very Bad Idea. And then he told himself that Christie wasn't being anti-Christmas per se – just apathetic about it. In fact, she seemed to find it hard to enjoy anything at the moment, but that was normal after bereavement. He just had to give her time.

The loft had a chilled, faintly animal smell about it. Paul knew there were mice up here – he and Christie could hear them sometimes, scuttling their way across the boards when they were in bed, and the noise the creatures generated convinced Christie they were rats, but Paul had persuaded her that it always sounded much worse than it was. Now he wasn't so sure. Mice he could deal with, but rats were filthy and spread disease. Even now he could hear scratching sounds – or was he imagining them? Perhaps he should get the pest-control people in. He didn't like the idea of killing things, but he couldn't let the situation get out of control. As he pulled himself to his feet, he flicked on the light and stared fruitlessly into the darkest corners. The air hung sullenly, shrouded in an orange dusty glow that emanated from the bare light bulb. At last his eyes adjusted enough for him to see that the Christmas decorations were over near the camping stuff, where he'd left them, the enormous tree they'd bought last year neatly in its box. Remembering how much Christie had loved that tree made Paul feel more confident. Doing this would make her happy, he was sure of it.

Being tall, Paul had to bend his head to cross the loft. Just as he reached the decorations, he heard the scrabbling noise again. It appeared to be coming from the corner nearest to him, just beyond where the boarding-up ended.

Paul stayed still, listening in the dim light.

Nothing.

And then he heard it again.

He bent down quickly, snatched at the loft insulation and ripped it back. He wasn't sure what he was hoping to find, or what he was planning on doing with whatever he did find. But it was too dark for him to see much anyway – he'd have to bring a torch up to have a proper look. As he removed another clump of insulation wool his hand hit something, and it made him jump. Thankfully the object was cold and hard, definitely not rat-like – and when he realised that it was a small leather suitcase, charmingly battered and stickered, he wondered what it was doing there. He'd found it in a similar place in their old house in Manchester, and he'd initially assumed that it had been left by the previous owners. But when he'd opened it up and started rifling through, a sick kicked feeling had begun building in his chest cavity – and so he'd closed the case and replaced it where he'd found it. Afterwards he'd pretended he'd never seen it, that it didn't exist – even to himself, it seemed, which had taken some doing. But now, mysteriously, here it was again, and he had no idea how it had got here – and, more to the point, when. To his knowledge he was the only one who ever came up here.

Just as Paul bent down to pull out the case, his head spinning with memories, he could dimly hear his mobile ringing downstairs, and then when that cut out, the annoying sing-song tune of the home phone – but he knew that by the time he got down to it he would have missed whoever was calling. A scurrying, scuffling noise started up once more, making him flinch. He pressed his hands to his temples, and he could feel his heart pumping through his fingertips. Still the ringing continued, hitting a frequency inside of him, scraping along the sheerest edges of his nerves. *When was it ever going to stop?*

Paul brought his hands down from his face and made them into fists, a slow-burning anger building inside him, one he hadn't even known existed still, as the phone carried on.

33

Eleanor

When she arrived home Eleanor still felt uneasy, and in a way she wished Alex were here, so she could tell him face to face about Rufus – but he wasn't, and if she called him, he'd probably be busy anyway. Instead she'd just have to make do with a cup of tea to calm her nerves, and again she marvelled at how English she'd become. But when she went to the fridge, inevitably there was no milk, and these days it wasn't her husband who drank it all.

Bloody Mason, Eleanor thought, not entirely benignly, as she slammed the fridge door. Her son might be a lovely boy, but he seemed to eat and drink more than the rest of the family put together. Peanut looked hopeful at the possibility of another walk, seemingly aware of the significance of the empty milk carton, and the cute way he cocked his head at her always got her . . . and so eventually she capitulated.

It had only just stopped raining when she left the house and between the rooftops further up the hill she could make out the faint stump of a rainbow. She couldn't remember ever seeing one there before, and somehow it reminded her of Rufus's garden in Hampstead, the bright primary colours . . . and she couldn't believe he had arrived, without warning, back into her life and, even more extraordinary, that she'd arranged to have coffee with him.

On impulse Eleanor carried on past the shops and continued walking, as if chasing the end of the rainbow, and it seemed it wasn't only the sudden reappearance of Rufus that was unsettling her. It was the country's ever-heightening security threat too, and this crazy weather, and her mind was refracting, streaming in and out of the past, bouncing between absent do-gooder husbands and cruel past lovers and evil murderous terrorists. She wished she could turn off her thoughts, but instead it felt like they were revving up, amplifying, and it was making her more anxious than she'd felt in ages. Even the humiliation she'd felt at being dumped by Rufus seemed fresh all over again.

Eleanor stopped and stared up at the sky. She'd been proud of herself, for coming through that. She'd been so lucky that Lizzie Davenport had taken a chance on her, as it could have all turned out so differently. Even now, despite the family having moved out to the country in recent years, she still sometimes saw Lizzie and the twins, who had turned from cheeky toddlers into young adults the Davenports could be proud of. 'And you should be proud too,' Lizzie often said to Eleanor. 'You were marvellous with them.' Despite the age gap, or perhaps because of it, Lizzie and Eleanor had remained friends, and in a way Lizzie had become the parent that Eleanor had never had. One who had been utterly consistent. Who was always there for her. Oliver, of course, had been another story, but even now Eleanor preferred not to think about that – or, perhaps more pertinently, about what Lizzie would do if she knew.

Eleanor's phone rang, and when she saw who it was, she found herself hesitating before answering.

'Hi, princess,' said Alex. 'How are you?' Normally Eleanor liked that he still called her that, but today it made her feel awkward. Their joke had always been that she'd been the princess trapped in the tower, who'd been rescued by her knight in shining armour – or at least one in a policeman's uniform. Having someone in authority who had looked out for her, who made her feel safe after her ordeal at the hands of Gavin

Hewitson, had been a powerful thing. But she'd been good for Alex too, Eleanor reminded herself. In a way it felt as if they'd saved each other somehow, and maybe that was why it had worked between them. And yet . . . lately Eleanor had found herself wondering whether she and Alex would ever have got together without such an impetus, a thought she would swiftly bury.

'I'm OK,' she said now, to her husband.

'What are you up to?'

She hesitated, tempted to be honest . . . and then at the last minute decided not to mention Rufus. 'Just out with the dog getting milk, seeing as Mason's drunk it all again. Like father, like son, huh?' She laughed. 'What about you? Taken out any terrorists or Russian spies this morning?'

'Ha,' said Alex, noncommittally. It had always been that way in this job, but it no longer annoyed her. In the beginning she'd tried to wheedle things out of him, had used every single one of her wifely charms, but he had argued, quite reasonably, that although he believed her *now* when she swore that she would never tell, what about if they split up because he ran off with another woman, or beat her up or something? She used to chastise him, retort that that wasn't a very nice thing to say, but he'd insisted that it was true, and she supposed it was. A woman scorned and all that. And although she'd sworn that she wasn't the vengeful type, he'd signed the Official Secrets Act, and so she'd had no choice but to accept it. (He hadn't seemed to mind bending the rules to find out where Gavin Hewitson lived though, she'd thought as he'd lectured her, but had decided not to mention it.)

'When are you coming home, Al?' said Eleanor now.

'I'm not sure, love.' She could feel the tension in his voice. 'It . . . it might be a week or so.'

'Oh. OK.' He'd never been away that long before. She wondered if he would be going abroad, to Turkey or Syria perhaps. She knew he carried his passport at all times, but he never said where he was.

'Alex?' she said.

'Yes, sweetheart.'

'Take care of yourself.'

'I will, love,' he replied. His voice was full of its usual tenderness, but there was tension too, and it made her feel bad that he was away working, putting himself at risk for the sake of the country, and she was planning a secret assignation with her ex-lover. She could hear the break in his voice as he added, 'I promise.'

34

Christie

By the fourth time Christie tried to get through to her husband, her early annoyance had begun to tip over into genuine worry. Where the hell *was* Paul? Why couldn't he ever bloody well answer the phone? Much as she loved her husband, he could be an airhead at times, and he'd get so caught up in whatever he was doing that she swore half the time he didn't even notice the phone ringing. But she'd been trying to reach him for over an hour now, and something didn't feel right. She'd originally wanted to talk to him about what to do about her poor father, who seemed frailer than ever today, and not quite with it, having deteriorated so fast since his wife's death it was frightening to witness. Her father had always been such a smartly dressed man, but now he wore the same old pair of trousers and jumper over and over again, and when Christie had tried to challenge him on it, he'd bellowed that it was the outfit he'd last held his wife in, and so he'd damned well wear it for as long as he wanted, thank you very much. It was so odd to see him like this. He'd never been fiery before, had never even cussed, but now he seemed consumed with something unmanageable, and it broke Christie's heart to see him so fragile and wretched. It was almost as distressing as watching her mother dying – and in many ways it felt as if she'd lost them both now. She would be the parent from now on, and it was a disquieting realisation.

'How *is* Paul?' her father said now, from his chair by the gas fire, as Christie hung up her phone yet again. A film of dust, interrupted only by footprints, coated the dark wooden floor, and yet whenever she tried to get the vacuum out, he'd get agitated and insist that he would do it later.

'Oh, I don't know, Dad. He won't answer the phone, as usual. I should put a bloody bleeper round his neck.'

'Hmmm,' said her father, and Christie wondered what he meant by that. His voice had a lucid tone to it suddenly that she neither liked nor recognised. Yet now she came to think of it, Paul hadn't seemed quite himself on the phone earlier. 'Shifty' was perhaps too strong a word, but there had been something he wasn't telling her.

'What's wrong, Christie love?' her father said. He struggled to his feet and shuffled towards her, and he had an old-man smell now, as though he never washed any more, and when he put his hand on her arm it was brown-spotted and wrinkled, and so much smaller than she remembered. He seemed to have been shrinking from the moment his wife had first fallen ill, and Christie wondered what he was doing for eating. It felt desperate, the thought that he might be starving himself to death, intentionally or otherwise. She wished she could simply take him with her back to Hertfordshire and be done with it, but she knew he'd refuse to come. This was his home, after all.

'Nothing, Dad,' she said. 'It's all fine.'

'If only your mother were here,' he said. 'She'd know what to do.' He took out his handkerchief, which was grey and stiff and unsavoury, and blew his nose noisily. As tears started streaming down his face, Christie realised that before her mother's stroke, she'd never seen him cry. Not even once. And yet these days he seemed unable to stop. She wished now that she'd let Paul come with her, especially as Alice had bailed out anyway – saying her husband had the flu and that she didn't want their father to catch it – but that was probably for the best anyway. Alice never had been able to handle the grittier parts of life. She preferred to exist in her midnight-blue astrological world, where the future was mapped out for her in the sun and the moon and the stars. And although Christie didn't mind having to shoulder the burden, she didn't know what to do, how to make her father feel better on her own. She stared at her mobile, cursed at the number of times she'd rung Paul.

'Christie, love, it's OK,' her father said now.

'What's OK?'

'*It's* OK.' He stared at her, and dust swirled and settled on a memory, and it was as if he were communing what he wanted to say to her through the power of thought alone. Her father's eyes were watery-grey and wise, and somehow she knew exactly what he was trying to tell her. It was about Paul. The blue glass bottles on the windowsill shone briefly through their layer of grime as the sun came out. Somewhere a dog exploded into a fit of hysterical yaps, too far away to dent the strange atmosphere of intimacy.

'I worshipped your mother,' he said now. 'Worshipped her. Like Paul does you. And so he should.'

'Oh, Dad.' Christie's heart was aching.

'Go home to him, love.' Her father's voice sounded stronger now, full of purpose again. 'He needs you. I'm just an old man. Nothing will bring your mother back, and that's all that I want. Go home to Paul. And please, Christie, don't feel guilty, love. About anything.'

35

Paul

Insidiously or otherwise, anger had played a large part in Paul's life. As he knelt in his neat, rodent-invaded loft, glaring at the leather suitcase he'd tried so hard to forget ever existed, the sound of the phone downstairs still ringing in his ears, he realised that this was the one secret he'd never confided in Christie about, nor confronted her with. He was surprised at how much it still hurt. Women were a mystery to him, and surely always would be. And despite the fact that he knew he'd always love Christie, regardless of what had happened in either of their pasts, this seriously pissed him off.

Paul continued to observe the suitcase, in the way you might study an old person to look for clues as to their health, or otherwise. The leather was ancient and battered, and he knew inside there were photos and letters and poems from a gorgeous young girl who'd once written with such promise and passion, and he'd found it hard to take that Christie had never written anything like that to him. And because he hadn't ever told her he'd found the case, he'd never been able to discuss it with her, what it had meant – and maybe that was why his jealousy had grown over the years, expanded into the air around the secret, constricting it, threatening an explosion. He could have simply disposed of the suitcase of course, and then denied all knowledge if ever challenged, but he'd felt conflicted. The letters were too precious to throw away, and yet too torturous to keep. The photos had been unbearable to even look at. And so he'd compromised, had put the case back where he'd found it – but he'd never been able to fully forget about it. And now here it was again, and he couldn't understand it. How had she managed it? *How much deception was she capable of?*

Paul took a deep breath and screwed up his eyes tight, so he couldn't see the images that he knew were in the case, threatening to invade his brain – of her, naked and young and supple, with a boy with floppy hair, as if he were out of *Brideshead Revisited*, bare-chested, sleek, leaning over her—

Paul turned sharply away, and tried to think of other, less distressing things. Christie would get home from Worcestershire later, tired and sad, and the house would unexpectedly be all Christmassy, and she'd be thrilled by it, and there would be mulled wine on the go, and he'd cook her steak and chips, her favourite, and they'd watch a new episode of *Peep Show* he'd recorded, and that would cheer her up. And then in a couple of days the kids would be home from university, and that would buoy her yet further. He'd missed the children too, of course, but especially Daisy, and maybe that's secretly how all fathers felt about their little girls.

Paul knew he was kidding himself. It seemed there was something about the loneliness of the house, the empty air in the rooms beneath him, that was making him feel like this. And yet he couldn't deny that he'd never been as close to Jake as he was to Daisy. After all, Jake had never looked like him. He'd never been like him . . .

And now he could feel the doubts resurfacing, jabbing at him, tormenting him . . . and Paul knew he needed to get the hell out of this loft. Yet still he sat there, rooted to the spot, lost in the past, remembering how Christie had fallen pregnant soon after she'd gone to a Cambridge reunion. Maybe she still hadn't trusted him back then, had been after revenge about his supposed infidelity. It wasn't beyond the realms of possibility . . .

And now Paul felt racked with the desire to just know. It was as if all the stress of the past few months had caught up with him. Perhaps he should force himself to study the pictures, X-rated or not, try to spot the resemblance. And if there was a likeness, maybe he could then get a few strands of Jake's hair, to make absolutely sure. There must be some kind of service he could find on the Internet.

Jesus Christ. He was being crazy. Stark raving bonkers. Paul knelt forward and punched his forehead, to get the demons out. It must be the suitcase that had unnerved him, on top of everything else. It had been a crap few months, but he didn't know what to do to make anything better. It didn't help that his own grieving was so far down the pecking order. Christie. Christie's father. The kids. They'd lost a mother; a wife; a cherished grandmother. All Paul had lost was a mother-in-law, and you're not meant to be sad about those. Paul had heard all the jokes. And yet he'd always had such a strong bond with Jean, and he missed her too. She'd been the mother he'd never had. And grief did funny things to people.

Paul shifted on his haunches, tried not to let it come, but as ever the memory invaded, with impunity, and he wished he could stop it. Unwillingly he pictured himself, back when he was five. Everything else was a blur, but that scene was still remarkably, traumatically, clear. He saw his pudding-bowl haircut, the mustard polo-neck jumper his mother had knitted for him but that was now on the small side. He could almost feel the wool rough against his skin, making his neck red raw where he couldn't help but scratch it. He could see his father coming home from the hospital, the bulk of his car coat, the smell of cigarettes. The feeling of excitement turning to one of utter dread. Of being taken into the front room, where all the brass ornaments were, still highly polished back then. Of being lifted on to the high hard couch and told, quite matter-of-factly, that his mummy had died and wouldn't be coming home, and neither would the baby for now. His father walking out of the room and disappearing upstairs, and it being rarely spoken of again. It seemed insane now, that Paul hadn't even got to go to the funeral.

Paul wiped his nose, forced himself back to the present. His mother-in-law had died too now, and she'd been the one person who'd always championed Paul to Christie. Even in the middle of the worst ructions, she'd told her daughter in no uncertain terms that one drunken escapade at a work do didn't mean he'd jumped into bed with someone else, no matter what some dodgy fortune teller had said. Paul was nothing like Christie's ex, thank the Lord, Jean had said, before telling Christie to stop stropping around and just get on with it. Paul would always be grateful to Jean for that, for believing in him still.

Paul sat on his hands, to stop himself reaching forward and yanking the case open, searching for the photos that might prove or disprove his suspicions. He'd never seen his rival's face – in the couple of photos he had looked at, it had been obscured in ways he'd rather not think about. He groaned then, a deep throaty agonising bestial call into the void. He needed to get a grip, gain some perspective.

Paul pushed the suitcase into the corner, unopened, and turned away from it. Now wasn't the time to be thinking about Jake's parentage. It was an outrageous suspicion anyway, one that would devastate both his wife and his son if they knew. Plus he needed to get on with trying to make the house nice for Christie. He adjusted his glasses, swallowed down the tense hard knot in his throat and started lugging the long oblong box that contained the Christmas tree across the breadth of the loft, towards the hatch.

36

Christie

It was only once she was on the M1 that Christie had finally managed to get through to Paul. She'd been deeply worried by then, as it was unlike him not to have got back to her for such a long period of time – but the initial relief that he was still alive had worn off now, and she was feeling unsettled again. She was sure there was something odd going on. He'd sounded out of breath and harried when he'd answered the home phone, just as she'd been about to hang up for the umpteenth time. Although over twenty years of marriage had put paid to Christie's doubts that maybe he was off shagging the neighbour, his manner just now had made her uneasy. She'd tried her best to seem friendly and relaxed, had simply asked him what he was up to, but he'd definitely sounded shifty and defensive, as though he hadn't wanted to talk to her, in case he gave something away. She wondered what it could be.

The traffic was sluggish, but there were no roadworks, no obvious signs of an accident. Sheer weight of traffic seemed to be the culprit, and the phrase made Christie picture obese cars with bulging tyres stuck in hot tarmac. She was bored, and sad, and worried about her father, who she was driving away from, leaving him bereaved and alone. And yet she was somehow serene too, as if she were floating above the motorway, looking down on all the stressed fed-up people who were trying to get home. She'd been up and down this motorway so many times of late, and its mood seemed to vary according to the time of day. In the mornings, there was a combustible mix of road users in various states of hurry, which resulted in a fractious atmosphere and a heightened chance of accidents. People stressed to the eyeballs that they were going to be late for something crucial – a meeting, or an interview perhaps – would huff and rev, chop lanes, drive far too close to each other, although Christie was sure it couldn't make more than a few seconds of difference to the lengths of their journeys. And then there were those who seemed quite happy to be crawling along, perhaps listening to Radio 2, for as long as it took, because that was better than sitting at their desks in the jobs that made them miserable. Finally, there were the people for whom driving was simply their job: the long-distance lorries and National Express coaches, the parcel-delivery vans, all clogging up the lanes, like cholesterol. All of them heading staunchly in the same direction, yet each with a unique destination, their own story to tell.

But in the evening, as it was now, the motorway seemed quite different. It was as if everyone had the same dull desire to get home, and so no one would ever let anybody in, but people were too tired to get overly het up about it either. Christie was glad she'd never had to do a commute like this every day. It would send her crazy.

As the traffic slowed to a crawl once more, Christie dropped down into second and yawned. Her mind felt vacant now, and bright somehow, like heaven. The car was too warm, and her eyes were drooping, as though she might actually nod off to sleep. It was a delicious kind of drowsiness, and it felt like a relief from the sadness of her current reality, and she'd barely slept last night, and she was *so* exhausted . . .

Wake up!

Christie shook her head, slapped her face, wound down the window. As a further diversionary tactic, she tried to call Daisy, but she couldn't get through to her daughter. She knew there would be no point trying Jake. His phone only ever went straight to voicemail, and it was clear that her son's idea of a phone was as an outgoing communication device only. Jake called the shots when it came to interpersonal engagement, and it was infuriating. She tried him anyway, predictably fruitlessly, and then shrugged her shoulders half-fondly, half-exasperatedly, and turned on the radio. After a couple of anodyne tracks, the opening tinkly piano notes of 'Driving Home for Christmas' finally released Christie from her soporific state. There was something about the fullness of the song, its heart-lifting expansiveness, the rich warm tones of the singer's voice, that caused a surge of emotion that had eluded her up until now. It was almost as if there just hadn't been any time to *feel* anything before this. When her mother had been dying, Christie had simply been coping – and then the death itself had been so brutal it had left Christie in shock that no one had been able to ease her mother's suffering. Christie hadn't known that in this day and age people still had to die like that, and it had been so dreadful to witness that it had taken something from her, something she was unsure she'd ever be able to get back. Nothing seemed to move her any more. Even the funeral, and the burial, and today, witnessing her father struggling to butter his toast, tears streaming down his sunken cheeks, had left her so impassive she'd stood silently, mutely useless, disconnected from her own grief, patting his arm as if he were a stranger.

And yet now, just because of one stupid song, the tears that had previously refused to fall were so blinding that Christie was forced to take one hand off the steering wheel and use her jacket sleeve to wipe her eyes. This was her favourite Christmas song ever, and it reminded her of happy times, of when she and Paul used to drive to Worcestershire with the kids, who would be going out of their minds with excitement about Santa, and seeing Granny and Grandad, and presents, and the possibilities of snow. But today Christie was driving home alone, and her children had grown up and left, and her mum was dead and her father was bereft and barely capable of looking after himself, and she didn't know how to help any of them.

As Christie sobbed her way through past memories, the music flitting randomly from decade to decade, from bitter to sweet and then back again, an Ultravox song came on that reminded her of her university boyfriend, and the memories shook her. Perhaps it was because her mum had taken such a shine to him, with his huge soppy eyes, his luxuriant hair, his flamboyant sense of style. 'He's the only one who ever *talks* to me,' she remembered her mother saying, but Christie hadn't known at the time of course that he'd shoved a whole load of cocaine up his nose to enable him to do so. But still, he and her mum had been fond of each other. Christie even wondered whether she should try to contact him, let him know her mother had died . . . and then she told herself not to be mad. He was a fake, who'd betrayed her. He didn't deserve to know. And anyway, he probably wouldn't be interested. Perhaps he was even dead himself. You never knew.

Midge Ure's voice was so yearning and yet so full of promise that Christie couldn't stand it any more. It seemed that her responses to *everything* were inappropriate right now. How could she weep like this over old songs on the radio, and yet stand helplessly by and watch her father sobbing, or her mother being lowered into the cold wormy earth, trying to force out tears purely to meet other people's expectations? What had that been all about? She squirmed as she remembered how the funeral had become quasi-farcical. Someone (Paul?) had given her a handful of earth and the act of flinging it had felt obscene, and she'd suddenly longed to jump into the grave and pull her mother out, take her home to Ware and tuck her up in bed in the spare room, where it was warm and safe. She'd felt Paul's hand on her arm, as though he'd realised how she was feeling, was worried she might actually do it. Perhaps it was normal to feel like that. She hadn't dared ask anyone.

And now this latest act of lunacy was to be howling in her car, semi in time to the music, and she knew she needed to sort herself out. She might even crash if she wasn't careful. And yet it seemed she just couldn't help herself. It wasn't only the loss of her mother. It was also the loss of her own youth and beauty, and the decreasing promise of what life had to offer, and the distressing decline of her father, the vision of his future dun and inevitable and pathetic. And when her shoulders started to shake even harder, she knew she needed to pull over before she killed someone.

Christie saw a sign for Services and, without even thinking, she veered into the nearside lane, causing a van to swerve and honk prolongedly at her. She left the motorway just in time, the grind of her tyres along the rumble strips adding to the panic rising in her. She was still trembling as she pulled into a parking space. Slade's 'Merry Christmas, Everybody' was blasting at her now, her heart thumping along erratically to its cheerful beat.

Nothing felt right. How she wished Paul were here, that she'd let him come with her after all. Why had she insisted on being all grown-up and brave about sorting out her mother's things? But it hadn't made sense for Paul to come and have to hang around all day, and besides, he'd had a doctor's appointment. She'd be fine, she'd told him, and he wouldn't be able to help her anyway. It was a heart-rending process, but it had to be done sooner or later. And her father had wanted it done sooner, soon, soonest – before Christmas, in fact, which had surprised Christie. But it was as if he couldn't bear to have his wife's things any more, if he couldn't have her too. Love was beautiful, Christie thought now, and then it was tragic and sad. Love always had to end, unless you died together, and hardly anyone ever did that.

Christie put yet another call in to her husband, ostensibly to ask him to take some chops out of the freezer for dinner, but more to hear his strong, steady voice, remind herself how lucky she was to have him. When again she failed to reach him she cursed him . . . and then somehow, suddenly, she knew. She could just feel it.

Of course. He was up in the loft, getting down the decorations, and she was absolutely, 100 per cent certain of it, and it made her feel better, that he would do that for her. Sometimes Paul knew her better than she did, and that was a gift he'd always had. Christie had an urge to let him know how grateful she was, without giving away that she knew his surprise, and so she left him a voice message that simply said, 'On my way home. Love you loads.' And then she wiped away her mascara, restarted the Volvo's engine and rejoined the motorway – and because the traffic had cleared at last, she found herself driving just that tiny bit faster, to get home.

37

Paul

At last the tree was done. Paul got down from the chair he'd brought in from the kitchen and stood back and admired his handiwork. The star was slightly wonky, and there were more lights on one side of the tree than the other, but it looked pretty good to him. It was amazing what a difference it made to the room. Hopefully Christie would be pleased he'd made the effort.

He rummaged in the box and retrieved a tasteful holly garland and draped it over the mantelpiece. He found matching red stockings that had 'Jake' and 'Daisy' written in glitter, that their great-uncle had once bought them from Macy's in New York. Paul hung them carefully on the mantelpiece, where they always went. He stood back and surveyed his work. That was enough, he thought. He didn't want to go overboard. It felt important to get the balance right.

Satisfied, he took the boxes upstairs to put straight back into the loft before he ran out of steam. He wanted the whole house to look tidy when Christie got home, so as not to stress her out. He held the Christmas tree box under his arm as he climbed the loft ladder, and then manoeuvred it above his head and neatly posted it up through the hatch. The still-half-full box of decorations was heavier, and therefore harder to negotiate on his own, but he managed it. Just as he was about to descend the ladder he heard the scratching sound again, and it was louder this time.

Little fuckers.

Paul climbed into the loft and clambered to his feet. He had his phone with him now and shone its torch into the corners . . . but all was quiet again. He knew they were there, though – he could feel them in the room. He could smell them. He imagined foot-long rats, like the one that had been found behind someone's dishwasher on the very next road, and decided that straight after Christmas they'd have to get someone in and be done with it.

Now, as if he couldn't help himself, Paul's thoughts returned to the suitcase. The kids were at university still, in Manchester and Leeds. It was odd how Jake had chosen to study back in his home town, and Paul wondered briefly just how the family's relocation down south had affected him. Maybe Jake had always felt like an outsider here. Maybe that was part of the problem . . .

Paul felt the compulsion pulling at him now. Christie wouldn't be home for ages. He had all the time in the world. He needed to know, insane or not, what the truth was. He retrieved the suitcase and brought it over towards the light. Tentatively he reached out and touched the battered old leather, felt the still-smooth vinyl of the stickers for hotels he'd never heard of and which probably no longer existed, toyed with the stiff rusty catch . . . until finally, against his better judgement and all his screaming instincts, he snapped it open.

38

Eleanor

'OK,' Eleanor said into her mobile, doing her best to keep the disappointment out of her voice. It was three o'clock in the afternoon, and the sky outside her window was darkening already, and she could see the single plant on the window ledge wilting after last night's frost. She needed to bring it inside. She hunched her shoulder towards her neck to hold the phone in its place while she continued chopping the fresh tomatoes she was about to have on toast, with salt and pepper and torn basil leaves and a drizzle of extra-virgin olive oil. Peanut butter and jelly was a thing of the past for Eleanor, especially as Alex had encouraged her to go on another health kick, seemingly determined for her to get back into her favourite jeans. It pissed her off that her husband could be so shallow, but she knew it would do her good to lose a few pounds. She'd do it for herself, not for him, and she'd told him so.

As Alex spoke, somewhere on the other end of the line, Eleanor felt a sudden stab behind her eyes, and she pushed her lips together, hard.

'Yes, that is a shame,' she said now. 'Well, hopefully Brianna will understand . . .' She paused, took a breath. 'You will call her though, won't you?'

'Of course I will,' Alex said, but as Eleanor hung up, she felt so sad for her daughter. Brianna might have a lead role in her university's charity Christmas show, but her father wouldn't be there. Alex hadn't even been able to tell his wife where he was going, and she prayed he'd be safe: she was almost certain it was something to do with the recent terror alert in Manchester. Alex never said, and it was just as well it was him doing this job and not her. It seemed that over the years he was getting closer and closer to the action, and there was no way *she* would have been able to handle the pressure of having to manage such difficult situations without being able to tell anyone. The stress would have killed her. But Alex seemed to have flourished since taking on this latest role. He had engineered himself from being a lowly bobby on the beat into one of the most prestigious units in the Met. She was proud of him. It was people like her husband who kept this country safe.

And yet.

Eleanor put two slices of rye bread in the toaster and turned and placed her head against the cool smooth surface of the American-style fridge that was nowhere near as solid as the real thing. The clunk of its opening was substandard too, but that was England for you. It was different. Not better or worse, she reminded herself. Just different.

Eleanor took a long, slow breath, and shut her eyes. For years she'd not known what it was, why there was such a pull in her stomach sometimes when she thought about her marriage. She could barely even confess it to herself, and it was only at times like these, when she felt irrationally cross with her husband, that she allowed herself to think it.

There was something missing.

Eleanor shushed the thought from her mind, like the mother duck she'd once seen shooing her babies away from the weir at Camden Lock. It wasn't true anyway. She loved England. She and Alex had been married for years. He was the father of her two children. He'd been her saviour. Her rock. And yet it didn't feel like that any more, or at least not at the moment – and maybe him being at work so much was beginning to affect how they were with each other. Perhaps it was inevitable.

Eleanor opened her eyes, turned and stared at the smiley family pictures plastered on the fridge, and acknowledged that it wasn't only that. The feeling was more fundamental, and therefore terrifying. The toaster popping startled her for a second, but still the hazy, unsettled feeling remained. As she put the toast on a plate and layered the tomatoes on neatly, another unwelcome thought, one she'd tried to bend out of all recognition, swooped and struck.

Rufus.

It still felt odd that he'd re-entered her life, even if it was entirely by accident – and it had rocked her. *How did she feel about him now?*

Eleanor picked up her plate and took it into the lounge, sat down stiff-backed on the chair by the window, and waited until the day had faded to grey before switching on the lights, rendering the glass instantly black, as if the outside no longer existed. The winter days were too short here. She needed light and air, to bleach the thoughts out of her, but in the meantime she was stuck with them. The tableau was pin-sharp in her mind, like a photo, and the rawness was vivid all over again. She saw herself lying alone on the floor in Rufus's flat, clenching into herself, coiling her body as tightly as she could, silently howling. And then afterwards, when she'd closed the door on his flat for good, it seemed she had shut the scene out of her mind so completely in her bid for survival that she'd almost entirely forgotten it. Maybe she'd never processed her grief. Perhaps that was why she'd never managed to truly get closure.

Closure. What a ludicrous word for a ludicrous thing. She'd spent her whole life being aware of closure, of course. Her father had treated film stars in their anguished bid for it, while his own family were busy falling apart. It was almost funny.

Eleanor stood up and stared out into the darkness, and there was nothing to see. Nothing going on. All the neighbourhood kids had grown up and moved away, and the road seemed sad in its quietness. It wouldn't be long before Mason went too, and it seemed that he and Brianna were the glue that had held her and Alex together. Perhaps they'd simply run their course as a couple, and it was nothing to do with Rufus at all, her thoughts about her ex-boyfriend merely a symptom, rather than the cause. Maybe it was simply time to face up to things, investigate new openings, into another, different life. After all, Eleanor acknowledged, Alex was a lone wolf in a way. His mother was long dead, and he had no contact at all with the rest of his family, which was hardly surprising. But maybe Alex was incapable of true intimacy; it was just that she'd never properly noticed it before.

Eleanor drummed her fingers on the wooden arm of the chair, tried to get the energy out. She wished she could talk to someone about how she felt, but who? Even the thoughts themselves felt like betrayal, as if she were impugning Alex, if only to herself. Alex had always been a good dad, and she had the kids to think of. She couldn't do it to them, make them feel like their whole lives had been a sham. She needed to try harder, for them.

Eleanor had always been a fan of diversionary tactics, in one way or another. Today's one, although somewhat prosaic, was to flick on the TV to catch the two o'clock headlines, but there was nothing of note being reported. It was amazing how much stuff went on behind the scenes, and it made her proud of Alex all over again. She'd been being an idiot, had overreacted about him missing Brianna's show. Alex was as good a husband and father as he could be in his line of work, but he had a job to do.

The phone rang. Alex. Again. Her heart lifted briefly – maybe there'd been a change of plan and he could make the show after all.

'Hi, sweetheart,' Alex said. He sounded muffled, as if it were windy where he was. 'I called Brianna. I told her.'

'How was she?'

'Fine.' Alex sounded upbeat now. 'She said my job might always have to come first, but at least I'm not a banker.' He laughed.

'Well, that's swell,' said Eleanor disingenuously, her mouth half-full of tomatoes on toast.

'What are you eating?' he said.

Mind your own business, Eleanor thought.

'Chocolate,' she lied.

'Oh,' Alex said. He tried to disguise the annoyance in his tone. 'I'll call you soon, princess. Love you.'

'Love you too,' she said, but it was an automatic response. A ritual. Afterwards she sat for ages glaring into her phone, willing it to tell her something . . . but no matter how hard she stared, the answer wouldn't come.

39

Christie

As Christie swung the car round the corner into her road, she could see the lights of the Christmas tree all the way down the street, and she smiled at the fact that she knew her husband so well. Thank God for Paul, she thought, as she parked up, watching the lights softly dimming and brightening through the open curtains. The decorations made everything feel more normal, and it would be nice for Daisy and Jake too, even if they pretended to scoff at the *Home Alone* look. As she pulled on the handbrake, she felt so tremendously grateful to Paul, to be coming home to him, her heart almost felt as if it would burst.

Christie got out of the car and approached the house. A wreath had been hung on the sage-green front door, and it was the one they'd had for years, with a fluffy owl in the middle that Daisy had always loved, and there was something about that gesture that made Christie's eyes smart again. What was wrong with her? She'd been frozen for weeks, and now it seemed that she was crying at bloody everything. She rang the doorbell, but there was no answer. Normally she wouldn't bother with her house keys because Paul would let her in, but now she scrabbled in her bag for them. Oh good, she thought, as the door opened with just the Yale key – he *was* home. He always double-locked the door when he went out, even if he was just popping out to the shops for five minutes.

It felt cold in the house. The hallway had a faintly musty, earthy smell to it. A stillness. There was a neat pile of unopened cards on the hall table and that was typical Paul too. He always left them for her to open, even though most were addressed to them both. 'Hellooo!' she called. She plonked her bag on the polished floorboards and poked her head into the sitting room. The Christmas tree was in its customary position, in the window, and he'd done such a good job with it. The lights were set to her favourite twinkling position and there was barely a bauble she would move. She smiled when she saw the kids' stockings hanging on the mantelpiece, yet still she felt uneasy. Where *was* Paul? It was almost as if something had become unplugged inside her, and on top of the crying jag in the car the world felt dangerous, and unstable, as if something was terribly, irrevocably wrong. She left the living room and went out into the kitchen, her heart thumping now.

'Paul!' she called. Maybe he was hiding in there for some unfathomable reason, to surprise her yet further – but no. The kitchen was empty, and in a mild state of disarray, although normally Paul would have been sure to have cleaned it up before Christie got home. There was no sign of dinner on the go either. Something must have happened. Perhaps he'd gone out after all and had forgotten to lock the mortise for once. Christie shrugged off her coat, hung it over the back of the chair. Her legs felt jumpy, as if she were standing on hot coals. For a moment she wanted time to stop right there, as she fidgeted in the kitchen, in her oldest jeans, her most comfortable jumper, her battered Converse. She didn't want the future to come at her. She wanted to hold it back, stay here in this moment, in the 'before' time . . .

Christie forced herself to stand completely still. She held her breath. She listened. But of course you can only hold back time for fractions of a millionth of a lifetime . . . and now it was coming. *It was coming.* Suddenly the future was crashing towards her, bringing with it the past and the present and the whole fucking shebang, and it was all mixed up and it was impossible. Impossible to stop. Impossible to start. Impossible to ever go on. And yet time stops for no man, and she had no idea who had said that, but it seemed it was true. Time was, right now, inevitably, racing towards her at top speed, like a double wave on the beach, coming, ever coming, and it was horrible and ghastly and nightmare-inducing, and too, too sad.

Christie leant against the worktop, her head feeling as though it were caving in, cracking from the enormity of the suspicion. *Maybe he'd left her*. His absence felt concrete, a permanence, as if he were never coming back.

Once more she called out into the silence, despite knowing it was hopeless. Eventually she moved. She needed to check for herself, look for the pulled-out drawers, the empty coat hangers, dangling like implements of torture. There was no time to lose.

'Pauuuuul!' she yelled, as she rushed back into the hallway and started up the stairs, two at a time, her footsteps thudding and rhythmic and ominous.

40

Eleanor

The demands of Alex's job were beginning to have an effect on their children, Eleanor was sure of it. It had been hard to witness Brianna's disappointment that her father had missed her Christmas show, even though she'd done her best to make light of it. Brianna was a daddy's girl, and would never hear a word said against him. But her husband's absence had been tough on Eleanor too, and she hadn't expected that. She'd hated sitting in the audience alone, and she'd wanted to turn around and reassure people that Brianna did indeed have a father, but that he was away on business – very important, secret business – but of course she hadn't. There had been something about the hall, and all the other parents, that had triggered memories of Eleanor's shame when her father had failed to come to her recitals. At least Alex had rung Brianna – her own dad would swear blind he'd be there, and then just not show up. That was partly why Eleanor had first been attracted to Alex – her future husband's devotion to her had been the diametric opposite of how her father had ever been. There had been something very secure about marrying a policeman, and it had suited her, at first.

Eleanor's breath was labouring as she marched up the hill towards Crouch End. Crappy hills, she thought. It hadn't been like that in Maine, where everyone drove everywhere anyway, nor in Manhattan, where at least the walking had been flat, punctuated by block after block, numerical proof that you were getting somewhere. In this part of North London there was barely a horizontal route to be found. She would have loved to have moved out to a nice Home Counties town, like Lizzie had, but Alex hadn't wanted to leave the city, had preferred to stay close to the action. Of course, Eleanor admired his commitment, but things had felt different in London lately. It wasn't merely the heightened security threat. It was also the fact of the family having to play second fiddle to it. After all, one day it might be Brianna's *wedding* that Alex failed to make, or the birth of his first grandchild – and Eleanor and Brianna both knew it. Only her son seemed genuinely sanguine about the situation.

'It's his job, Mum,' Mason had said, when she'd retorted this morning that the reason the bathroom door lock was still broken was because his father was never around to bloody well fix it. And then she'd felt mad at herself that she'd said 'bloody well', like an English person, and it had made her feel unfathomably homesick for a second. For America. For her mom. For an American summer camp where she'd fallen in love with—

Eleanor pulled herself up. She had to stop thinking about Rufus like that. It was hardly surprising, given recent circumstances, but still – it wasn't on.

She crossed the side road, strode up past the hairdresser's and the art gallery, and hurried along the crowded street, head down, trying not to be noticed. It seemed like wherever she went she'd know someone, and there were advantages and disadvantages to living in the same place for years on end. The middle-aged woman in designer gym wear passing her now looked familiar, but then most of the women from her spin class looked the same – thin, honed, hard of face. The well-dressed woman with the round pretty face just coming out of Waitrose loaded down with shopping looked like one of the mothers from back when her kids had been in primary school – or maybe her familiar, homely features meant she was someone off daytime telly. It was hard to tell sometimes, whether you knew them, or they knew you.

Eleanor stopped a few yards from the coffee shop, breathing heavily. It was the place of the moment and invariably rammed, despite being decked out like an old lady's house – and Eleanor had no idea why that would be trendy, and it seemed she still struggled with the idiosyncrasies of English culture.

She peered in through the lace curtain. The man with his back to the window looked just like Rufus, and her heart jammed, and then jolted. She dithered, thought about fleeing – and then took a sharp, sniffy kind of a breath, and told herself to get a grip. When she entered, she saw that the man wasn't Rufus at all. Despite his dark hair and somewhat louche demeanour, he was clearly far too young. He must have felt her staring at him though, as he cast a brief uninterested eye over her, before returning his attention to his MacBook.

Eleanor realised that Rufus himself was in the far corner, beyond the serving counter, and it was still the weirdest thing, seeing him again after all these years. She felt naked, and devious, and utterly disloyal to her husband – and then she reminded herself that it was only a coffee with an old friend, and it was the middle of the day in the middle of Crouch End, and so there was no harm at all to be done. Besides, she was here now. She swallowed hard, gave her demurest smile and approached the table.

41

Christie

It had been impossible to stay in the house for a single second longer once Christie had found her husband. She'd run from her home, shrieking, her hair flying, her arms flung wide, like an aeroplane. She'd never known whether to be disappointed in herself, for not going to him, or whether that was the normal response to happening upon such a scene. Beyond that single grisly image, imprinted on her consciousness forever, she had only fragments of memory, intermingled and broken, like crushed shells on the beach, about what had happened next. She recalled a blanket being wrapped around her, and she could still feel the scratchiness of it against her cheek, as if, despite the horror of what she had witnessed, all that could get through to her now were physical sensations. Rough wool on skin. Hot, sweet tea. She knew that someone must have called the police, because she could recall blue lights whirling and swirling, intermingling with the fairy lights. She'd heard sirens wailing too, although that might well have been the noise she'd been making. Daisy had turned up at some point, but Christie couldn't remember seeing Jake. Had Jake come? She didn't know. All she knew was that the people opposite must have taken her in, as she was upstairs in Karen Sampford's house right now, and there was someone in the bed behind her, and it couldn't be Paul, because he was dead.

As Christie continued staring out of the window, it felt like she was watching a scene from the twenty-four-hour news, about their street, their house, *them*. Blue-and-white fluttery tape had been wrapped around the house, as if it were a Christmas present to the local press, as well as to those neighbours who lived vicariously through other people's tragedies. The sight of the tape, juxtaposed against the soft-glow tree lights that no one had thought to turn off, made Christie's legs give way. As she clung to the window ledge, the shock was filling up her whole vision, leaving no space even for grief. It was as if she were sinking, and the water was coming over her head, and she couldn't breathe . . .

'Mum?' came a voice, and it sounded too old for its body. 'Are you OK? Come and get back into bed.'

Christie dropped to her haunches on the carpet, which was as soft and springy as moss, and put her head in her hands. Poor Daisy. How could they have done this to Daisy? Her daughter was still only twenty-one. She didn't deserve to have that note of despair in her voice, as if nothing would ever be right in her world again, no matter how hard she tried to disguise it. It wasn't fair. None of this was fair, but for this to happen to her children . . .

Christie heard Daisy get out of bed and come over to her. She felt her lie down and put her head in her mother's lap. Christie smoothed Daisy's hair, stroked her forehead, as if her daughter were a little girl again, and the connection was not a relief exactly, but at least a reminder to Christie that she was alive. That she was real flesh and blood still, and so was her daughter. That had to mean something.

'Jake,' Christie said now. Her voice was that of a stranger's. 'Daisy, love, where's Jake?'

She could feel her daughter cease breathing for a second or two. The waiting was stressful, but somehow Christie didn't want to know the answer either. Maybe it was better in this in-between time, before the facts unfurled themselves, as they surely would.

'He's . . . he's in Turkey, Mum,' Daisy said at last. 'He's on his way home.'

'Turkey?' Christie couldn't compute it. 'What's he doing in Turkey?' In her mind's eye she saw a puffed-up black-and-brown bird with a beady red eye wearing a festive hat, and then she saw the machete coming down, slicing through air and feathers and bone, and then just a body, running in circles. It was Christmas, after all.

'I . . . I'm not sure, Mum. He's coming.'

'OK,' Christie said. Her brain felt curiously adrift from her emotions, as if none of this was real. But it was real, which meant it must all be true. The realisation knocked the last of the strength out of her. Gently she shifted Daisy's head off her lap and shuffled herself down to lie on the carpet, with her arms round her daughter, and the two of them remained there, mute and unmoving, until the house grew quiet again and their bones ran cold, but not as cold as Paul's.

42

Eleanor

'Nelly!' said Rufus, standing to greet her, and even that made her cringe. *She shouldn't have come.* Rufus held out his hand formally, and she held out hers. The touch of his skin was like a memory, a creeping, insidious impression of the past. 'Thanks for coming. How are you?'

'I'm good, thanks. You?'

Rufus was studying her, and it was unnerving. 'You're looking well, Nelly,' he said softly.

'So are you,' she replied, but he wasn't, not really. His face was still attractive, but it had the haunted, harried look of someone who has struggled, and Eleanor wondered with a pang how Rufus really was. She'd only ever thought of him as having made a success of his life, without her. But he'd once been a troubled youth too – perhaps he'd never managed to settle to anything. She had no idea. She had cut him from her life as ruthlessly as an infected limb in her bid to survive, and she'd been proud of herself. And in those days it hadn't been possible to stalk people the way it was now, through Facebook, which was probably just as well.

'So, what are you having?' Rufus asked. As he picked up his coffee cup she noticed that his hands trembled slightly.

'Oh, just a latte, thanks,' she said.

Rufus gave the tiniest nod of his head, and immediately the young waitress was there, and she took their order (two lattes, one chocolate brownie for Rufus) and then giggled. There was something about Rufus even now. There always had been, of course. He'd been Eleanor's first love. He'd broken her heart.

'So,' Eleanor said, 'what's new with you?' And then she laughed, and so did he. Where on earth were they meant to start?

'Well, I got married,' said Rufus. He put his hand to his forehead and swept his hair back on to his head, and it was an unconscious gesture, and she remembered it being one of the things she'd first noticed about him. She was glad he still had a full head of hair at least, even if it was shorter now and streaked with grey. 'And then I got divorced.'

'Oh,' said Eleanor. 'Sorry to hear that.'

'And then I got married again.' He grinned wryly. '. . . And then I got divorced again . . . And then my business went bust.'

Well, he's really selling himself, Eleanor thought. Maybe he wasn't hoping for an affair after all. Perhaps he just wanted to repair old wounds, make amends to her somehow. It didn't matter, though. It was all in the past.

'That's too bad,' she said. 'Do . . . do you have any children?'

'Two,' Rufus said. 'From my first marriage. You?'

'Same,' Eleanor said. 'A boy and a girl.'

'Me too,' said Rufus. 'I don't see much of them these days, though. My first ex-wife isn't, shall we say, my greatest fan.'

Oh God. Although Eleanor felt bad for Rufus, she wanted to get away now, reverse her decision to see him. She wanted to go home to her husband, who had saved her in her hour of need, had protected her when Rufus hadn't . . .

And then she remembered that Alex was away still, so there was no point in rushing home at all. That was partly why she was here, after all.

'So, you're still married,' Rufus said, looking at her wedding ring. It wasn't a question, and yet it felt uncomfortable as a statement, and there was something about it that bothered her. He turned his gaze upwards to her simple grey jumper, her necklace, the smooth shine of her hair, her wide-set eyes. It felt like a calculated look, as if he were deciding whether to buy her.

'Yes.'

'And what's his name?'

'Alex,' said Eleanor, but she felt even more unnerved now, as if she were compounding the disloyalty. She wasn't even sure why Rufus had asked; what was it to him? She put her hands to the nape of her neck and played with the two drop pearls of the necklace Alex had given her, for each of the children she'd borne him. *She shouldn't be here.*

'Rufus,' she said now. 'Why did you want to have a coffee with me?'

Rufus looked wistful suddenly, and ever so slightly ashamed. And then his expression became unreadable again, and she felt the urge to reach out, touch his cheekbone, check whether he was real. She put her hands in her lap and gripped her knuckles.

'Nelly, why did you leave that day?' His voice was soft, like mud. She felt stuck in the question, as if she couldn't escape it.

'What do you mean? You told me to go.'

'I didn't mean for the conversation to end up like that. I meant to tell you that I was confused, and that I didn't know what I wanted, but Nelly, I was wrong. I got it so wrong . . .' His voice started to break. 'I searched for you, but I could never find you . . .'

Eleanor stared at Rufus, her mouth open, a hollow feeling in her throat.

'And so now, well . . . look, when I saw you again, I just knew . . .' His voice lowered even further, so she could hardly hear him. 'Nelly, it was always you.'

'*No!*' Eleanor stood up. 'Sorry, Rufus, but no.' It wasn't only what he was saying, which she scarcely believed anyway, or what Alex would think about the situation. It was something more profound than that. Had she been right all along, that she and Rufus had been made for each other? Had her fear of rejection, born out of being a ping-pong kid, never quite wanted anywhere, been so strong back then that she'd overreacted to what Rufus had been trying to say? Had she simply bolted without listening to the full story? Should she have stayed in that sunny little flat in Hampstead to hear it? Where would she and Rufus be now? What was this parallel life that might have been theirs? It didn't bear thinking about.

'Eleanor, I'm so sorry.'

Her heart was hammering, although she strove not to show it. She had to stay strong. 'Rufus, it's been great catching up with you but, well, I'm married now, and I don't think us seeing each other again is a good idea.'

'All right,' said Rufus. He seemed a little hurt, even as he cocked his eyebrow. And then she decided that it wasn't that at all. Maybe he was pleased he was having this effect on her. Perhaps he found her more desirable now she wasn't available, saw her as a challenge. Once an arsehole . . . she thought.

'It was good seeing you, Nelly.'

'And you, Rufus,' Eleanor lied. 'And you.' She turned then and made her way between the cramped tables as quickly as she could manage, and it was only once she got out into the busy choked air of the high street that she realised she hadn't paid. Never mind, she thought. After what Rufus had done to her all those years ago, buying her a latte was the least he could bloody well do.

43

Alex

Alex was pretty sure that Eleanor didn't know his mother had died on the fourteenth of January. But then again, why should she? The anniversary of her death felt like a private thing – not a secret as such, but just something that had no meaning to his wife. And seeing as Eleanor had virtually no relationship with her own parents these days, albeit partly because there was an ocean in the way, why would she be interested in his? Secretly, though, Alex always felt edgy at this time, as if the very day of the year, the position of the sun in the sky, the alignment of the stars, did for him. He could feel his teeth aching at the back of his mouth. Another year gone. Surely that must mean something.

Brianna's silence was noticeable as she sat in the passenger seat, playing on her mobile. Alex was dropping his daughter down to Euston, so she could catch the train back to Coventry after the Christmas holidays. It still seemed unbelievable that she'd left home already, that she was at university now. Where had the time gone?

'So, you looking forward to going back, Brianna?' he proffered, as a potential opening. The name still grated on him a little, and maybe it was just too American for his northern roots. Eleanor had loved it, though, and Alex hadn't minded enough to object.

'Yeah, it'll be all right,' she said.

'Looking forward to seeing everyone?'

Brianna wasn't biting. 'Hmmm.'

'And how's the love life?' he persisted. He turned on to the Camden Road and switched into third.

Brianna sighed. 'Fine.'

'So, when are we going to meet him?'

'Oh, Dad, you are so embarrassing.' Brianna paused, and Alex could feel the tension in her body, resonating through the car seats. '. . . And anyway, Mum's already met him.'

'What? When?'

'When she came up for the Christmas show.' She didn't need to follow up with, 'You could have met him too, if you'd come.' The thought was as good as audible.

'Oh,' Alex said. He was furious that Eleanor hadn't told him. A pang of remorse hit him, that he seemed to be always missing things lately, but that was the nature of his situation. He couldn't be in two places at once. It couldn't be helped. He kept his eyes on the road as he made his way across the roundabout, nipping in front of but perilously close to a school bus.

'Hey, careful, Dad. You're not on a blue light now, y'know.'

Alex kept his voice as even as he could. 'It's perfectly safe, Bree. You're just like your mother.' He patted her knee in an attempt to be conciliatory, but inside he was roiling still.

'Yeah, right,' she said.

Alex pulled up outside the strip club just along from the side entrance to the station. He always stopped here when he was dropping someone off at Euston.

'See you in a few weeks,' he said. 'Be good.'

'Bye, Dad.' Brianna leaned over and pecked him on the cheek. 'Thanks for the lift.' As she jumped out of the car and sashayed across the street Alex felt a pull of poignancy. His little girl, away at university, sleeping with someone. She looked so like her mother had once done, and it made him feel old somehow, and sad, and as if life were passing him by. As if Eleanor were passing him by. It was a tortured kind of a feeling, as though he didn't know what his wife wanted any more. What she was thinking. *Who she was seeing.* He needed to sort it out. He put the car into gear and pulled out into the traffic, preparing to do a U-turn.

'Hey, Dad!' yelled Brianna, from across the street.

He pressed the brakes, wound down the window, rolled his eyes. What had she forgotten now?

'I forgot to say happy birthday!'

Alex grinned, blew her a kiss and then, only when his daughter was gone, did the sudden, entirely unexpected, tears come.

44

Christie

In the weeks after Paul's death Christie found it hard to be on her own for any length of time. She still missed her husband so badly it was as if the world had come undone, split right apart at the seams, spilling out unknown, unmanageable gunk from its deepest core. Christie found Paul's absence disorienting, unreal even, to the extent that, whatever she was meant to be doing, she'd often think, *I'll just check with Paul about that*, and sometimes she'd even go to her phone to call up his number, before remembering all over again that he was dead. She hadn't realised how dependent she'd become on her husband, until it was too late. It hadn't ever felt unnatural or weak for her to be like that; it was just the way things had been between them, after so many years together. You either grew together or drifted apart, she'd thought, and unlike many of their friends, in her and Paul's case they'd very much grown together. They'd been a team, in the best possible sense of the word. *Hadn't they?*

Christie was still in shock, the doctor had said, perhaps in an attempt at being reassuring, as he'd put her on ever-increasing doses of Valium. But the drugs weren't helping. The nights were interminable, with pictures ingrained and framed in her memory, coming and going, waxing and waning . . . and then pouncing, like rabid monsters. Her husband hanging, dead, in the landing, dead in the middle of her mind's eye, dead in the centre of her universe. A picture lying beside him. There was no coming back from death: not from any death, let alone this one. And yet despite her nocturnal terrors, Christie never wanted the nights to end, to have to face another day without him. Daisy had tried her best, but she was in pieces too, and Jake had barely spoken to his mother since the funeral. Christie tried to understand, pretty sure that both her kids felt almost as distraught at the way their father had died as at the fact of his death itself, even though they'd never say so. But there again, Christie couldn't face talking about it either, and although her memory of that night was slowly returning, she was not at all sure it was helping. It was hard recalling the moment she'd first set eyes on her drawn, newly fatherless daughter, who'd rushed from university to be with her. Christie's response had been primal, and nothing else. There had been no room in her innermost psyche for any kind of play-acting, of even attempting to fulfil the role of mother that night. She'd been a wounded animal first and foremost, and no daughter should have to witness that. The excruciating nature of the pain and remorse had felt like Christie's stomach had been ripped out – and it was still like that now, as if nothing would ever knit the wound back together. She had no idea how she felt in her head either. Calmer certainly, but not better. There was a strange kind of vacant sensation that followed her wherever she was, whatever she did. Neither here, nor there. Neither this, nor that. Time had become abstract, as random as unformed, half-finished sentences.

And so now, before Christie had known it, it was January and she was currently staying at her father's house, ostensibly to help look after him, but also so she didn't have to be at home, and she wasn't at all sure it was doing either of them any good. It was grief doubled, quadrupled, multiplied by sixteen, expanding, ever expanding, into every hole and crevice of both of their lives, suffocating them. It was unhealthy.

Christie winced as she opened a jar of jam she'd found in the back of her father's fridge to find the surface covered in white clouds of mould. Her father shuffled into the kitchen, which, although neat and sunny still, was where the dust danced now. He was clutching the copy of the *Sunday Times* he had delivered each week and which he'd just picked up from the doormat, and his back was stooped a little from the newspaper's improbable weight, and his face was so sad and bewildered it made Christie want to weep. Just six or so months ago, everything had been great in her father's world. He'd been about to go on holiday with his wife to a nice hotel in Malta, like they did every June – it had become a pleasurable habit for both of them, as reliable as Christmas. Yet last year they hadn't made it to their sunshine island after all, as Jean's stroke had put paid to that – and then she'd died in the November, and his son-in-law had died too, just before Christmas, and now it was the New Year and his daughter was one step away from a breakdown, albeit doing her best to hide it from him. Poor Dad, Christie thought. He was too old for such tragedy.

Christie took the proffered pages of newspaper, and although she wasn't remotely interested in the Money section, she didn't have the heart to tell her father, who used to know full well that Paul had managed the finances and that Christie barely knew what an ISA was. After a while she picked up the Driving section, but even the act of thinking about cars led Christie to recall the abysmal events of the last night of her husband's life, which kept looming out of the fog to get at her, knock her down again, just when she thought she was ready to get back up. The ordeal of the drive home. The brief interlude of brightness, when she'd twigged what Paul had been up to, had seen the proof sparkling down the road at her. Those last twinkling seconds, when she'd still thought everything was OK.

And after that, darkness.

Christie put down the Driving pages and turned to the Culture section. A famous actor was on the front, reluctantly plugging his latest film. The look in his eyes betrayed him, and she didn't need to read the interview itself to know how he felt about the movie the critics had already savaged. It made her feel wretched for him. Her own eyes glistened, and that feeling was always there now, as though sorrow was forever lingering, looking for an opening. Seeking a foot in the door, even a vicarious one. But if she was going to feel sorry for anyone, it certainly shouldn't be for an insanely rich A-lister with a new block-buster out.

The phone on the countertop had a shrill old-fashioned *tring-tring* to it. When Christie picked it up, she was surprised to hear her sister's voice, although she shouldn't have been. Of course Alice would be ringing to see how their father was. She sounded awkward somehow.

'Christie, sweetheart, how are you?'

'OK,' said Christie.

'How's Dad?'

'He's OK.'

'How long are you staying with him?'

'I'm not sure,' said Christie.

'OK,' Alice said. 'Well, look, let me know if I can do anything.'

'I will,' said Christie, on autopilot. It's what everyone said, and what she said to everyone.

'Er, is Dad there?' Alice said now.

'Yes, he's just reading the paper. I'll put him on.'

As Christie listened to her father's half of the conversation with Alice she was struck by how animated he sounded suddenly, and it made her realise that she was failing him, bringing him down. They were both stuck in this in-between time, in this in-between world. Neither knew how to communicate with the other, without the buffer of her mother, or the steadfastness of her husband. She needed to do something to break the impasse.

When her father hung up the phone he sounded more cheerful than he had in weeks.

'Christie?' he said.

'Yes, Dad?'

'Go and ask your mother if she wants a cup of tea, would you, love?'

Christie stared at her father.

'Dad,' she said at last. 'Mum's . . . Mum's not here.'

'What, love?'

'Mum's not here.'

'No, of course she's not, love. Don't be silly.' And then her father started to cry, and his nose was running clear, thin mucus, and it was awful to witness. As Christie went over and helplessly patted her father's shoulder, she decided that this couldn't continue. Something had to be done.

Christie stood up, interlaced her fingers, stretched them, looked out of the window, put her palms to her cheeks. There was nothing going on. Literally nothing. Even the bare branches of the trees, robbed of leaves and birds, were motionless. The air was crisp and unmoving, as if all breath had left the planet. It was unnerving. She didn't know what to do, how to move on. This wasn't helping anything.

It came to Christie then, and it seemed obvious to her suddenly. Before she could be of any help to her father, she needed to be brave – go home at last, sort out the lovely house she and Paul had bought together, face up to things. *Face up to her feelings of guilt.* Of course, she'd known he was dead the second she'd gone upstairs. He'd been hanging upside down, trapped by his right ankle, his accidental fall broken, but sadly not in time to prevent the clean snap in his neck, which had rendered his body so inapt, physiologically speaking, the sight so catatonic in its ghastliness, that the image lived with her and would surely do so forever. No blood – just broken angles, the maths of her husband's body all wrong. The horror swarmed and gathered again. The banality of the death seemed to make it worse somehow. The fact that it appeared to be the end result of Paul trying to provide her with a lovely, heart-warming surprise made the pathos almost absurd. But it seemed that one minute Paul had been standing in the loft, and the next he'd taken a step back into thin air, and he must have misjudged it, and he'd been unable to save himself, had had no time even to put out his arms to break his fall. The post-mortem had shown that he'd died almost instantly – and at least that meant he wouldn't have felt any pain. Thankfully her children hadn't had to witness what she had, and she would never tell them the truth of how dreadful it had been, or what might have caused it, or how it may well have been all her fault anyway. She was grateful to the police for that, for being discreet. The fact that the truth was a burden she would therefore have to bear herself was better than her children ever having to know.

Christie moved away from the window and tossed her head, as if the images in her mind were like those of an Etch A Sketch that could simply be shaken clean, but they couldn't. The house she and Paul had loved was forever tainted with tragedy, and there was no heart to it now, and there never would be again. Not for her anyway. Maybe a new family would make it a home once more, but Christie couldn't. She needed to accept the fact that Paul was dead, and that nothing could or would ever change it. She needed to deal with it, for her father and her children, if not for herself. The wallowing needed to stop.

Christie turned away from the window, certain at last of what her new truth was. Paul was in the past. Her mistakes were there also. That was then. The only place for Christie was now.

45

Alex

The prospect of seeing his father for the first time since he was twelve years old was an odd sensation for Alex. All he knew was that he'd once tried so hard to make his father proud of him, but he'd failed miserably. And now that it was all too late, Alex was coming today for . . . what? 'Closure' was the first word that came to him. 'Peace' was the second.

Alex was going to the funeral alone, in fact hadn't even told Eleanor about it. He tried to settle back in his seat, but he felt cramped and on edge. He'd decided to take the train up north, as it was quicker than driving, but now that he was squashed into a window seat in a cramped, far-flung carriage he almost regretted it. There was an oversized table in front of him that contained a white coffee and a huge chocolate muffin that belonged to the dispirited-looking businesswoman opposite, and Alex couldn't help but think how Eleanor would have insisted on having one too, and how fuller of face she had become, especially as he thought she was meant to be on a diet still. Was it so wrong of him to care how his wife would have looked to the family he hadn't seen in years? Even the thought made him feel ashamed. Eleanor had been such a beauty once – but he was pretty certain that if she walked into his police station now, he wouldn't be bewitched by her, which was another thought he immediately tried to bury.

Alex sighed and turned his face to the window. He hated funerals at the best of times, and it made the thought of his own mother's death feel raw all over again. But perhaps that was normal; he didn't know who to ask. He hadn't felt able to confide in Eleanor, and maybe that was where things had started to go wrong. He had felt too mortified.

'You sure you're OK, Alex?' Eleanor had said this morning, before he left. He'd said he was working, as it felt easier than trying to explain himself, but she'd obviously picked up that something wasn't right.

'Yes, fine,' he'd replied, despite knowing that was just about her least favourite of his expressions. It wasn't a response as such. It was a firewall, when he didn't want to have to talk about his feelings. Or anything, for that matter. Fine. Yes, fine. Eleanor had raised her eyebrows, but she hadn't challenged him, and he couldn't work out whether it had been apathy, discretion or else genuine lack of awareness of his turmoil.

Alex watched the woman opposite devour her muffin, and then wipe her face free of dark soily crumbs, before settling down into her seat and shutting her eyes. She appeared normal, and content enough, and successful, but who knew what people's truths were, what dark secrets they harboured? He gazed out of the window at the trees and the fields rushing by and it was easy to forget how much empty space there was between the towns. He was miles away still. There was plenty of time to turn back. He hadn't even been invited – and then he remembered that people didn't get invited to funerals as such. They were open to anyone. It was only because he'd been left something in the will that Alex had even known about it. But maybe this was the moment to see his family again; try to right some of the many wrongs that percolated in his brain, mixing and thickening, slowing his thoughts down. Perhaps facing up to the past at last would unlock something in him. Even be the making of him.

Alex put on his headphones and played Nirvana, loudly. He contemplated how he'd once thought about putting a gun in his mouth, sure that he would never make it past the age of twenty-seven either . . .

But instead here he was: mid-forties and alive. Married. A father. On a journey back to the town of his birth.

As the train pulled into Crewe, Alex felt an urge to get off, turn around, head back to London, but he didn't. He sleepwalked through the rest of the journey: the arrival in Preston; the long trudge along the platform in the biting wind; the sharpener in the station bar; the queue at the cab rank. It was only once he was in the taxi, and red swirling weals were springing up on the backs of his hands, that he woke up. He scratched at his wrists and felt the thick lines of the veins, and everything was itching on the inside now, as though ants were crawling through his internal pathways, making their way to his nerve centre, ready to invade his brain. When the taxi turned the final corner and he saw the church, and the people milling around outside, waiting for the coffin to arrive, he ducked down, turned his face away.

'Can you carry on, mate?' he said.

'Didn't you want St Swithin's?' the driver said grumpily. 'This is it here.'

'No, just drop me round the corner,' Alex said, in such a way as to make the driver not question him again. He got out and hovered on the pavement, watching the taxi drive away up the road, unsure what to do next. When he finally slipped into the back of the church fifteen minutes later, the service had already started. There were so many people in there, and some of them were his family . . .

And then Alex found himself remembering the man who'd come to take him away, the one whose face he had spat in, whose shins he had kicked, whose arms he had tried to shrug himself free of, while his father and brother had watched on impassively. As if it weren't even happening.

And now here at the funeral it was the same thing. The eulogy itself was extraordinary, not least because it was as if Alex had never existed. It was one thing not being part of a family any more, but to be airbrushed out of history, as if you had never even been born . . . now that was something else.

Confusion curdled and churned. Alex bent his head, pretended to pray, prayed that no one would recognise him. And then he decided that he couldn't do this, after all. It was too much. The hurt was too overwhelming. The rage was yet to come. And so, as soon as the service was over, he stood up quickly and left, without having said hello or goodbye to anybody.

Alex's mood darkened further on the train home, especially as when he tried to call Eleanor, she repeatedly failed to pick up. He was probably being irrational, but he kept thinking about who she might be with, what she might be doing, and after the fourth attempt to get through, his mind was awash with potential scenarios too abject to countenance – and so he gave up, convinced in that moment that he'd been abandoned by her too.

46

Christie

It was Daisy who'd first suggested that her mother book a holiday, insisting that it was time, and that everything would feel slightly easier now that the one-year anniversary had passed. And it was true that Christie had been forced to stop thinking: *this time last year Paul and I were in Cornwall.* Or *this time last year we were driving home from dinner when we got the call about Mum's stroke.* Or *this time last year it was Mum's funeral and Paul was being fantastic, and I'd wondered what on earth I would do without him.* Well, now Christie knew – and she'd got through it. She'd survived. At last enough time had passed for every memory with her husband in it to be more than a year away, making it feel like too much of a stretch for Christie to continue trying to relive it. Christmas had been the worst time of course, but at least it hadn't been as bad as the first one. Christie and Daisy had got through it this year courtesy of Waitrose and the TV schedules, and it had been more manageable than Christie could have imagined. She'd been sad that Jake hadn't come home, but in a way him going to a friend's in Manchester had made it less stressful, and she couldn't say she blamed him. Death at Christmas, *for* Christmas, *because of* Christmas, felt especially cruel. Maybe she and the kids should scrap the whole thing in future, and just do summers together. Yes, perhaps that was the answer.

And so now it was February, and the days were inching themselves longer, and maybe planning a holiday was a good idea, would give Christie something to aim for. She had to at least attempt to enjoy life. It was surely what Paul would have wanted.

Christie knew she was deluding herself. God knows what Paul would have wanted after he'd found that suitcase. She could feel a constant fear now, but of what she wasn't sure. It wasn't as if Paul could come back and get her. She still felt mortified about the photo the police had found next to her husband's body. She'd been horrified when they'd given it to her, albeit in a brown envelope, awkwardly saying they didn't need it, and that they thought she ought to have it. Was that the last thing Paul had seen before he died? She wished now with all her heart that she'd thrown that suitcase out, but it had been hers, part of her history. It hadn't remotely changed how she'd felt about Paul.

'What's up, Mum?'

Christie realised that she'd been staring into space, picturing the cream walls, the beige carpet, the innocuous backdrop to the horror. Daisy was home from university for the weekend, again, and although Christie would have loved to unburden herself at last, there was no way she could confide in her daughter. She wished now that she'd been honest about the case's existence, the nature of its contents. Yet Paul had always seemed jealous about her time at Cambridge, as if he'd felt inferior, not just to her ex-boyfriend but to the whole experience somehow, and so it had felt easier to simply not tell him.

Yet now Christie bitterly regretted it. If she hadn't hidden the case up in the loft, Paul would never have found it, would never have seen the photos, might even still be alive. The idea that Paul had died feeling betrayed by her was overwhelming. Her poor husband.

'Mum?'

'Yes?'

'I said, what's up?'

'Oh, nothing, love.'

Daisy's eyebrows were lifted, and since she'd had them tinted they gave her a rather arch look, so that Christie felt as if she were being told off. It was odd how Daisy looked so much like Alice at times, with her straight sleek hair, the colour of old bronze, yet didn't have even a smidgeon of Alice's eccentricity. Daisy knew something, though, Christie was certain of it, and for the millionth time she wondered what she might have said to her daughter the night Paul had died, when she'd been incoherent with grief.

'Ooh, this one sounds good,' Daisy was saying now. She was sitting at the kitchen table, on her iPad researching adventure holidays for older singles, but despite the convivial tone her daughter was striking Christie could tell she felt uncomfortable being in the house now. And yet somehow Christie hadn't been able to bring herself to move after all, as if this was all she had left of Paul. As if even the horror were worth holding on to. Instead she'd simply made do with having the landing repainted a classy blue-grey and the carpet changed. *One step at a time*, she thought.

'Mum!' Daisy said. 'I said, come and look.'

Christie walked over from where she was loading the dishwasher, holding her greasy rubber-gloved hands behind her back. She looked over Daisy's shoulder at the page that had just loaded.

'Horseback riding through Chile?' she said. 'You have *got* to be kidding.'

'Well, what about cruising down the Amazon then?'

'No, Daisy.'

'Oh Mum, it would do you good . . . and I could always come with you, if you like?' Daisy's face, with its delicate pattern of freckles, looked anxious for a moment, almost as though she were scared of her mother's rejection, and she never used to be like that. Both mother and daughter seemed to be experiencing inappropriate levels of distress now, in peculiar, unpredictable ways. Silly things, like running out of stamps, would cause panic verging on meltdown in Christie, and yet whenever something awful came on the news, another terrorist incident perhaps, she'd feel blocked in her grief, seemingly unable to process the trauma. It was as if her responses to things had become utterly random, and it was making it hard for her to even go out, be with people. She didn't want to risk having a public breakdown over something trivial, like not being given milk with her tea, if a bomb had just gone off somewhere.

Daisy's foibles seemed to be manifesting themselves in different ways. She had become noticeably more worried about her appearance, although Christie had told her over and over that she had nothing to be unhappy with. Daisy had inherited her father's tall frame and was now convinced her legs were too thin, too long, too pale. Christie tried to tell her daughter to be happy with what she had, and that everyone looks beautiful if they feel beautiful – but, as Daisy pointed out, it was pretty hard to feel great, whatever your appearance, when your father has fallen out of the loft and accidentally killed himself. And, put like that, it was no wonder Daisy was struggling.

Conversely, Jake, on the surface at least, seemed to be largely unaffected by the tragedy. He'd gone back to Manchester immediately after the funeral and, aside from a text to Christie every now and again, he'd mostly cut himself off from family life, perhaps trying to pretend that Paul's death had never happened. It almost certainly hadn't helped that Jake hadn't made it home from Turkey until two days after Paul had died. It meant he'd been more removed from the situation from the start. Poor Daisy had been the one who'd borne the brunt of it.

Christie looked over at the fridge, where there was an ancient school picture of the two of them, gap-toothed and gawky. They looked so different, *were* so different, but they were brother and sister. Christie longed for the three of them to bond again somehow. It felt important to bring what was left of her little family together, but she didn't know what Jake was doing, why he kept going to Turkey, how he could even afford it. It made her anxious about what he wasn't telling her, but when she'd asked him, he'd shut her down so harshly she hadn't dared broach it again. She wondered now what she could do to bring him back into the fold, keep him safe from trouble.

Reluctantly Christie's focus returned to her daughter's holiday suggestions, which Daisy was currently doing the hard-sell on. She was dressed in a blue-and-white-striped T-shirt dress and Vans, and she looked about twelve, and her enthusiasm was endearing, Christie had to give her that.

'Well, what about the three of us going away somewhere?' Christie said, a rare flash of animation in her voice.

Daisy looked confused for a second. 'Oh, you mean with Jake?' she said. 'I . . . I'm not sure he'd be up for that, Mum.'

'Oh yes, of course,' Christie said. She felt stupid for having even mentioned it.

'It's not personal, Mummy.' Christie blinked in surprise. Daisy never called her that. She pulled at a chunk of her hair, but her scalp felt numb. If only she could *feel* something.

'It's OK, Daisy. It was a daft suggestion.'

'Well, we could always ask him.'

'No, no, it's OK.' Christie had often wished that Daisy and Jake were closer, but it seemed that her children had grown further apart than ever lately. Perhaps it was just one of those things – after all, Christie thought, you can't choose your family and all that. And yet she was concerned about her son. The last time she'd seen Jake before Paul's death he'd seemed low anyway, but Christie had put that down to the fact that he'd been in one of his 'off' spells with his girlfriend, on top of having exams coming up. Christie tried to remember how she'd felt as a student, where exams and lovers and friendships were the only things that mattered at the time, and nothing else invaded from the outside, not even the news. Maybe that's how it was for Jake too. It was hard to know with him. So when she'd been unable to get through to her son in the run-up to this Christmas, she hadn't been too concerned.

He was tired, she'd told herself. Tired, and newly dumped – as well as bereaved, of course.

But now? Christie wasn't so sure. Perhaps it was easier for Jake to imagine that Paul wasn't dead if he stayed up in Manchester. He'd always stayed there throughout the holidays anyway, and he'd hardly ever come home for weekends because he worked in a nightclub. In fact, his behaviour now wasn't all that different from how it had been since he'd gone off to university in the first place.

And yet something else didn't feel right with Jake, and although Christie didn't know what it was, what she did know was that it would do no good to pry. Jake was an adult now. He had his own life to live.

'Hellooo,' Daisy said, turning and waving her arms in front of Christie's eyes in flamboyant criss-cross patterns. 'Anybody there?'

'Sorry, love.' Christie put her hands over her face briefly, pressed the heels into her cheekbones, and breathed out. She smiled. 'Shall we walk into town soon? Pick up something nice for dinner?'

Daisy ignored her. It seemed she was not to be distracted from her mission.

'Corsica,' she said now. 'You like French bread and cheese. You like walking. What about a walking tour in Corsica?'

Christie curled her lip for comedic effect.

'Oh, come on, Mum,' Daisy said. 'There'll be no long flights, no jet lag . . . it's cheaper than South America. And apparently the scenery is spectacular – look at this.' Daisy pointed enthusiastically at the laptop's screen, where a rugged-looking silver-haired man was perched proudly high up on a rock, overlooking a sparkling sea and a white sandy beach. 'Honestly, Mum, it would do you good.'

Christie gazed at the picture, marvelling at how much she adored her daughter, and how that was the one stable part of a world whose sands shifted a million tiny times a day now, where horror and terror seemed to have become a permanent part of the backdrop. Parental love was rock solid. You would love your children, no matter what they did, no matter how much they neglected or betrayed you. No matter what sins they committed. It was hard-wired. It wasn't the same with husbands. There was always the opportunity to withdraw your love for your spouse – or vice versa. It happened all the time.

And yet, Christie thought now, parenthood wasn't easy to get right either. Daisy and Jake needed entirely different types of love, and it baffled her at times. Daisy was the faithful dog, with her endearing eagerness, her constant desire to please, her natural tendency to mischievousness tamed by metaphorical treats and tummy rubs. Jake was the cat, with his long absences, his defensive, couldn't-give-a-damn demeanour. Was that how her son *really* felt? Christie was pretty sure it wasn't. But she needed to give him time. Even if he didn't call her for a year, she would wait for him, to come back.

When Christie's phone pinged behind her, she knew it was him. She could feel the connection, and she felt sad at the irony, that she'd been longing for Jake to get in touch, but now that he had she was scared at what he might want. For a moment she imagined herself running up the stairs again, and instead of finding her husband dead on the landing, discovering Jake there. His short, squat body hanging, rather than Paul's long, lean one . . . And then she told herself she was being overwrought. She was a single mother now, and they were all grieving, so it wasn't surprising how things were with Jake. And he'd always been a handful, especially with Paul, which she still felt bad about. At last she turned, reached for her phone, steeled herself to look at the message – find out what her wayward son had to say for himself this time.

47

Eleanor

The Heath was looking as lovely as it ever had, and it was such a treat to be out on it, on a Sunday lunchtime, with her husband. The rhododendrons were at the peak of their show-offishness, their huge, intricate flowers smothering bushes that were the width and height of small ships. Families were ambling across the tidy green lawns, and lovers strolled, and dogs strained on their leashes as they headed towards the West Heath, where they knew they would be allowed to run free. Everything seemed so bright and sparkling in the fresh spring sunlight, and it was easy to forget here that evil existed, that terrorist attacks seemed to be an almost daily event now, somewhere in the world. Instead there was an expanding feeling in Eleanor's heart, which she got purely from beauty itself, and she wondered if other people felt it too. Impulsively she took her husband's hand, and squeezed it tight, tried to get every last thought of her ex-lover out of her mind, stop the emotions flowing and swirling, risk drowning her in guilt. Alex turned and looked at her, and there was an expression she couldn't read on his face. And then he stopped and dropped a kiss on the tip of her nose. He seemed more relaxed than he had in weeks.

'This is nice,' Eleanor said.

'What's that?'

'Just hanging out with you. Doing something normal.' She immediately realised she'd said the wrong thing, as he extracted his hand from hers and carried on walking. 'I didn't mean it as a criticism, Al,' she said. 'It's just been hard lately, what with you being away so much, and me worrying about you, when I don't know how you are . . .'

'I know, Eleanor,' Alex said. He paused. 'But it's not easy for me either.'

'I know it isn't. I was being selfish. I'm sorry.'

'That's OK,' he said. But he was walking a little in front of her now and Eleanor wondered just how much he couldn't tell her about what went on, and what toll it must take on him. Eleanor was so rubbish at keeping secrets, there was no way she could do such a job. And then that reminded her of her meeting with Rufus. What had she been thinking? And in such a public place as a café. What if someone who knew her and Alex had seen her?

'I . . . I met my ex-boyfriend,' she said to her husband's back, and it felt desperate almost, last-ditch.

Alex stopped dead. He turned around and stared at her.

'You what?'

'For a coffee. I bumped into him on the Parkland Walk. A few weeks ago.'

As Eleanor stared out her husband, giving as good as she got, she wondered what she was doing. Why had she told him? Was she trying to make him jealous, or just clearing her conscience? She was a grown woman. Why was she acting like a teenager?

'What boyfriend?'

'The one I had when I first came to London.'

Eleanor didn't like the way Alex's body flinched. She thought for a moment that he might even hit her, and the fear was so alien it felt as if she hardly knew him.

'So?' he said, at last. He had a strange look in his eyes now, as if he might just walk off.

'I . . . I just didn't want you to get the wrong idea, in case . . .' Eleanor was visibly squirming, wishing she could backtrack.

'Why did you?'

'What?'

'Tell me.' Alex had started walking again, and she wasn't sure whether he wanted her to follow or not – but she fell into step beside him, almost running to keep up.

'What do you mean?' she said.

'Why did you not tell me before, that you even *had* a boyfriend in London, but you're telling me this now?' Was his tone threatening? She wasn't sure. It was so unlike him.

'Well, maybe if you'd been around more I would have told you before.' Her voice had raised itself, just a notch too loud, and she could hear the American twang creeping into it. People were looking. She and Alex rarely argued, but for Christ's sake – did he not even care that she might be about to embark on an affair? What was the matter with him? He'd been acting so oddly lately, and she was sure it must be because of the stress he was under. She hated his job suddenly, hated that they were in this position.

'And?' she said.

'And what?' Alex's eyes were black, his pupils huge, despite the sunshine. It was unnerving.

'Well, aren't you even going to reply to that? Am I just expected to be the little wifey, and wait around for you at home?' Still Alex stayed silent. She grabbed his arm, and when he shook her off there was no gentleness to his touch. She didn't care.

'Alex, Brianna's gone, and Mason will be off to college soon too. *I need more than this.*' And as she said it, she immediately regretted it, although she knew it was true. Peanut was straining on his lead and so she let him off, even though she wasn't meant to here, and he tore away with a joy that she thought she herself might never feel again. Her eyes were bright with unshed tears. 'Alex, what are we going to do?'

Nought to one hundred. That was her. She had taken this ship of a marriage, the one that had steamed along innocuously for years and years, and had just rammed it into one hell of an iceberg.

'I don't know,' said Alex. His expression was unreadable. 'Maybe that's up to you now.' He fished in his pocket and tossed the car keys at her. 'I'm out of here,' he said, and then he turned and strode manfully across the lawn, past a couple pushing a child in a wheelchair, out past the magnificent Georgian house, towards the bright green fields – and Eleanor was so stunned by their altercation, at what she might have unleashed in her husband, she truly wondered if he would ever come back.

48

Christie

Christie had finally capitulated and booked a holiday, mainly to appease her daughter, but also partly because Daisy might actually be right that it would do her good. And it was only for eight days, in Europe – it wasn't as if she was going all *Eat, Pray, Love* on anyone. She'd ended up choosing the walking trip to Corsica, as the least risky option of those Daisy had suggested – but the closer the trip got, the greater the dull throb of anxiety that grew in her stomach, as if she were constantly waiting for a lift to bottom out. Christie even considered not going, but if the worst came to the worst, she could always bail out halfway through and fly home.

Christie wasn't leaving for almost another week, but she'd already nearly finished packing. She always packed early. She always wanted to get to the airport early. Paul had been the exact opposite and she hadn't been able to bear the stress of it, so at least that was one bonus of travelling alone. She went through her list, which she'd printed out on a sheet of A4 paper, and all she needed to do was make sure she had every item on it. Passport – check. Walking boots – check. Waterproofs – check. Water bottle – check. Plenty of layers – check. Swimsuit – check. Sun cream – check. Underwear – check. She had everything laid out on the bed in the spare room, and she was trying not to think about the fact that the last time she'd done this was when she and Paul had gone to the Highlands; and that if she stepped out of the door to go to the bathroom she would walk over the exact spot where she had found Paul, hanging, broken, and irretrievably lost to her.

Almost immediately a low swirl of air seemed to sweep across the room, invisibly moving, and she felt her shoulders lift towards her ears in an involuntary shudder. She didn't believe in ghosts, but it was eerie, and it wasn't the first time, and she knew that when she got home from Corsica she needed to sell up and move. *Why hadn't she moved?* No wonder her nights were peppered with screaming dreams, waiting, circling, ready to pounce, whenever she did manage to snatch some sleep. No wonder Daisy hated coming here. No wonder Jake refused to come at all.

Christie opened Paul's Swiss Army knife and studied its stumpy sheen blade, thinking about her son still. She didn't know what to do about him. She'd been appalled that he'd dropped out of university at the end of the Christmas term, without even consulting her, and was in Turkey yet again. She still had no idea where he was getting the money to afford it. He hadn't even come to see her to say goodbye.

Christie sniffed, grabbed a tissue, blew her nose and then threw the tissue on the floor. It just compounded her grief, having lost her husband, that she appeared to be losing Jake too. But what could she do? He was a grown man, with a beard. All she could do was look out for him, love him from afar. Pray for him. And yet it worried her where he was, what he was doing. Volunteering, he'd said, on one of the rare times she'd managed to speak to him on the phone. What kind, she'd asked. But Jake had been vague, had refused to tell her, and Daisy wasn't telling either, although Christie was pretty sure she knew something. Yet surely Daisy would have told her, if it was something dodgy. *Wouldn't she?*

Christie snapped the knife shut and put it on the bed, next to her passport. As she stood up, she could hear the loneliness clanking through the pipes. The house was too big for her. It used to be such a fun, noisy, messy kind of a place. Now nothing ever moved from where she'd last put it, which still felt weird. But it was the house where Paul had drawn his last breath, and so perhaps that was why Christie had wanted to stay close. She longed to tell Paul that he'd got it all wrong about her, and that she loved him, and was sorry about the photos he'd found, and always would be. But of course she hadn't told him any of that, because when she'd found him she'd run away, out of the house and down the street, and he'd been cold and dead anyway. And she couldn't do it now because he was still cold and dead. She'd never be able to do it. She'd never know how he'd felt when he died, exactly what had caused his fall – so why was she prolonging the agony?

Christie felt her blood rising up through her body, as if it were being sucked up through the top of her head. She took one last unseeing glance at her list, screwed it up and tossed it on the floor, next to the snotty tissue. Then she placed everything into her suitcase and snapped it shut. Enough was enough. She'd put the house on the market as soon as she came back from Corsica. It was time. She was ready.

49

Eleanor

Driving home alone from the Heath, the air in the car felt compressed, oppressive, maybe close to detonation. Eleanor was numb, and troubled, and she wasn't exactly sure what it was that had upset her so. She looked in the rear-view mirror to catch a glimpse of herself, but it was like looking at a person much older than her. How had that happened? *When* had that happened? She changed gears and switched lanes, and steered adequately enough, but she felt like an automaton, a shadow-person. It had been so unlike her to make demands on Alex and, if she were to be honest with herself, that was odd in itself. All these years, she'd put up with the fact that his job came first and, aside from feeling bad for the kids that they didn't see enough of their father, Eleanor had been fine about it. What had changed? Was it that Rufus had unexpectedly come back on to the scene and it had unbalanced her, forced her to think about how her own life was? And so now she minded that Alex was away so much? Now she missed him. *Was that it?*

Eleanor sat outside in the car, looking up at the house where she lived. It was a typical English Victorian terrace, small and poky and outwardly tatty, a complete contrast to the smart houses of Maine and the brownstones in Manhattan where she'd grown up. She had an English husband. She had half-English kids. Her life was here. But was it enough? Had it ever been enough? Had she ever fulfilled her potential? Achieved anything of note? It was almost absurd that she didn't even know what 'enough' meant any more.

Eleanor got out of the car, walked up the weed-sprouting path, opened the front door, which was cracking and in need of a paint. She breathed in the air, and it felt empty. She felt the need building in her again, the one that had been sleeping for years. For excitement. For the forbidden. It was there. Still there. It was coming to get her. Perhaps *he* was coming to get her. Eleanor tore up the stairs, into the bathroom, locked the door behind her, and put her face under the tap.

50

Christie

The cab to the airport had turned up a full twenty minutes late, and despite her rising stress levels, Christie wryly wondered whether it was Paul ordaining so from above, just to freak her out. As the driver hurriedly grabbed her suitcase and put it in his pristine, fur-lined boot, she still felt ambivalent, although she managed to resist the urge to tell him to take it out again. But then when they drove off she couldn't remember if she'd locked the front door or not, which only made her anxiety worse. It was too bad, though – they were running late enough as it was. She'd just have to ask Karen Sampford across the road to check for her. Karen wouldn't mind. She'd been the most brilliant friend and neighbour since she'd taken Christie in, the night Paul had died. Thank God for Karen.

Christie settled herself into the back seat and was just taking her phone out of her bag to text Karen when a loud bang reverberated down her backbone and she was thrown forward. There was a curiously satisfying crunch of concertinaing metal somewhere behind her. When Christie looked up from her phone to see what had happened, she saw they were at the traffic lights at the end of the high street, which had just turned red.

'Fuck's sake!' the driver said. He pulled on the handbrake and jumped out of the car as Christie turned around to see a man get out of his own car behind them. Even as Christie registered that she was fine, he was fine, everyone was *fine*, she could feel the stress ramp up, begin to thrum through her fingers, up into her temples, down through to the back of her throat, across the cave of her mouth to the skin above her lip, which was dampening. Little stress soldiers, patrolling her body, checking for weak spots, places to manifest themselves. *She had a plane to catch*. Without thinking, she opened the car door and got out to see for herself how bad the damage was, just how likely it was she'd miss her flight.

'Oh God, I'm so sorry,' said the other driver, turning to her. 'Were you in the back seat? Are you all right?'

'Yes, I'm fine, thanks.' She walked around past him and glanced at the back of the taxi. The bumper was badly dented, although the car was clearly still drivable. But even so, perhaps this was another sign that she shouldn't be going away. That it was too soon, after all.

As Christie watched the two men exchange numbers, she noticed that her driver was wearing grey socks and slippers under his long white tunic. The other man was smart-casually dressed, and he had a nondescript black car, and as he turned and looked at her she felt a thrum of recognition somehow – as if they were both desperate, in their own ways. She wondered where his mind had been. Perhaps he was drunk, she thought.

'Look, can I get your number?' the man said to Christie now. 'In case I need a witness.' Christie hesitated. She wasn't sure what she could add. Wasn't crashing into the back of another car always that person's fault, regardless of witnesses? As she gazed at him, stupefied by the morning's events, she decided not to argue, and she wrote down her number on the piece of paper he thrust into her hand. He had blue eyes, like Paul. He was attractive, like Paul, yet in a different, more muscular way. It was a shock to even think it, but it was the way he was looking at her. The intensity of his gaze, for the count of one, two, three . . . And then he turned, and it was over.

The driver opened his boot, and tutted at the wrinkles on the paintwork, but Christie's suitcase was intact.

'You going on holiday?' the stranger persisted.

'Allegedly,' Christie said. She smiled nervously.

'Alone?'

'Er, yes.'

'Oh, well . . . have a good time.'

'Thanks,' said Christie. He crinkled his eyes then, and she was unsure whether he was apologising to her still, or coming on to her. That was the thing she would always remember about him, the ambivalence. How she felt about him. How he felt about her. She took a look at his ring finger, but it was bare, although that meant nothing with men. Loads of married men didn't wear wedding rings. Paul hadn't – and the memory of her husband was like a low blow to the stomach. *Guilt.*

As Christie got back into the taxi and waited for her driver, she was aware of an odd feeling spreading inside her, like heat turning on, thinning her blood. She looked at her watch. They were running seriously late now, and her throat tightened.

'Airport?' the driver said when he returned to the car at last, but he seemed angry, as if he felt like this was all Christie's fault, which was completely unfair, in her opinion. She hesitated. Perhaps she should simply ask him to take her home, and she could hide out there for a week or so, just pretend she'd been on holiday if anyone asked. She'd been in a car crash, after all.

The cab driver was still craning his neck to glare at her, his mouth a thin straight line nestled amongst the grey-black of his beard.

'Well?' he said. 'You going, or not?'

'Yes,' she replied. 'If that's OK with you?'

◆ ◆ ◆

Although the North Circular had been slightly quieter than usual, almost as soon as they'd joined the motorway the traffic had drawn to a near-standstill. And although Christie had been convinced the gods had ordained she was going to miss the plane after all, the driver had worked hard, if somewhat erratically from a lane-changing point of view, to redeem the situation. When he'd finally pulled up outside Departures, she'd given him a pretty hefty tip for all his trouble, but he'd still been tetchy, which had been fair enough in Christie's book.

And so now Christie was finally inside the terminal, a mere fifteen minutes before the flight was due to close, and the board telling her where she should be checking in was immediately in front of her, but it was as if her nerves had taken over her mind and signals were being scrambled, and the flight details might as well have been written in Japanese. *If only Paul were here*, she thought now. It was the firsts that seemed to confound her. First night as a widow. First Christmas without him. First birthday. First car crash. And now first airport.

Christie realised that she was daydreaming. *She was going to miss the plane.* She studied the board and at last managed to work out that she needed to go left, and she turned on her heel and ran, weaving her way through the luggage trolleys and kids with Trunkies, the general dawdlers. Yet when she reached the desk to find the queue snaking around the block, she thought she might actually pass out. Fortunately, a roving member of the check-in staff must have noticed her panic, and it seemed that Christie wasn't the only person to have been stuck on the motorway.

'I'm so sorry,' she said to the couple she'd just been ordered to push in front of. They nodded politely but failed to raise a smile, and she could feel pairs of eyes on her back as she handed over her passport. She was unable to meet their glances afterwards, and instead mumbled a thank you as she walked quickly away. It was only when she finally reached the gate, out of breath and panicked, to find a load of other people still queuing to board, that she began to calm down. At exactly that moment her phone rang. The number was withheld, but she answered it anyway.

'Hello?' she said.

'Hi, this is Piers Romaine,' said the voice. 'The incompetent driver from earlier. I, er, just wanted to check you made your plane OK.'

'Oh. Yes, I did, thanks. I'm just boarding now.'

'Oh good. Look . . . can I buy you dinner when you're back, to say sorry?'

'Oh, really, there's no need for that.'

'Well, maybe I'd like to,' the man said.

Christie hesitated. What a weird day this was turning out to be.

'Well,' she said at last. 'I'll be back in a week, so why don't you call me again then?'

'Deal,' Piers said. 'And in the meantime, have a great holiday.'

'Thanks.' She stared at the phone as it rang off, feeling the colour rising in her cheeks. She was unsure what to make of it. It was flattering, certainly, but she hoped he wouldn't call back. She had enough on her plate right now. She was a widow in mourning. She had grown kids to worry about. She had fifty miles of walking to do.

51

Eleanor

The *rat-tat-tat* of the knock was unmistakeable. It was strange how that was the case, that Alex had always knocked in such a unique way that it could never be anyone else. Sometimes he had come back from a trip when she'd least been expecting it, and that exact combination of raps had made her heart leap. Today Eleanor was unsure how to answer it. She'd had plenty time to think, but the fact remained that he'd stormed off from the Heath and then had been shitty with her for days afterwards, before buggering off on a job, leaving her feeling disproportionately let down. As if the one time she'd dared to complain about him not being around enough, he had turned it on its head and acted as though *he* was the wronged partner. She was worried too about how he would be with her, and maybe that was more the nub of it. After all, Alex had no relationship with his own family. He'd fallen out with friends too. In fact, he had a capacity for cutting people out of his life when it suited him, and it was a tendency that had always concerned Eleanor. She knew she wasn't close to her family either, yet that was circumstance more than anything. But perhaps he'd turn her loose too if she weren't careful.

'Hi,' Eleanor said, as she opened the front door, more gingerly than usual. She tried hard not to sound sulky.

'Hello, Eleanor.' He stared her down as she stood in the poorly lit hallway, and it was as if neither of them knew how to act somehow. Her feet were bare and the nail polish was chipped, but he didn't notice. He lifted his hand, took hold of a soft strand of her hair.

'I've been an arse,' he said. 'I've been working too hard, neglecting you. I'm going to take some proper annual leave. Let's go away together. Just the two of us. Somewhere nice.' He touched her cheek then, and his fingers felt strong and warm. He had never sent shockwaves through her, not like Rufus once had, but love came in all shapes and forms. She looked into her husband's eyes now, and they were blue and beseeching. He could act so selfishly at times, and then he would do something like this. She didn't know what to say.

'I'll book it,' Alex continued, 'for in a month or two, when things have hopefully calmed down at work.'

Eleanor raised an eyebrow, looked at him. 'Is there something going on?' she said.

'No, nothing to worry about,' Alex said. And that was enough for Eleanor. Sometimes he'd ring and casually suggest that she stay out of central London, and then it would be conversation over, and that was the closest he ever got to giving anything away. A 'nothing to worry about' now was reassurance enough for her.

Alex put his arms around her and pushed her back against the wall. 'I'm going to make it up to you,' he murmured, 'and we're going to have an awesome time.' He bent his head to kiss her.

Eleanor pulled away for a moment. 'Alex, what about what I said on the Heath, though, about the fact that I saw my ex-boyfriend?'

Alex gave her a look she would remember a long time from now.

'Why didn't you ever tell me about him?'

'I don't know. It was over. I was more traumatised by my stalker by the time I met you. And I so wanted to forget all about my boyfriend it never seemed relevant to tell you. I'm sorry.'

'How did you feel about seeing him?' Alex asked at last.

'A little sorry for him.'

'Anything else?'

Truth waxed and waned, tried to unveil itself. She stood up a little taller, faced him off.

'No,' said Eleanor, at last. Their eyes were searching, both searching, for secrets.

'Just don't see him again,' Alex said. It was undoubtedly an order, but his voice carried a tinge of something else too. It was as though he might be struggling to control a deep river of rage somewhere inside him. 'Eleanor, you're *my* wife,' he said. 'That was years ago. You're mine now.'

Eleanor nodded, and Alex duly kissed her, but he was rough and needy and she had to make her excuses for it not to go any further. And then afterwards, locked in the bathroom, she worried about him, wondered whether the stress of his job was getting on top of him finally. And she couldn't work out whether she was OK with her husband being so territorial of her suddenly. Or whether she was scared.

52

Christie

Fireworks were exploding in Christie's chest, and a stitch was stabbing her in the fleshy part of her stomach, and in the privacy of her own head she was fully cursing her daughter now. This wasn't a gentle walking holiday at all – it was a full-on sodding climbing expedition. Christie had had no idea that there were such high mountains on a little island in the middle of the Med, and she really wasn't fit enough for this kind of exertion. She kept her eyes focused on her feet and willed them on. Count to fifty, she said to herself. And then do fifty more steps after that, and then another fifty, and *then* you can stop for a drink. Break it up into chunks. One foot in front of the other. Never give up.

Today, the third day, was the hardest yet. The incline was steep, forcing her to lean into it, and the sun was pressing down on her back, and sweat was pooling in her cleavage, and she thanked God that at least she didn't have to carry a rucksack. That was one good thing about this trip at least. Some time late this afternoon she'd arrive, dishevelled and dirty and utterly worn out, at some charming hitherto-unknown hotel, where she'd be shown into a clean simple room, with an awesome shower, most likely with a stupendous view, and almost magically her luggage would be already there, waiting for her. The anticipation almost made the pain of the hike worthwhile. In the evening she'd enjoy a hearty meal and a few drinks with her fellow hikers, at which point she'd decide that she'd had the most wonderful, amazing day ever – and then before she knew it she'd wake up the following morning and dread having to do it all over again.

Christie trudged on, breathing heavily. She briefly looked up and the air was hot as it blew at her. The whole sky was blue, and there were no clouds to save her from the unremitting sun. Right now, she was in the very centre of the worst part of her daily cycle. Conflicting emotions rang through her brain and threatened to undo her. She'd have to stop. She was determined to keep going. She was doing it for herself. She was doing it for Paul. She was getting on with her life. Moving on. As Paul would want her to. As she walked she found herself wondering about the man who'd crashed into her taxi. *Piers Romaine.* She thought how unusual the name was, how romantic it sounded, almost like a matinee idol. She wasn't sure whether he would ring her but, assuming he did, what would she even say to him? Should she agree to go out with him, if he asked? And if so, how should she describe her status to him? She was a widow, of course, but she'd resisted ever referring to herself in that way before. 'Widow' was such a weird word. An alien state. It was something she'd never imagined becoming . . .

Christie groaned and made one last effort as the path steepened yet further, and then at last she reached the top. She stopped and put her hands on her hips, panting. Beyond her, far below, the water was a bold blocky patchwork of indigo and turquoise, as though a child had coloured in the sea with two different pencils. A crescent-shaped beach of white sand was flanked on one side by a ruined castle, and on the other by a smattering of pink-tinged boulders. Dots of yachts swung lazily on their anchors in the bay. Christie reached for her water bottle, pressed it to her lips, felt her heart soar with the eagles . . . *Paul would have loved this.*

'Oh wow,' said Helen, one of her fellow climbers, as she reached the top too.

'Indeed,' Christie said, and they smiled at each other, and for the first time since Paul had died Christie felt truly at peace. Friendship and beauty were all she needed for now. She didn't need to go on dates with strange men who back-ended her taxi. This was the start of her recovery.

This was enough.

53

ALEX

It was a quiet day at work for once, and Alex was in a reflective mood. He could hardly believe Mason would be turning eighteen this weekend, and he didn't know where the time had gone. He could still recall every moment of his youngest child's first birthday – perhaps because it had happened to be the self-same day that Alex had finally fallen in love with him. The memory made Alex smile even now. Eleanor had bought Mason a checked collared shirt and a pair of smart beige cords for his party, and proper little leather shoes, and a few days previously she'd had his softly ringleted curls cut for the very first time. Mason had spent the afternoon fiendishly surfing the furniture, grinning triumphantly, looking like a miniature person at last, rather than a scrunch-faced blob, and the relief Alex had felt had been greater than he could have imagined. It must have been so hard for Eleanor, Alex thought now, for him to have rejected his son like that, especially as he hadn't been like that with Brianna. He'd tried to hide it, of course, but mothers knew. Babies knew too, and it seemed that Mason had picked up on it, as whenever Alex had gone near him, Mason had started bawling. Father-son relations had got better after that, thank goodness, and since then family life had mostly been fine. Until now.

As Alex stared absently at the CCTV camera footage, searching for that one elusive clue that he knew must be there, he felt an almost dangerous mixture of agitation and resentment about this Rufus character. Jealousy had nearly been the undoing of them once before, back in the early days, and the memories were prodding at him again, teasing him. There was one particular time he remembered that seemed pivotal now, pin-sharp in its apparent innocuousness. They'd been sitting in the kitchen together, Brianna bouncing on Alex's knee, giggling, when Eleanor had asked him to mind the kids for a couple of hours on Saturday, so Lizzie could take her for afternoon tea as a belated birthday present. Alex had raised an eyebrow, yet kept his voice even.

'Lizzie who?'

'Lizzie Lizzie,' she'd said. Had that been a note of sarcasm in her tone, as though she'd thought he was stupid? He still wasn't sure.

'I'm working this weekend,' he'd said.

'Oh. I thought you said you were off?'

'Well, I'm not,' he'd replied, and he still didn't know why he'd lied about it. What had been so wrong with Eleanor wanting to see Lizzie again? Alex had known that Eleanor loved her ex-boss, so why had he been so hostile about it? Perhaps he simply hadn't liked his wife's increasing independence. Or else he'd been worried that she'd be seeing the husband too. Even all these years later, Alex was convinced there'd been something between Eleanor and Oliver Davenport. But still. He'd behaved like a prick.

'Maybe next weekend,' he'd said, as if by way of appeasement. Eleanor had scowled at him, but he'd refused to bend, and his only excuse was that things had been getting him down at the time, and the situation had panicked him. The easiest option for him would have been to have told her he'd got off work after all, but he hadn't. He regretted it still. Of course he did.

As Alex half-heartedly surveyed the ghostly images on the screen his mind was in turmoil. It kept turning backwards, wending and winding into dark forgotten places that made him angrier than he knew he was capable of becoming. Surely it was because of the funeral. He swore now he'd gone there to make peace, but it most definitely hadn't turned out like that. As he'd slipped out of the church into the brittle winter sunshine, he'd felt an isolation that had shrunk him to nothing, rendered the world giant and throbbing around him, with him playing no part in it, almost as if he were dead.

'Oi, you still here, Al?'

Alex jumped. One of his colleagues was at the door, a large clear plastic bag full of clothes in his arms.

'Seen a ghost, have you?'

'Ha,' said Alex, mirthlessly.

'You all right?' Gary persisted.

'Yes, or else I would be if I got some sodding peace.'

As Gary's florid face fell, Alex felt bad for him, regretted his rudeness.

'Sorry,' he said, but Gary had already lumbered off and Alex knew he'd made an error. Stay undercover; that was his motto. Never draw attention to yourself. Being arsey with the most genial bloke on the team was not the way to go.

Alex felt a weight pressing on the back of his throat now, as if someone had him on the ground, with a boot to his neck. *Eleanor*. He could still recall the effect she'd had on him when she'd walked into his life, how much he'd wanted to look out for her. It was almost as if they'd been saving each other. Those early months had been heady in their strange mix of danger and romance, what with the salacious packages and anonymous phone calls, the fact that as well as being the police officer she'd first made the report to, he'd entered into a romantic relationship with her. And yet she'd never ever told him about this Rufus. Or that they'd apparently bonded over a mutual level of screwed-upness. Fuck's sake. How much else about his wife didn't he know?

As Alex felt his mind glazing over, he had to force himself to concentrate on the CCTV images. They were so grainy, and he wondered moodily why technology hadn't moved on to make them not so, a thought he'd had myriad times before. He yawned. Tapped his leg. Cracked his knuckles. *Nothing*. This was a waste of time. After another ten minutes he flipped off the screen and stood up. His shift was nearly over anyway. He needed to go home, try to get a grip on what was going on in his life. Before he did something he regretted.

54

Eleanor

Rufus had somehow managed to get hold of Eleanor's number, as she definitely hadn't given it to him. When they'd first bumped into each other, they had simply arranged to meet for coffee a few days later, and part of why she'd ended up going was because there had been no way for her to cancel. But now she felt unsure what to do. It seemed she had made Alex jealous, which was perhaps no bad thing, but her and Rufus's meeting had threatened to open up doubts in her mind about all sorts of issues. Seeing him again wasn't worth the potential trouble. The past was the past.

Eleanor put on her raincoat and sighed when the buttons felt that little bit tighter. She needed to do something about her weight, but she'd gone off the idea of running along the old railway line for now. She didn't want to risk bumping into Rufus again, or at least not somewhere so secluded and romantic, where who knew what she might be tempted to—

Eleanor pulled herself up. Those thoughts were out of line. And yet it seemed she still couldn't help thinking about Rufus, mourning the boy he'd once been, the love they'd once shared – especially now she knew that his life hadn't turned out remotely how she'd imagined, with him swanning off into the sunset with his old girlfriend and living happily ever after. It left her confused. Rufus was in the past – but the past was no longer how she remembered it. Alex was in the present – and yet it wasn't the same between them any more either. Mason was about to leave home, and even the thought of it was highlighting Alex's absences, compounding her loneliness. It seemed that circumstances were ripping open a chasm-sized gap in Eleanor's life, in her history, and she felt untethered somehow. Neither here nor there. Vulnerable again. Getting out in the air, moving, would hopefully help in more ways than one.

Eleanor left the house and walked Peanut past the shops and then up into the little park that sat on the brow of the hill. She was just letting him off the lead when her mobile rang. Even all these years later, after suffering Gavin Hewitson's telephonic onslaught, the sound of a phone unnerved her. Involuntarily she recalled her stalker's sick obsession with her – how he'd sent her a bullet through the post, and then another time a dead mouse. The harassment warnings hadn't worked, but of course it was hard when he'd lived next door to her, especially as the police never seemed able to pin anything specific on him. By the end she hadn't known whether she was imagining things, and that was how much it had messed with her head. Even having a policeman for a boyfriend hadn't been enough to quell the terror she'd felt, every single time she'd left the house, or answered the door, or at the way Gavin had peered at her from behind his curtains. It had been such a relief when she'd moved out from Lizzie's to live with Alex and the harassment had stopped, overnight. Presumably he just hadn't known where to find her.

But today it was Rufus calling, again, causing Eleanor's memories to sweep backwards, ever backwards, even beyond those days of being stalked, to when she'd been in King's Cross still, alone and desperate. It almost made her feel tempted to answer, if only so she could ask him what had happened to the girl he'd left her for. That was the only piece of the past she still didn't know. The face that had haunted her for years. She pictured the girl now – red-headed, Asian, blonde, brunette, black – the images flicking through Eleanor's mind as if in a fruit machine, never stopping, never revealing her nemesis's identity. Who knew? Who cared? It made not one iota of difference.

Eleanor sighed, stared at her mobile, as if willing it to stop, before at last it cut out. She felt close to tears suddenly. She made the next call before she had time to decide not to, but inevitably it cut straight to voicemail. Jesus. Where *was* Alex when she needed him? Didn't he realise how close she was to—

Eleanor stopped herself. She couldn't even articulate what it was that she was close to. It was far too dangerous. Instead she switched off her phone and put it back in her coat pocket – and then she cleared her throat and called Peanut to her.

55

Christie

Christie came home from Corsica tanned and half a stone lighter, and happier than she'd been since her husband had died. Her hair had been streaked by the sun and the style had softened from when she'd last had it cut, too short, as if in penance. Now loose strands fell around her face, and she knew that the misery-induced sagging around her jowls had lifted a little at last.

When Piers rang the day after she got home, it was odd to hear his voice. She'd assumed he wouldn't call, and now that he had she wasn't sure why. Perhaps it was to do with the car accident.

'So how was your holiday?' he said.

'It was great, thanks. How's your car?'

'Oh, it's fine. I've had it fixed.'

'And the taxi?'

'Yeah, it's all in hand,' Piers said. Christie didn't know what to say. She felt a jolt of uncertainty, at what he wanted. Who he was.

'So, are you going to let me buy you that dinner?' Piers asked. His voice still had a tone to it that she couldn't put her finger on. She wondered where he was from.

'I'm not sure,' Christie said. 'I don't mean to be rude, but . . . well, I don't know anything about you.'

'So what do you want to know?'

'Well, what you do, for a start.'

'I'm a management consultant – as well as a bad driver, of course.' He laughed.

'Oh,' Christie said. She didn't know much about management consultancy. All she knew was that Paul had always referred to them as a bunch of leeches, but she chose not to mention that fact to Piers.

'Really, there's nothing to worry about,' said Piers. 'Look, I'm going to be in London next Wednesday, for a conference. I could easily come up your way afterwards?'

Christie hesitated. Her holiday had done her the world of good, had helped her finally realise that maybe there was life after Paul after all. But that didn't mean she was ready to go on a date. She wished she had a genuine excuse not to see him, let something external make her decision for her. But she was free that evening. As she listened to his steady breathing down the line, she felt extraordinarily conflicted.

'Hello?' Piers said.

Christie pulled herself together. He seemed nice, and it was only dinner.

'Yes, OK,' she said.

56

Alex

'What's brought this on?' Mason said, as he stood at the bar with his father. 'Taking Mum to Venice? Bringing me to the pub?'

'Well,' Alex said, 'you're of the age now to come to the pub with your old man, and you'll be off to university soon, so why not?'

'Because you're usually far too busy.'

'Well, I'm not now,' Alex said, trying not to get annoyed. He didn't need his son doing the guilt thing on him as well. He was feeling wound up enough about Eleanor.

'Dad, I'm kidding,' said Mason. 'It's cool to have an undercover cop for a dad.'

'Shush,' Alex said, looking around nervously. They were in one of his favourite pubs, with its huge-paned leaded lights and ornate ceilings, dark wood everywhere, full of old silent men and a terrific selection of real ales. It was a proper pub still, which were few and far between around here these days. But you never knew who was listening, and he was sure the barman had half-cocked an ear, and he wished Mason would keep his voice down.

'Sorry,' Mason said, grinning amiably and taking a slug of his pint. Alex didn't know why his son drank cider, but each to their own, he supposed. Mason was what Alex would call a strapping lad now, tall and broad-shouldered, and he was proud of him. He was one of those people who had so much natural charm and self-assurance it was as if he'd been born with it, and Alex knew his son would make a success of his life, whatever he chose to do. Eleanor had done a good job with both kids, that was for sure.

'Dad . . .' Mason said now.

'Yes?' Alex was wary, could sense the unease in his son's voice.

'How much danger are you in these days . . . with all this shit going on?'

'Oh, Mason,' Alex said. Mason might be innately, sunnily confident, but it seemed that he too was anxious about his father. Alex felt instantly terrible, that he was doing this to his family.

'Well?'

'It's fine, son. The training's top-notch. We . . . we have each other's backs.'

'OK,' Mason said. 'Look, I'm sure you're right, but it's just I know Mum's really worried about you these days.'

'Well, there's no need for her to be,' said Alex. He picked at the crisps that were lying on the bar between them, the foil bag gashed open so they lay in a pile in the middle. 'Why? What's she said?' He could hear that his voice had grown unintentionally menacing, and he felt his Adam's apple pulsing as he stared his son down.

'Nothing, Dad. Chill out.'

'Sorry.'

'Look, Dad, what's up?'

It was the kindness of the question that got to Alex. He could feel the agitation sloshing around inside him now, rising and falling, threatening to spill over, and he felt so fraught suddenly he longed to confide in his son, tell him what was going on, but of course he couldn't. The stress might be killing him, but he'd made his choices, and so this was just how his life was right now. Mason was watching him closely, and Alex struggled to think how to answer. To buy himself some time he stuffed a handful of crisps in his mouth, chewed slowly, drily. And then he managed to wink at Mason, crack a smile.

'Nothing, son.' He finished the last of his pint, looked at Mason's still half-full one pretend-disdainfully. 'Same again,' he said to the barman, his mood thankfully back to equilibrium now, although it had been a close call. He knew he mustn't let himself weaken like that again. There was no use feeling sorry for himself, as what was the point? What in hell could he do about it now anyway?

57

Christie

Swept off her feet. That was what people called it. Christie hadn't experienced anything quite like it. The closest she'd come prior to this was with her old boyfriend from Cambridge. With Paul her feelings had been far more rational. They'd grown to love each other deeply, and had made a good team, but they hadn't exactly rushed dizzily into things. It had never been an impulsive thing for Christie with Paul. They'd been friends first and foremost, and Christie had simply enjoyed spending time with him, enjoyed his passions, his humour, until things had developed between them organically.

With Piers, though, right from the start all Christie's senses had been highly charged, in one way or another. Perhaps it was because their love affair was just so unlikely – if her taxi to the airport hadn't turned up late, it would never have been involved in an accident with Piers, who she would never have met, would never have given her number to . . . Surely it was fate. (Good grief, Christie thought, she was beginning to sound like Alice.) She even considered ringing the cab office to say thank you, and that's how crazy she felt. Her feelings were heightened by the fact that she and Piers couldn't see each other regularly, as he was based in Bristol, but he came to see her as often as he could, and although he'd always got a hotel, from the third occasion onwards she'd stayed there too. Yet she still couldn't bring herself to let him come to her house, take him upstairs, past the spot where her husband had died, even though she'd tried to tell herself that that was ages ago now, and that Paul would have understood. Yet the truth was, she and her husband had never talked about such scenarios, and so she had absolutely no idea *how* Paul would have felt. His death had slammed itself at Christie in the most bizarre and violent way possible, and it had left her untethered from how she'd used to be. Changed, forever.

Christie opened the door to the restaurant, which had the chic sleek lines of an old-fashioned cruise liner, and a rush of warm air came at her. Piers was already there, at an intimate table in the corner, and it was such a strange feeling, that before all this she used to be a married mother, the linchpin of a happy, buzzy household who spent half her life in jogging bottoms, and now she was a widow, with a lover for whom she'd gone to Agent Provocateur and bought underwear, the likes of which she hadn't worn in years. Her perfume was French and heady and expensive. She'd blow-dried her hair specially.

And yet. Despite the hot-and-cold rushing feeling in her spine, the tingly thrill of seeing him, Christie had a strong desire now to back out of the restaurant, carry on up the street to where she was parked, and reverse her Mini Cooper all the way home. She found herself seeing her life as a cine reel running backwards, ever backwards, to dry grey earth travelling up into her hand, a coffin being exhumed from the ground, cars speeding in reverse along the M6, Paul magically flying upwards into the loft, his body fixing itself mid-air, letters and photos leaping back into a suitcase, the lid being shut again forever. *That* was the pivotal point of her life, undoubtedly.

Piers gave Christie a little wave of greeting, but she remained at the door of the restaurant, immobile. He looked familiar, and yet like a stranger too, as if she couldn't possibly even know him, let alone have been sleeping with him for the past six weeks or so. Confusion rose in her throat, like a stifled scream. In one way she longed to go to her lover, let him kiss her cheek in greeting, prove he was definitely real. But in another she wanted to turn around and flee the restaurant and never ever see him again. It was too soon. It was disloyal. *It didn't feel right.*

And so it was in that exact golden-hued moment, with the benefit of physical distance – as if she were looking at a picture of someone, rather than seeing the flesh-and-blood person they were – that Christie realised. She hadn't made it through yet. She still wanted Paul. And yet now she wanted Piers too. The dichotomy was killing her.

'Good afternoon, madam,' said the maître d' softly, breaking the impasse. Christie startled a little, but finally began to walk, ever so slightly too slowly, across the black-and-white chevron-tiled floor, past the smooth fluid lines of the mirrors, ensuring she didn't catch a glimpse of herself, of her painted, traitorous face, towards her lover. Was he her future? It was too soon to tell – but for the moment he was helping plug the empty pit of despair in her heart, and surely, please God, that was reason enough, for now. Wasn't it?

58

Alex

It had been humbling for Alex to finally realise just how much his family worried about him these days, and it made him feel guiltier than ever. But at least he was doing something to treat Eleanor for once, and he was enjoying their trip to Venice. In a way it had been a relief for him to be reminded that he didn't like other men sniffing around his wife, that he loved her still. Yet sometimes he wondered where the passion had gone, that burst of emotion that had been ignited the very first time she'd walked in off the street, to be saved by him. Perhaps it had merely been the thrill of the chase, the impossibility of going out with a crime victim, the anger he'd felt towards that weaselly creep who'd had the temerity to think he stood a chance with her. It was hard to tell now, and maybe it didn't matter anyway.

Alex had booked the fanciest hotel on the Grand Canal, and it had cost him a fortune, but that was what unexpected inheritances were for, weren't they? And it had been over twenty years since he and Eleanor had married, and they'd made do with a honeymoon in the Lake District, as that was all they'd been able to afford at the time. He'd still enjoyed it though, had relished taking this blonde goddess with the film-star drawl down the pub to meet his so-called mates from school who'd spent years laughing at him and calling him a dumb prick. They'd still been idiots, even then. Punching above his weight, Mark Hughes had said, within earshot of his new wife, and Eleanor had actually put out her hand to restrain Alex, as if she thought he was going to flatten the wanker, and maybe he would have.

'You OK, Al?' Eleanor said now. They were wandering through the narrow, cobbled streets, crossing canals on ancient bridges, going nowhere in particular, just seeing where they ended up. She had her hand through his arm and when Alex turned to look at Eleanor he could see the girl she'd once been. She was still so pretty, and she was the mother of his two children, who she might have insisted on naming badly but had almost single-handedly brought up to be fine young adults. He'd missed out on so much. He had a sudden pull of gratitude towards her, but it didn't help alleviate the shame.

'I'm fine, love,' he said. He stopped and gazed down at the pavement, found himself wondering how they'd built this place in the middle of a huge lagoon, how long it would take to finally sink.

Eleanor put her hand under his chin, gently tilted it upwards, forced him to look at her. 'How are you feeling about work, Al?' she said. 'Does it scare you?'

Alex pushed her hand down, jerked away from her.

'For god's sake, Eleanor,' he said, 'you're a shrink's daughter through and through, aren't you? Can't you ever think about anything else other than people's sodding "feelings"?'

He watched as Eleanor's expression turned from surprised, to hurt, to 'fuck you'. She always had worn her emotions on her face . . . and then he remembered that she'd managed to have a secret boyfriend, so she wasn't that open after all. What else had she kept from him?

As she veered away, her hair aglow in the stone-soaked sunshine, somehow he knew that he was losing her. That it was only a matter of time.

'Eleanor,' he said.

She stopped, turned back to him. 'What in hell's up with you, Alex?' she said. 'I know your job's tough, but that's not my fault. There's something else wrong. I know there is.'

He thought about telling her then, but where to start? How far back did he need to go to explain it? It was everything or nothing. There was nowhere in between.

'I'm fine.' That expression again. The wrong one.

Eleanor's eyes flashed. Her temper snapped, almost audibly. 'Fine,' she mimicked. 'Shall we head back?'

'Fine,' he said.

'You got it.' As she led him through the labyrinthine canals, with a seemingly expert sense of direction now, Alex told himself that he needed to be careful. He mustn't fuck everything up. They turned right at the end of an alleyway and suddenly they were stomping across the vast main square of one of the most beautiful cities in the world, and people were milling, and violinists were playing outside one of the grand cafés, and pigeons were taking off and landing en masse, to the delight of an angelic-looking little boy who was chasing them, laughing. The arches of the surrounding buildings were shimmering in the sunlight, dancing with the shadows, promising something. Eleanor had been the very first thing he'd ever fought for, and he still had her now. He needed to make sure he didn't lose her. He grabbed her hand again, swung her round to face him, took her in his arms, almost forcibly.

'Eleanor,' he said, into her hair. His eyes were glassy with tears. 'I'm so sorry.'

59

CHRISTIE

Now that Christie was settled in her seat in the restaurant, a glass of red wine in front of her, she was feeling more relaxed. Piers was being as charming as ever, and in fact was opening up a little at last. He was half-French, he told her. His mother had been forty-five when she'd had him, his father a decade older. He'd been their little surprise, apparently. He'd been a judo black belt, and had got into university, and then after graduating he'd travelled through Australia for a while, and then had worked all over the world ever since.

'I've always wanted to go to Australia,' Christie said now. She refrained from adding that she and Paul had been planning a trip there, and that the memory was searing. Instead she took a mouthful of sea bass in lemon chervil butter and tried not to think about it.

'Well, why don't we go there together?' said Piers now.

'What?' said Christie. 'When?' Her throat felt tight suddenly, and she struggled to swallow.

'Yes, why not?' Piers continued. 'I'd love to take you to the Whitsunday Islands. I never made it that far, and they're meant to be beautiful.'

'Piers,' Christie said now. It felt important to know for definite if they were going to take things on a step. 'I know this is a weird question, but . . . are you sure you're not married?'

A look flashed into Piers's eyes for an instant, and then it was gone. There was a flush at the base of his neck, where his button-down shirt was open. He looked wistful, and yet closed-down at the same time, as if he were struggling to control his emotions.

'Of course not,' he said, at last.

'Oh,' she replied. The atmosphere was uncomfortable still. 'Divorced?'

'No . . . What's with the interrogation anyway?'

'Nothing. I was just asking.' She stared at his wrists, the soft blue of his shirt sleeves.

'What? Don't you trust me?'

'It's not that.'

'Well, what is it then?' Piers seemed angry now, a low-down, pit-of-the-stomach kind of pique that she hadn't seen in him before.

'Sorry,' she said, not as an apology as such, but more to diffuse the situation.

'That's all right.' Piers put down his knife and fork, gazed intently into her eyes. His own eyes were so blue, his hair fell across his forehead, and yet she found her thoughts drifting back to Paul somehow. She hardly knew the man across from her. He was a mystery to her, an unread tome, and possibly a dangerous one at that. His hands were resting on the table, and they were bronzed and shapely, and she remembered where his fingers had been, and how gentle yet strong they were. Who was he? What was he capable of?

'Christie,' Piers said then. His voice was low and layered and sad, as if he were hiding some kind of terrible secret. 'You're the only woman in my life. There's nothing else I can say.'

As Christie sat opposite her lover, she felt pity for him then, could see how much he was struggling.

'OK,' she said, at last. And then she smiled the smile that could light up a thousand rooms, even now, and allowed herself to relax again.

60

Eleanor

The toaster popped, and Eleanor took out the perfectly browned bagel, smothered it in butter, followed that up with a thick slathering of cream cheese and a slice of smoked salmon. After a squeeze of lemon juice and a final flourish of black pepper she placed one half on top of the other, put it on a plate and took it over to the kitchen table. And then she sat down and stared at the bagel, almost as if it were an adversary, knowing that it would taste delicious but that it wouldn't be enough to quell the craving in her soul.

The house was too empty.

Eleanor missed her children. She missed the fact that when Alex had been away working, there'd always been someone to look forward to welcoming home, at least once a day. Even after Brianna went off to Coventry, her son had provided the clockwork routine to the house. Mason used to get up, spend an age in the shower, come down to have breakfast reluctantly foisted upon him, rush off to school, come home again. They would nearly always have dinner together, albeit laconically, and then he would disappear up to his room and talk animatedly to his friends over the computer while allegedly doing his homework, until she'd yell at him to go to bed. It had given a rhythm to the house. Provided her with a purpose.

But now Mason was gone too, and so when Alex was away there was no need for her to get up at a certain time, no need for her to cook. No need for any routine at all.

Eleanor knew, though, that she couldn't put too much pressure on her husband at the moment. It wasn't Alex's fault that Mason's going off to university happened to coincide with possibly the tensest period in recent times in terms of national security. It felt to her now that you couldn't turn on the radio in the morning without hearing of another atrocity in Paris or Brussels or London or Manchester. It was no wonder that Alex was having to work harder than ever, nor that he seemed more on edge these days. Ever since their trip to Venice she'd known her husband was struggling somehow, and she even wondered if he might need some kind of counselling – but she knew not to go there, as he'd only tell her again that she took after her father. Yet she wished Alex was allowed to open up to her at times. It might make his life less stressful – and, in so doing, hers too. It might make continuing to resist answering Rufus's calls that little bit easier.

Eleanor took a bite of her bagel and almost enjoyed the forbidden feeling it gave her as much as the taste itself. *Screw Alex*, she thought mildly. How dare he tell her to maybe lay off the eating for a bit. She'd spent years watching her weight, letting it yo-yo, and for what? He wasn't even here to tell her not to. He was lucky she hadn't resorted to a bottle of wine a night, like more than a few of her friends had. Eleanor smiled. At least she had her annual afternoon tea with Lizzie to look forward to later. She and her old boss were as close as they'd ever been, possibly because Lizzie's twins had moved overseas, albeit supposedly temporarily, and so both women felt lonely. They spoke at least once a week on the phone, and met up regularly in town, where Lizzie would insist on doing something nice, like going for lunch somewhere old and stately, like the Goring, or else to one of the season's events, such as the Hampton Court flower show, or perhaps Queen's Club for the tennis, and Lizzie would always insist that it was 'her treat'. And although

Eleanor would try to object, she had to admit that it was a welcome respite from the unheralded role of undercover policeman's wife.

Eleanor finished her bagel and stood up. It would be good to see Lizzie. Perhaps Eleanor could tell her oldest friend how she was feeling, try to ease the pressure building inside of her. She'd definitely tell Lizzie that she'd seen Rufus again, perhaps even confess what was bothering her about him, now that she'd finally realised.

Eleanor crossed the kitchen and put her plate and knife in the dishwasher. Still she couldn't stop thinking about it, going over it, trying to make sure that she wasn't mistaken. But no, she definitely wasn't.

What was bothering Eleanor was this: when she and Rufus had bumped into each other, he'd told her quite definitely that he knew she was married. And yet she never ever wore her wedding ring when she went running, and her finger rashes were long gone – so if they really had bumped into each other entirely by accident, how on earth would Rufus have known?

61

Christie

It had taken Piers another three months to finally tell Christie. It was a Thursday evening, and he'd just returned from a business trip to Hamburg. It was the second or third time he'd come to the house, and Christie had cooked dinner, and now they were in front of the TV, sharing a rather nice bottle of red wine. She was lying lengthwise on the couch with her feet in his lap, and he was giving her a foot massage, something Paul had never done. She tried to suppress the comparison, but it was too late. It was out there.

'Christie,' Piers said. 'There's something about me that you need to know.' Christie tensed, as if she were driving and her car was slowly planing and all she could do was wait for the collision – perhaps into the back of *him* this time. This was it. This was the moment the dream was about to be smashed. It was a relief in a way. She could go back to being just nice, normal Christie Ingram, one-time history teacher, mother of two, recovering widow.

'My wife died,' Piers said.

'Oh.' Christie was sideswiped, didn't know what to say. It seemed so weird that he hadn't told her before. That she hadn't asked. She'd asked him if he *was* married, or divorced, the answer to both of which had been an emphatic no, but she'd never asked if he'd *been* married. And whenever she had asked, it had felt awkward somehow. Clearly this was why.

'How?' Christie said finally. As she swung her feet off his lap and sat upright on the couch, her heart felt as if it had been overfilled, stretched too thin, and was in danger of rupturing. Piers looked like a little lost boy, and she almost wanted to put her arms around him, tell him that it would all be OK. But not quite.

'How did she die, Piers?' Christie repeated, when he still hadn't said anything. Suddenly she dreaded the answer. Thoughts flitted through her mind, flickering in and out of sharpness, the possibilities varying from inane to hopelessly tragic to frighteningly gruesome. Nothing felt right.

'She died in childbirth.'

Christie could feel her mouth slacken and hang half open, like an idiot. Of all the options she'd considered, this wasn't one of them. She didn't know what to say. What *could* she say? Her mind was melting into a morass of conflicting feelings, stuck in the middle of the before and after . . . until at last everything started to fall into place. No wonder he'd not wanted to tell her the truth at the start of their relationship. She would have run a mile, as how can a man ever move on from *that*? But what had happened to the baby? Had it been a double tragedy, or had the child lived? She could hardly bear to ask.

Christie stared at the TV, the canned laughter of the American sitcom discordant to the scenario, trying to find the words, the feelings, that would be appropriate. It was almost surreal. How *did* she feel? She was a widow. And yet he was a widower. Did that make them right for each other? It certainly seemed they were both tortured souls, in their different ways, who had been brought together entirely by accident. And although Christie felt so sad for Piers's wife, who'd been cut down in the very act of giving life, it changed everything. How could Piers ever love Christie as much as he'd once loved his wife, when she'd died in that way? Weren't the most dangerous ex-lovers always the dead ones?

'I'm so, so sorry,' she managed at last. Piers was looking down at his shoes, his hands tightly locked together between his thighs.

'It was a long time ago,' he said. He turned and gazed at her, and the hurt in his eyes was something she'd never seen before, almost as if his wife dying had been some kind of rejection of him. It left an impression on her, made her want to look out for him, shield him from any further pain.

'I never talk about it,' he said quietly.

'So why are you telling me?'

The air grew still, and thick. The moment could have gone one way or the other.

'Because I love you.'

Christie felt a tightness in her chest. Hope mixed with fear, coagulated.

'What happened to the baby?'

Piers appeared perplexed for a second, as if he couldn't handle even the memory. She watched his eyes glisten, the lashes long and dark, as she waited for him to reply.

'He died too,' he said at last. He spoke quickly now, his words running one into the other, as if, now the story was out at long last, he couldn't hold it back. 'He only lived for an hour, and he was tiny, and beautiful and . . . well, it was horrendous.'

Christie stood up and walked over to the window. She was freaked out now. It was all too much.

'Christie, I'm over it, honestly,' Piers said, standing too. It always surprised her when he stood, how much shorter he was than Paul. Not short, exactly, but shorter. It was a visual tic, a reminder of the past. 'I've had other girlfriends since, of course,' he continued. 'I even lived with one for a while. But it was when you got out of the car, and I saw you . . .' He paused. 'It was almost as if I knew you.'

Christie looked at Piers, who had taken hold of her arm, a fierce intent in his eyes.

'And?' she said. She wanted him to leave now. She didn't want to fall down this rabbit hole, where the world would be odd-shaped and twisted, and unlike anything she'd ever known before. She wanted life to feel certain again, anchored into the solid dark earth.

'Christie,' Piers said. 'Will you marry me?'

62

Eleanor

Lizzie and Eleanor were meeting for tea in a grand old hotel in Piccadilly, and it was one of Eleanor's favourite places, with its golden splendour and overt, yet relaxed, Britishness. And even though Eleanor was early, Lizzie was earlier. She looked tired, though, and her hair had been cropped short, and instead of making her look more youthful, it aged her. Her manner was spiky. Eleanor was immediately worried for her friend's health, although she tried to disguise it.

'And so how's Alex?' Lizzie asked, after Eleanor had settled into the padded satin chair the waiter pulled out for her. Lizzie picked up the menu and perused it in the manner of someone who knew exactly what was on it. Her nails were long and expertly painted a pearlescent shade of mushroom.

'Oh, he's fine,' said Eleanor. 'Busy. Working all the hours.' She sighed, took a sip of sparkling mineral water. 'But it's the way it is in the police at the moment – it just seems to be one thing after the other . . .' She trailed off, the recent catalogue of horrific incidents requiring no mention.

'And the children?'

'Oh, they're good. Brianna's doing well on her art course, and Mason, well, he's just Mason.' She grinned. 'I hardly hear from him, but I guess that's normal . . .'

'Hmmm,' said Lizzie, and her tone was dubious. There was something wrong, Eleanor could feel it.

'And how's Oliver?' Eleanor said now, to ease the silence.

At this, Lizzie's smile faded completely, and there was a pain in her eyes that Eleanor had never seen before. Eleanor looked at Lizzie's hands, as if by instinct, and noticed the fat ruby engagement ring was gone, as was the wedding band.

'I'm sorry to have to tell you this, Eleanor, but Oliver and I are separating.'

Eleanor blanched, unsure what the story would be. Whether it had been Lizzie's decision or his.

'Oh, Lizzie, I'm so sorry,' she said. She leaned across and took the other woman's hand. 'That's too bad.'

Lizzie shrugged Eleanor off. 'I wanted to tell you in person,' Lizzie said, 'rather than over the phone.'

'Of course. But that's awful news.'

'Well, not really,' said Lizzie. 'There comes a time when you tire of your husband's affairs.'

'Lizzie!' said Eleanor. She looked about her, to check that no one had heard. Lizzie had never once admitted to doubting her husband, although Eleanor knew, from the rows she'd occasionally overheard when Oliver had come home late and drunk, that Lizzie had.

The waiter bustled by, and Lizzie ordered two champagne cream teas, without asking Eleanor what she wanted. It was clear to Eleanor now that the older woman wasn't ill, after all. She was furious. But at whom? Eleanor felt a low spiral of dread start in her stomach, work its way up, around and through her internal organs, towards her heart, stabbing it.

'Eleanor,' said Lizzie now. 'I took you in. I gave you a job. I supported you throughout all that business with your stalker. I let you look after my children.'

'Lizzie . . .' said Eleanor, horrified at what her friend was about to say, trying to stop her saying it.

'Don't you "Lizzie" me!' She took a breath, looked about the shimmering room, and raised the volume even further, so it won out against the clatter of teacups, making the couple at the next table turn their heads in barely concealed glee.

'Look, Eleanor, I just need to know. Did *you* ever sleep with my husband?'

Eleanor dropped her gaze helplessly to the table, noticed that the jam for the scones looked too red, too shiny – and it reminded her of clotting blood. She didn't want to have to explain herself. Not here. She needed time to work out her response. Lizzie was her oldest friend, and yet she'd hurt her, was in danger of losing her. She still felt ashamed at what had happened, but it was so long ago. She'd been so young. How could she possibly explain it all now?

63

Christie

'You're *what*?' Jake had stood up and gone over to the butler sink, and was standing against it, staring at his mother, shaking his head like a disappointed teacher at a mildly errant child. Daisy was still sitting at the solid kitchen table, trying her best to look neutral, but Christie could see that her lip was quivering. A freshly baked cottage pie was steaming in the middle of the table, a gash out of its end, the remaining contents seeping inexorably into the dish, settling.

Christie dolloped the portion she'd been holding mid-air on to Jake's plate and put down the serving spoon. She tried again. 'I said that Piers and I are getting married.'

'But you hardly know him, Mum,' Daisy said quietly. She picked up her glass of white wine, took a sip, patted her glossy lips delicately, perhaps playing for time. 'Don't you think it would be better if you waited a while?'

'Waited for what?' said Christie. 'If there's one thing I've learned since your father's death, it's that you never know what's just around the corner . . .' She trailed off as the triteness of what she'd said bounced around the walls and then settled uneasily, somewhere in the steamy air. Neither of her children offered a response, as Jake continued to glare at her. He was home for the first time in over a year, purely because Christie had effectively summoned him, and when he'd turned up, he had tattoos up both his forearms and his beard was longer than ever. Christie had been shocked but had known better than to cast judgement. It was so hard to get through to her son now, and it felt as if they might as well have been absolute strangers. When she'd opened the front door to him this afternoon, he'd looked too big, alien almost, as though he were standing too close to her, invading her personal space. Their greeting had been brittle and brusque. It broke her heart, but she didn't seem able to find a way back to him. Sadly, now she knew how Paul must have felt.

'Well, Mum, if you're sure you know what you're doing . . .' Daisy said at last.

'And what's *that* supposed to mean?'

Daisy looked as if she'd been punched. Christie paused, took a breath. 'Sorry, love,' she continued. 'I just thought you two might be happier for me, that's all. You've both got your own lives, after all, and Dad's been gone for nearly two years now . . . It's not as if it was yesterday.' She wiped a stray tendril of hair out of her eyes and tried to calm her breath.

'Well, where are you going to live?' said Jake. 'Isn't he based in Bristol?'

'He's going to move in here for now.'

Daisy started to cry. 'Oh, come on, Daisy love,' Christie said. 'It'll be all right.' As she put her arm around her daughter, Christie felt Daisy shrink away from her, and it exacerbated the strange feeling of foreboding she'd had ever since Jake had arrived home. She could feel the beginnings of a migraine. *Was* she being selfish? Was that why she felt so uncomfortable, because the reaction of her children was highlighting that fact? Or were *they* the ones thinking only of themselves? Jake was busy doing God knows what and had almost nothing to do with her these days. Daisy had graduated and was trying to get her career going. Paul's absence didn't stare them in the face every single day, like it did her, where every morning when she opened her eyes he wasn't there next to her, even when he'd been there in her dreams, until that very last moment. Somehow Christie had found those light-filled, flower-strewn hallucinations, where she and Paul were barefoot hippies running hand in hand through meadows, even worse than the nightmares. The realisation upon waking that the dream wasn't true was always a terrible stomach-punch of a blow, whereas being jolted from the nightmares at their most depraved point was an unmitigated relief. Fortunately, the nights were rare now that she'd wake up shuddering and screaming, as she plunged down a well into hell, or saw Paul hanging, swinging, his skeleton head mouthing rebukes at her.

Christie pressed her hand to her temple, tried to push the images down. She longed to get up from the table and flee the kitchen, flee the mental images that tormented her still. She couldn't think about the past any more, it was too wretched. She had to get a foothold on the future. Piers was her future. At least he'd made the nightmares go away. Her children needed to understand that.

'Oh, Mum, are you sure you know what you're doing?' Daisy said.

'I do, Daisy.' Christie's voice was steadier now. 'Piers will never be your father, but he's the most interesting, amazing person, and he loves me.' She took a breath, and stared her children down. 'The thing is, your dad and I adored each other, and he gave me the two most beautiful children I could ever wish for.' Did Jake roll his eyes? She was sure he did. She ignored him. 'But he's dead. And it's been difficult for all of us, but now . . .'

'Now what?' said Jake. His left hand was shaking slightly, and again Christie wondered what was going on with him, but she didn't dare ask. It was probably all in her head anyway. She took a breath, and her eyes were shiny. Soft spirals of steam were still emanating from the cottage pie, as if it were an injured beast, slowly dying. She felt irritated suddenly. Her children needed to trust her.

'You two have your own lives to live,' she said. 'You shouldn't have to be worrying about me. And now you don't have to, because I've finally met the person who accepts that I'll always love your father first and foremost, but who wants to look after me anyway.' She paused, took a breath. 'And you know what?' She smiled then, the same wide gorgeous smile that spread all the way to her eyes and which her husband had fallen in love with so many years ago. 'I'm happy to let him.'

64

Eleanor

'Oh my gosh,' Eleanor said, stunned, unsure whether Lizzie's question was attacking or not, what Oliver might have said about what had happened. 'What on earth do you mean?'

'It's a pretty straightforward question, Eleanor.' Lizzie picked up her champagne glass, and she was gripping it so hard, Eleanor swore it might implode under the pressure. 'And Oliver said you did.'

'Lizzie, no . . .' Eleanor's head was wheeling now, as if she were the sun and the globe lamps in the room were the planets orbiting her, spinning, whizzing, creating a kaleidoscope of colour and confusion. She thought she might even be sick.

'The thing is, Eleanor,' Lizzie said now, 'I could forgive him the girls in the office, at conferences, the hook-ups when he was away on business. What the eye doesn't see and all that. But under *my* roof . . . With the person who looked after *my* children, who became *my* friend . . .' Lizzie trailed off, and it was as if the anger had dissipated. She'd come up to London, had asked the question, and the effort had clearly exhausted her.

Eleanor didn't know how to explain it. She remembered the night so clearly now, although she'd done her best to forget it for all these years since. Lizzie had been away on business, overnight for a change, and

Oliver had been out for the evening. Eleanor had got the twins into bed, watched a bit of TV downstairs, and then had settled in for the night in her loft room, in bed, reading a book. She'd just been drifting off to sleep when she'd heard clattering up the stairs, had smelt the whisky breath, before he'd even reached her.

'Hello, Eleanor,' he'd said from behind the door. 'Banished up to the attic, are you? Come down and have a nightcap with me.'

She'd giggled nervously. He might be attractive, but she knew a come-on when it was one, and he was her boss's husband – and paralytic at that. 'I was almost asleep,' she'd said. 'It's too late.'

'It's never too late,' Oliver had said. He'd come fully into the room at that point, sat down on the end of her bed, had reached over and put his hand on her thigh through the duvet. She'd frozen – in shock, yes, but more than that. In fear. If she called out, the only people who might possibly hear her were her stalker next door, or Oliver's four-year-old twins.

Eleanor had thought quickly. Under the covers she was safe enough, but if she got out, tried to escape, she'd be vulnerable. Somehow she'd known to stay still, try to keep the situation calm.

'Well?' Lizzie said now. Her face had aged in an entirely natural way, and she was usually an attractive woman, but now she looked depleted somehow, as if someone had booted her in the stomach and knocked all the breath out of her. As if she were slowly deflating, like a balloon after a birthday party.

Eleanor needed to think fast. She decided on a version of the facts, one that would be the least hurtful for Lizzie. 'Oliver made a pass at me,' she said. 'When you were away once. I rejected him.' She stared the other woman out. 'I didn't want to have to tell you.'

'Are you sure you rejected him?'

Eleanor didn't reply straight away. She recalled the unedifying struggle, his sour hot breath, how she'd had to beat at him until he'd seen sense. She'd been lucky. She should have quit after that, left immediately, but Oliver had apologised, said he was drunk, had never come near her again. She hadn't wanted to leave Lizzie in the lurch. But more than that, where would she have gone? The one person who'd tried to befriend her had turned out to be a stalker; she'd had no family in the UK, nowhere else to go . . .

And yet, it occurred to Eleanor now, maybe *that* was why she'd reciprocated Alex's advances mere weeks later: because she'd needed an escape route – not just from Gavin, but from Oliver too. Maybe she'd just never put two and two together, had never confronted the truth of her marriage before . . . That maybe she'd ended up with Alex because she'd needed him. Had been vulnerable. Alone.

Surely not?

Long-pent-up tears were rolling down Eleanor's cheeks. Lizzie was still studying her, waiting for her answer. But how could she possibly tell Lizzie that Oliver, her husband, the father of her children, was not only a serial cheat but a sexual predator too? She took a deep breath.

'Lizzie, I *promise* you nothing happened, but, yes, he did try it on once, I admit that.' She chose not to go into detail. 'And after that I only stayed because of you and the twins. Maybe I should have told you, but I just didn't know what to do for the best . . .'

Neither woman spoke. Emotions flitted and bounced about the room, as the waiters continued their rounds with silver teapots and delicacy-laden cake stands. They simply stared into each other's eyes, searching for the truth. At long, long last Lizzie's face softened. 'Oh, you poor girl,' she said.

Lizzie took Eleanor's hand and they continued gazing at each other, tears flowing down both women's cheeks now, as far-distant memories continued to percolate within Eleanor, of all those early traumatic times in London . . . and as she sat there, she doubted herself all over again, about how she should have handled the situation with Lizzie's husband . . . but, worse, far worse, she doubted whether she'd ever truly loved her own.

65

Christie

Morning rushed at Christie sometimes, and it was as if her head were being forced back against the pillows and she would never be able to get out of bed again. It was an irrational feeling, and not necessarily related to the weather, or the latest depressing news story, or even how well she'd slept the previous night. It was more primal than that. More fundamental. Even the act of opening her eyes made her heart hurt. What was the saying? You could never be happier than your least happy child. But there was nothing to go on, nothing to pin her worry to, and so some days the world just seemed that little bit heavier, for no apparent reason at all. Yet how could it be that the baby boy she'd once carried, had suckled and cooed over, had been there for, through the joys and pitfalls of childhood, was now a virtual stranger to her? It was the loneliness of it, the fact that she could never articulate her fears. They felt too impossible. Too ridiculous.

Christie bit the top of her lip, pulled it towards her mouth, thus stretching the skin beneath her nose, as if she were preparing it for a waxing. She held her breath as she leaned over and grappled on the floor for her iPad. She propped herself up with pillows and rested the tablet against her knees. How did this innocuous device have so many answers inside it? She could ask it anything – except what her son was up to. She'd tried googling his name, but it was fruitless. If there was something, it would be underground, on the Dark Web, whatever that was. And so mainly Christie made do with constantly scanning her emails, watching for something from him, which rarely came.

This morning there were no messages from Jake, as usual. In fact, amongst the normal unsolicited rubbish, there was only one email of interest. It was from a luxury holiday company, with her personalised wedding quote, and even without opening it, it made her feel guilty, although she was sure Paul would have understood. She remembered how happy Paul had been for one of his workmates who, much to other people's disapprobation, had married his late wife's nurse. Surely Paul would have felt the same about Christie moving on too. And maybe it was better that she and Piers go to the other side of the world and do it quietly, just the two of them, with no fuss. Her children had made it clear they didn't want to come to the wedding anyway. This would give everyone the perfect excuse.

Christie shifted in the bed, scraped her hair away from her neck and twisted it into a topknot. She leaned back again, so the bun was held in place by the pillows, and gazed around the room. It was a warm shade of caramel, accented with vanillas and creams, the fabrics sumptuous and comforting, and the conflicted feeling was unnerving. She missed Paul. And yet she let another man sleep in his bed now. One she had agreed to marry.

She needed to move house.

Christie rubbed her eyes with the heel of her hands. It didn't help that she and Piers still hadn't worked out where they should live. She wouldn't go to Bristol, as it would be too disruptive for Daisy and Jake, even if they pretended not to care. It would be yet another change foisted upon them through no fault of their own. Maybe she should simply sell the house anyway and be done with it. Paul was dead, and there was nothing she nor anyone else could do about it. She could buy somewhere else round here, create a new home that worked for everybody. Yes, surely that was the answer.

When Christie finally opened the email, the cost of the trip was even more extortionate than she'd predicted. But, she tried to tell herself, it *would* be sensational, and the money didn't really matter anyway. She could afford it, which still surprised her, even now. She had never imagined, when she'd married Paul, that they would end up so well off.

'Everyone needs packing cases, Christie, love,' Paul had said, when he'd tried to convince her that it was a good idea for him to quit his job and put money on the mortgage to start his own business. 'As sure as they need nappies and coffins.' He'd laughed then, and she'd thought he was mad, but the eventual size of his bank balance had been no joke. It had come as yet another shock after Paul's death. When the business had first taken off, she hadn't wanted much to change anyway. She and Paul had liked living in Ware – neither of them had seen the need to move back up north. And although they'd upgraded to this place, it was by no means a mansion, and their only extravagance had been to decorate throughout before they moved in.

So now, unfathomably, not only was Christie a widow, but a wealthy one. She was about to spend an absolute fortune marrying a handsome management consultant, having turned into a giggling, orgasm-infused parody of herself. Shirley Valentine perhaps. And put like that, maybe that was why everyone else seemed so fed up about it.

Christie sighed. Her thoughts were dragging her down, into the soft, accommodating pocket springs of the mattress. She needed to get up, but it was almost as if she couldn't. She felt paralysed by dread. She shut her eyes and saw Paul, beckoning her from afar; and then she pictured Daisy, sad-eyed and thin, the epitome of heroin chic these days . . . and then the face magically melded into Jake's, and there were palm trees behind him, a look of hate on his face . . .

No.

Christie sat bolt upright, her heart roaring. As she clambered out of bed her knees creaked and felt weak, but they were always like that first thing in the morning. She tried to normalise her breathing, render her mind blank, at least until she was ready to paint it again. Would she pick red for terror, or blue-grey, like the sea, for frigid, pointless fear? *Get a grip, Christie. Get a grip.*

Christie went into the shower, stood under the fierce tepid water for five minutes or so, her face pointed into it. She didn't bother with soap. When she'd finished, she wrapped herself in a clean warm towel and returned to the bedroom, hair dripping. She sat down on the bed and reached for her phone. She was addicted to it. She was addicted to trying to find out about Jake. She looked at her calls first, in case she'd somehow missed one. And then she checked her email again, her social media feeds.

Where was her son? He'd told her that he'd stayed up in Manchester for the summer. But whenever Christie had tried to call him, his phone had been switched off. She'd just got the odd email, saying that life was fine, and that he was working hard at the Dime Club. But she knew he'd been lying. When she'd rung the nightclub one evening last week and asked to speak to him, they'd said that Jake didn't work there any more, and Christie didn't know what to do. What *could* she do? Jake was nearly twenty-one now. She had no hold over him. He had no father to tell him what to do.

Christie leaned over, picked up a mug from the bedside table and took a gulp of cold tea. Perhaps she just needed to move forward, get on with her own life and let her children get on with theirs. As she clicked on her most recently bookmarked web page again, of a paradise resort on a tiny island off the coast of Australia, the thrill of anticipation was both a relief and a source of shame. The image the computer served up to her, like a sorcerer's trick, was brash in its infinite blue-and-whiteness. She'd always wanted to go to the Great Barrier Reef. The fact she would be going there to get married felt surreal. She would treat it like a holiday first and foremost. The wedding itself would be low-key, incidental almost. She imagined herself barefoot, loose-haired, in a simple white dress. Just her and Piers. Nothing fancy.

Don't be ridiculous.

Christie vigorously towelled her hair and wondered whether it was time to get it cut to something more age-appropriate. The skin around her eyes was creased now, and her jawline had slackened, but she wasn't going to meddle with her looks, like some of her friends had. She put her head back, stretched her neck. She could feel the bones in the base of her head crunching, cracking, popping. Why was life so complicated? Why couldn't her family be pleased for her? She didn't buy any of the platitudes about how worried everyone was on her behalf. *She* knew what kind of a man Piers was, how happy he'd made her.

Christie's phone pinged.

'Hi, C. What do you think of the resort? Shall we do it? It's up to you, my darling. We can always go to Skegness if not. P xx.'

Christie smiled. Her senses were dialled up, and as she pressed reply it was as if there were energy waves coming from her lover, emanating up from her fingers, through her arms and into her spine. Joyfulness flowed from somewhere deep within her, lava-like, reaching the surface at last. Henry, her first love, from Cambridge. Paul, her late husband, from home. And now Piers, her soon-to-be second husband, from out of the blue. Third time lucky, she was sure of it. Her happy ending was here, right now. All she had to do was take the chance to reach for it.

66

Eleanor

It was a text from Mason that first alerted her. It read: 'Hope Dad is OK? Keep me posted. X'

Eleanor rushed across the kitchen and flipped on the radio. The newsreaders' tones had that quite unique note of sombreness that they reserved for only the most abject of breaking stories, when no one was quite sure what was going on, or knew who had died, and people were worried that it could even be someone they themselves knew personally. It seemed this latest strike had been in the heart of the West End, and it was another terrorist attack, and scores of civilians were dead or injured.

Eleanor tried to call Alex, but his phone was switched off, although of course that wasn't out of the ordinary, and she wasn't allowed to have his work number. Now she cursed the police's policy. Where was he? *Was he OK?* She'd been so proud of him, before, and although she'd always worried about him, fundamentally she'd believed that he'd be all right. But these days it truly frightened her, not knowing where he was, what he might be doing, how close to danger he actually was. Alex was always so circumspect about it and, as Eleanor tried to reassure herself, what he was working on right now might not even be related to this attack. He'd always insisted to her that he was perfectly safe, and that his training was rigorous, and he'd been on enough courses for her to know that that must be true. Sometimes she wished the cops had guns in Britain, like they did in America. It seemed to her that the police here were sitting ducks, especially in this day and age.

Eleanor went into the living room and turned on the TV, but despite the non-stop coverage all she found out was what the radio had already told her. She tried Alex once more, but again his phone went straight to voicemail. She opened Twitter and already the amateur videos were being posted. She couldn't stand it. She picked up her phone again.

'Just text me that you're OK. Love you,' she wrote. After she'd sent it, she went upstairs to sort out the washing, but that felt too trivial. She needed to call the bank, but it felt like too much of an undertaking when her husband might be dead or dying. She tried not to think about it. She knew Alex would call or text her soon enough – he always did when there was any kind of story that made the news, knowing that she had a tendency to think the worst these days. She simply had to not worry about it until then. She kept telling herself it would all be fine. There were thousands of police officers who worked in London, and so the chances of Alex being directly involved were surely minuscule. She just had to pray that the numbers would work in her favour.

And yet, as the minutes dragged on, and she still hadn't heard from him, somehow Eleanor knew. She could feel it. Something was badly, mortally wrong – but she just didn't know what to do about it. All she could do right now was try to keep the hard, tight ball of panic in her stomach contained, keep checking the news, keep waiting. Keep hoping. What other choice did she have?

67

Christie

Lonely. That was how Christie was feeling, and it was such a strange sensation. She'd got married today, and it had been idyllic, and she was in a place akin to paradise, and her handsome new husband was lying snoring softly beside her, and they'd drunk champagne and made incredible, passionate love. And yet now she felt lonely. The answer was gut-wrenching in its obviousness.

She missed Paul. It was a terrible, terrible realisation. Australia had always been their one-day destination, when the kids were through university, when the mortgage was paid off (or at least before Paul's business had taken off, and they'd had one to pay off). They'd planned to travel around in a camper-van. Paul wasn't meant to have found her old suitcase, and then fallen out of the loft and killed himself. Jake and Daisy were meant to be safe and secure still, with parents who loved each other. They weren't meant to be hurt and upset by her actions, by her going to the other side of the world to marry someone she'd met in a car crash.

What on earth had she done?

Christie sat up in bed, her heart racing. She didn't know how it had come to this. On the beach earlier, the moment had been gloriously azure, and perfumed, and Piers had gazed into her eyes and made her feel so special, and she'd felt truly grateful that happiness had come for her again. And now she felt like a traitor. It was as if her first marriage had ended so suddenly, so abruptly, so *violently*, that even though nearly two years was a just-about-acceptable amount of time to wait, the guilt refused to leave her. It had followed her here, to the other side of the world, to her second honeymoon. Grief and joy. Joy and grief. The polarity of her position was killing her.

As Christie got out of bed, she could feel the soft swoosh of her silk nightgown as she walked. It was the most decadent item of nightwear she'd ever owned and she'd loved it. She'd felt like a forties movie star. Now she felt like a silly middle-aged woman in a negligée, bought for a husband she barely knew. Mutton dressed as lamb. A pig in lipstick.

Christie walked on to the balcony and gazed out to sea. The moon shot slivers of light across the water's shimmering surface and the wind was so light and warm it felt like someone was out there, whispering to her.

Paul. What was he trying to say? The feeling of dissociation was searing. She turned sharply and went back inside. She found her iPad by the side of the bed, locked herself in the bathroom and typed in: 'guilt at remarrying when husband has died'. A host of articles popped up about how normal her feelings were, how there was room in her heart to love both men, how what she had done wasn't a sin. It must be true, she told herself. It said so, on the Internet. Yet still she remained sitting on the edge of the bath, her mind in overload, her memories flicking back and forth between the past and the present, trying to understand every last thing that had led her to here.

'*Till death us do part.*'

And that's when Christie realised it. Death *ended* a marriage – that was the vow. She needed to pay heed to it. She came out of the bathroom and stared across the room to the bed, watched her new husband sleep. He looked so innocent, and it was endearing. It was done. She had him, and he had her. Everything would be all right. Everything would feel better in the morning.

Christie slipped back into bed, and instinctively put her hands to her new husband's face, kissed him gently. He jolted, and when he opened his eyes in the half-light he looked panicked, as if he didn't know where he was for a second. And then he smiled sleepily.

'Hello, Mrs Romaine,' he said. He yawned. 'What time is it?'

'I don't know. I couldn't sleep.'

'Hmm, so you thought you'd wake me up?'

'We-ell . . .' said Christie. 'We are on honeymoon.'

'And what's that supposed to mean?' said Piers. His voice had a gentle mocking tone to it now. He reached across and pulled her to him. 'We-ell . . . I suppose if you're going to insist . . .'

68

Eleanor

Anxiety was infecting everyone, making the whole world nervous. It was three and a half hours since Eleanor had first heard the news, and she still hadn't heard from Alex – and she'd long stopped believing that everything would be OK. Now she was certain that the news would be bad . . . she just needed to know how bad. It was no good. She couldn't wait any longer.

The odd thing was, it was only once she'd finally decided to do it that Eleanor realised she didn't have a clue how to contact her husband at work. All she knew was that his office was based somewhere near London Bridge and that he worked in counter-terrorism. When she tried googling it, no numbers came up, but she supposed that was hardly surprising. It wasn't as if they were going to advertise their services. In the absence of any other ideas, she called 111, the non-emergency public number.

'Hello, Police.' The voice was distinctly London, coarse, no-nonsense, female.

Eleanor tried not to sound out of breath. She deliberately slowed down her words, so they wouldn't run into each other, become blurred. She adopted the most English version of her accent.

'Hello, I'm trying to track down my husband. I'm . . . I'm worried that he might have been caught up in the recent incident in the West End.'

The woman didn't skip a beat. 'Madam, you need to call the victims' helpline.' She started to rattle off a long freephone number.

'No, my husband's a police officer. He was on duty, and I can't get hold of him.'

'Oh.' The woman paused. 'What division is he in?'

'Anti-terror.'

The operator seemed a little more cooperative now. 'OK, I'll see if I can get a number for him. What's his name?'

'Alex Moffatt.'

'And he's based at London Bridge?'

'Yes.'

'Hold the line, please.'

Eleanor waited, her lips pressed together, her breath edgy. She drummed the fingers of her left hand on her jeans. She knew the chances of Alex actually being dead were slim, but she couldn't explain this feeling, of just needing to know. She felt his absence, and it was a visceral thing, as if he were far away, dead already.

At last the operator came back on the line. Her tone had changed again, but Eleanor couldn't pinpoint it. Was it thinly disguised sorrow? Pity even?

'Mrs Moffatt? I'm sorry, but I can't get hold of anyone who can help you.'

'Oh.' Possible outcomes danced in front of Eleanor's eyes. Did the operator know something that she wasn't telling? All Eleanor wanted to know was that her husband was safe.

'I'll have to give you another number to call.' The woman's voice had resumed its barely concealed impatience, as though her switchboard was jamming and she needed to get Eleanor off the line, no matter how parlous the other woman's plight might be. 'Good luck,' the operator said, and then she hung up, leaving Eleanor staring at her useless, mute phone, bewildered and full of foreboding.

69

Christie

Piers was dead to the world, post-coitally snoring, but Christie still couldn't sleep. She was thinking about Jake again, and no matter how much she tried to reassure herself that all was well, she couldn't rid herself of the feeling that there was something badly wrong with him. Even from Australia she kept calling him and emailing, but he still hadn't got back to her. The feeling she had was ominous, and it was similar to how she'd felt when he'd first started secondary school. A mother's intuition was surely too strong to deny, and so it had proved back then. She'd fretted endlessly, an uneasy feeling in the pit of her stomach whenever Jake was out of the house. Once she'd even gone and waited for him after school, on the pretext that she'd been passing by on the way home from shopping, and she'd parked up outside the ugly blue building and watched the children coming out, in straggles at first, and then on a wild surge of hormones and semi-hysterical behaviour. Just as she thought she must have missed Jake amongst the throng, she'd seen a group of boys, with loosened ties and scuffed shoes and shirts hanging out, laughing and joking and jostling each other as they spilled out on to the pavement. And then behind them had come Jake, alone, leaden-legged, and he'd seemed so sad and timid Christie had longed to get out of the car and rush over and give him a hug, but she'd known that would have been social suicide for him. Instead she'd waited in the car, watching impotently through the windscreen as one of the boys in the group had turned, said something unknown, making Jake visibly shrink into his blazer – and there was something about the instant and habitual manner in which he did it that made Christie realise that this was not a one-off. The other boy had proceeded to walk back towards Jake and barge into him, and Jake had cringed, tried to ignore the incident, keep on walking. Next, another of the boys had come over and grabbed Jake's bag from his shoulder and thrown it to the ground, and then all the boys had crowded around the bag and stamped on it, laughing, before walking off without even looking back. Lastly Christie had witnessed, in the dumb silence of her car, Jake scrabbling on the ground, picking up his pencil case and wind-strewn, trampled-on papers and books, and she'd been too distraught to even go and help him. She'd always hated herself for that. That she'd let those boys do that to her son. That she hadn't stepped in and rescued him. That maybe that might have made all the difference. But it had all happened so quickly, it was as if it were happening to another boy, one she hardly recognised. And that had made her feel even sadder for Jake – *that he hadn't trusted her enough to tell her*. So when she'd finally wrenched open the car door and rushed to him, the humiliation on Jake's blotched, teary face had instantly amplified a million-fold, that she'd witnessed it. And instead of letting his mother comfort him, he had begged her not to go to the school, and once he'd got into the car he had taken his anger out on her, yelling at her to stay out of it, turning his head towards the passenger window, his fists clenched as if ready to punch someone. Her baby. Her poor, tortured baby. Christie still felt sick at the memory. She'd never been able to get close to Jake after that, and maybe that was where this had all started.

What had all started?

Christie shifted in the bed, and listened to the noise outside the hotel window, where the sea was emanating its rhythmic, primeval roar into the midnight blackness. She found herself longing for everything to be all right again. But of course that was impossible. The future was out there, as sure as the sun would soon be rising, seeping its way into this little corner of paradise. There was nothing on earth that she could do to stop it, no matter what desolation it would bring. She could feel its dread thrum, coming at her.

Christie shivered, reached out a hand to touch Piers's firm, warm body, as if to prove he was there with her. As she felt his breath rising and falling, she did her best to convince herself that she was wrong, that more hurt and pain wasn't due to engulf her family – and then she shut her eyes, and tried her hardest to go to sleep.

70

Eleanor

It was now more than five hours since the attack and Alex still hadn't been in touch. Eleanor had failed to track down the unit he worked in, and no one had any news about him, and the only explanations she could think of were that he was either one of the as-yet-unidentified injured, or else he was already dead. Maybe she was being melodramatic, but what else could explain it?

Eleanor forced herself to consider other, more plausible, options. Perhaps he was somewhere where there was no access to phones for some reason. Or the monstrosity of the attack and his busyness in the aftermath had made him completely forget to contact her. If that was the case, and he wasn't actually dead, she'd damn well kill him for it when she finally saw him.

Eleanor looked at her watch, again, but only three minutes had gone by since the last time. *Why hadn't he been in touch?* She watched the news endlessly, to see if she could spot Alex, even though she knew she was becoming obsessive.

As Eleanor checked her phone, for the zillionth time, she found herself picturing a tiny shiny line of something that might take the edge off her extreme anxiety, and that made her think of being holed up at fifteen years of age in some squat on the Lower East Side, mooning over a Kurt Cobain lookalike. She'd only done it a few times before her father had gone mad and packed her off to summer camp, but even so. Teenagers seemed so different now, so straight almost, and Eleanor thought it might be because there was nothing to rail against any more. Her kids had been able to do pretty much what they wanted, when they wanted, and she and Alex were still together, and stable enough, to boot, and so there had been absolutely no need for Brianna and Mason to rebel like she had as a teenager. But how would they cope in this scenario, if her worst fears were realised?

Loneliness invaded Eleanor, marbled through the fear. She tried Alex again, and then made the next call before she'd had time to think. And yet, as she waited for it to connect, she didn't hang up. Hearing the single long beeps felt like coming home. Suddenly time rolled back, and she was desperate to talk to him, prayed he would answer. He'd saved her once. Maybe she'd misjudged him, should have asked him to help her all those years ago, after Rufus had dumped her. Or later, when she was being terrorised by a love-crazed stalker. She wouldn't be here now if she had done, with a missing husband she was no longer sure she loved anyway.

'Hello?' said the voice.

'Hi, Dad,' said Eleanor.

71

Christie

Waking up on the other side of the world to find out that her capital city had been under attack was difficult for Christie to process. She'd woken early, a feeling of unexplained tension still in her chest, which had made further sleep impossible. There'd been something in the air. She'd left her new husband dozing in bed and had stepped out on to the balcony, to sit overlooking a balmy bay with a single white yacht swinging, with all the time in the world, on its anchor. She'd taken her phone with her, to check whether there were any messages from Jake, but there hadn't been, of course. There was one from Daisy, though – 'Mum, I'm safe' – and that was how Christie had found out. Safe from what? Christie had immediately loaded the BBC website, and her revulsion at what had happened, the people who must have been killed, all those injured, was almost instantly superseded by thoughts about Jake. *Where was Jake?*

Christie stood up, and then remained motionless for a minute, unsure where to go, what to do. She studied her hands, the new ring that blinked at her, jaunty in its insouciance. She blew out her cheeks, flattened them with her palms, like a child, covered her eyes, drew her fingers down her face, pulled her bottom lip into a comedy pout. And then she turned and walked back inside, where the room was draped with soft light, making the atmosphere gauzy, dreamy, ghostlike. Her head was pounding with trepidation. She tried to ground herself, make sense of where she was, in a honeymoon hotel on the other side of the world, with a handsome new husband in the capacious bed. It felt even more wrong to be here now, when people were suffering and dying at home. Even the hotel itself felt inappropriate. It was luxurious, in that muted way, with high-thread-count linens and clean, neat lines, and she wished that the room had more heart, more personality to it. Nothing felt real.

Christie went over to the bed. 'Piers, wake up,' she said. She nudged him then, and when he opened his eyes, she got that feeling again, as if he were a sweet little fawn. It was confusing. But it was the hope in his eyes that was so endearing, that made her love him. She had to remember that.

'There's been another terrorist attack,' she said. 'In London.'

Piers's expression changed slowly, and she didn't know the word for the look on his face. Horror didn't even begin to describe it.

'Shit, that's bad,' he said at last, the master of understatement. 'Are your kids OK?'

'Daisy's fine; she texted me.' Christie cleared her throat, but still her voice was low and raspy, nervy. 'I can't get hold of Jake.'

'Oh?' He raised his eyebrows at her, and there was something about the look that made her sure he knew what she suspected. Yet how could he know? She'd never confided in anyone, not even Daisy. The unease had grown and festered and expanded inside her like rising dough . . . and maybe it was beginning to show on the outside at last.

Piers said nothing more. He got up and went into the bathroom and shut the door. Christie sat down on the bed and hung her head between her knees, said a prayer for the victims. She tried to call Jake again, and then she rang Daisy, but Daisy hadn't heard from him either.

Christie sat quietly, scrolling through the headlines on her phone. When Piers still hadn't come out of the bathroom, she knocked gently.

'Piers. Are you all right in there?'

She heard a kind of grunt of acknowledgment, and then after a few moments Piers opened the door. He had a towel wrapped around his midriff, although he didn't appear to have showered. His face was white.

'I'm OK,' Piers said. 'Sorry, my stomach is a bit dodgy. Any news from Jake?'

'No. Not yet.'

Piers took Christie by the shoulders and stared into her eyes. It was as if he were trying to convince himself, rather than her.

'Everything will be all right, Christie,' he said. 'D'you want to go in the shower first?' The question was a non sequitur.

'OK,' she said. Her mind seemed to be floating about three feet above her head still.

He kissed the tip of her nose.

'I love you, Mrs Romaine.' The name jolted her. *Her* name jolted her.

'I love you too,' she managed. He passed by her then, and as he did so he gave her a tiny shove, towards the bathroom. It was subtle, but deliberate. As Christie locked the door, she no longer had the remotest idea what was going on in this deviant, messed-up world. All she knew was that it was no longer fear she was feeling. It was something much more complex and cosseting and dread-inducing than that.

72
Eleanor

It felt surreal speaking to her father again. Since she'd been in England, aside from a couple of trips home, communication between them had mostly comprised of greeting cards and the odd email. Phone calls had never been their thing, which was curious, seeing as talking was meant to be her father's business. He'd been her hero when she was little, but her disastrous spell in New York had put paid to any closeness between them. Being thirteen and buck-toothed and lispy, with gangly legs and unexplained mood swings, was not the time for your mom to decide to send you to live in Manhattan with a father you barely ever saw. Eleanor had never thought of it quite like that until Brianna had gone through puberty herself, and she'd made sure she'd been there for her own daughter every step of the way – on the tear-sodden night Brianna's periods had started; during the times when the other girls at school had acted like bitches; when her daughter's spots had started erupting so fast it was practically happening in real time. Eleanor hadn't wanted Brianna to go through what she herself had experienced – and yet, Eleanor realised as she heard her father's voice, the irony was that in a way Brianna had. Brianna too had an absent, unengaged father who continually broke his promises, no matter how admirable the reason. Eleanor had been patient, but now, even if Alex did turn out to be safe, she wondered whether she might finally have had enough. Jeez, his job might be important, but sometimes she and the kids needed him too.

'How are you, Eleanor?' her father said, from the other side of the Atlantic. His voice had a vague thread of irritation in it, as though he had no idea why his daughter might be calling him and that now wasn't a good time, if it wasn't a bona fide emergency.

'I'm OK, thanks.' The bright pink gerberas on the mantelpiece were just starting to droop, and it occurred to Eleanor that they'd be dead soon. She couldn't decide whether to cut them off in their prime or leave them to wither naturally. As she eyeballed them encouragingly, perhaps trying to coax some life back into them, she kept the phone hunched between her ear and her shoulder.

'How's Alex and the kids? Everyone safe?'

Eleanor hesitated. She'd only rung her father because she'd convinced herself that Alex was dead or injured, but now it felt stupid to say so – as if she were just being hysterical.

'Er, yes, I think so.'

'Good to hear . . . Hey, did that old friend of yours manage to track you down?'

'What?' she said. 'Who?'

'Robert? Rupert? I forget his name now.'

'Sorry, Dad, what are you talking about?'

'A guy called the practice, with a real posh English accent, saying that he was arranging some kind of reunion, and asking for your address so he could mail you the invite.'

Eleanor felt her knees bend, just a little. *Rufus*. Was *that* how he'd found her? How he knew she was married? Did he even live in Crouch End – or was that merely his excuse for running into her? *Surely not.* And if so, why? What was wrong with him?

A new thread of disquiet, about what Rufus was up to, entered Eleanor's throat, but she swallowed it down. She'd deal with that later.

Right now, the father of her children was missing. She had other things on her mind.

'Dad, can I ask you a question?'

Her father paused. 'It depends what it is.'

'Were you and Mom ever happy?'

'What?'

'Just that.' She needed to know now, whether her very being was a lie.

'Well . . . of course we were.'

Silence rang between them, through the invisible phone lines, over the ocean, the falsehood expanding and amplifying. There was nothing else to say.

'Eleanor.' Her father's voice sounded concerned at last. 'Look, is everything OK?'

73

Christie, nearly a year later

It was the twentieth of December, and Christie was even more stressed than usual for this time of year. Her father had refused point-blank to come to Ware for Christmas, so she and Piers had travelled to Worcestershire to give him his presents, and it was pitiful to see her once-proud father, his skin slack and wrinkled and pulling away from his bones, his cardigan hanging off him. He was sitting in his chair with his head resting on his chest as though he'd given up on the world, and Christie wasn't sure whether he was asleep or simply pretending. She sat down on the sofa next to him and put her hand on his arm.

'Dad,' she said softly. 'It's me, Christie.'

'Oh. Hello, Christie love,' he said, opening his eyes, and she was so happy he'd got her name right for a change. The curtains were open and thin winter sunshine was slanting through, glinting against her mother's prized brass on the hearth, and it was good to see how spotless his carer kept the place. The only thing that differentiated the house from before was the presence of a walking frame, and a high-backed easy chair with a plastic seat, and the strong smell of bleach that permeated everywhere now, covering up something even more unpleasant.

'And who's this?' said her father.

'It's Piers, Dad. Remember? My husband.' Christie kept her voice even and calm, so as not to risk upsetting her father. She couldn't even say 'new' any more, for fear of offending Piers. It had been more than a year, after all.

'Oh, have you got a husband? I thought he'd hanged himself?'

Christie drew in her breath at the baldness of the statement.

'Paul died, Dad, that's right, but not . . .' She tailed off, as what was the point? She tried again. 'But this is Piers, Dad. He's my second husband. Remember?' Christie shot a look of apology at Piers, but he just shrugged and gave her an understanding smile.

'So who's this then?' said her father, grumpily. 'What happened to Paul? Did you divorce him?'

Christie sighed inside. Fortunately, the carer rescued the situation, as she bustled in with a tray for lunch, and Christie was grateful to her.

'So, Stanley,' said Piers now, as the sports highlights flashed on to the always-on TV screen, 'have you been watching the football?'

'Ridiculous game, Paul,' said Christie's father. 'Overpaid bunch of morons.' Again, Christie cringed, and she didn't know whether *this* was her real father, or if *that* had been him. It was hard to gauge who he really was – and therefore who she was. She felt conflicted, and part of her wanted to bundle her father in the car and take him home with her so that she could look after him, and the other half wanted to leave him there and never come back. She didn't dare discuss it with Piers though, not until she'd got her own head straight. Christie wasn't quite ready to admit it, but she was finding Piers's moods hard to gauge, and it was stressing her out. He seemed to have changed so much since she'd married him. Now he'd get irritated over such silly things, like if she bought the wrong type of apples, or if she wore a dress he decided he didn't like. He'd pretty much banned Karen across the road from the house, saying that she was too nosy, and he barely mentioned Christie's children any more, as if they didn't even exist, were a threat almost. It was making Christie doubt herself. Paul had never been like that.

Christie's father was eating his lunch now, and he had a trail of beef stew dribbling from each corner of his mouth. He seemed to have forgotten that she and Piers were even there, and when the news headlines came on he grabbed the remote control and turned the volume right up, and it was remarkable how he seemed to have such trouble with his cutlery, yet was still an absolute whizz with the remote control.

'Bloody terrorists,' he said now, as the images of yet another security alert filled the screen. 'I'm glad your mother and I live in the country.'

'Well, yes,' said Christie. 'But life goes on, Dad. We can't let them beat us.'

'Oh Jean, that's a stupid thing to say. Every time they kill us they bloody well get the better of us. Round 'em all up and hang the lot of 'em, that's what I say.' Christie looked at Piers, but he gave nothing away. Did he even know how anxious she was, how overriding her fears were, and how they seemed to be growing by the day . . . Already Christie could feel the stress start to rise in her body again, as if someone were physically pumping it into her.

Piers leaned forward and took the remote control from the old man, who let him. He even failed to complain when Piers turned off the TV, leaving a haunting black hole in the room, still and silent, like death. It was almost as if Piers were being deliberately cruel, and it was unnerving to witness the power play unfolding. Finally, her father harrumphed and said mildly, and with a grudging hint of admiration, 'I was watching that, Paul.'

74

Eleanor

Alex had booked a hotel in the South of France for the whole family for a week, almost certainly in penance for failing to contact Eleanor during the last terror attack. His phone had been dead and there'd been just too much going on, he'd explained when he'd finally rung her, but Eleanor had been angrier than she'd ever been. This was his final chance, she'd yelled down the phone at him, and she'd been so shocked at her outburst she still didn't know whether the fact that Rufus had reappeared in her life had anything to do with her sudden ultimatum, or whether she'd meant it. But either way, she was becoming tired of her and Alex's situation, was seriously beginning to imagine a different future for herself. One without her husband in it. Even the thought made Eleanor feel disloyal.

As Eleanor double-checked that she'd turned off the boiler before they left for the airport, she told herself that she needed to give her marriage one last try. She owed Alex that and, to give him his due, he'd been way more attentive lately. Maybe he was even becoming aware of his own mortality at last. Times felt wild and dangerous, and unprecedented, with apparent terror threats almost daily, making it feel like nowhere was safe. But Alex was right. You had to just get on with it – and he knew better than anyone else.

Eleanor called up the stairs. 'Brianna, hurry up, sweetie. We need to leave.'

'All *right*,' came the reply, which was uncalled for. Brianna was always late, and it drove Eleanor mad. In a bid not to harangue her daughter further, as all it did was make the situation worse, Eleanor went and waited in the living room, which was where she'd once sat for hours watching the TV news, trying to spot Alex – dead or alive.

Eleanor checked her phone. Twenty past five in the morning. Twenty minutes later than she'd announced they would be leaving. Ten earlier than they actually needed to. Mason and Alex were already in the car. Alex would go berserk if Brianna took much longer. *Hurry up.*

'For Christ's sake,' said Eleanor, to no one in particular.

'What?' said Brianna, thundering down the stairs and bursting into the room, a huge handbag slung over her shoulder. She was what Eleanor had heard being called a slip of a girl, with a tiny waist and delicate bones, and yet she managed to make more noise than Mason.

Eleanor ignored her. She was standing stock still now, too shocked to move, fixated by her phone.

'I thought you said we were in a hurry,' Brianna said.

'There's been an incident, in Nice.'

'What kind of an incident?'

Eleanor looked at her daughter, at her long smooth hair, her open expression, Brianna's skin as plump as her own had once been. It was a face that didn't need corrupting. Not now.

'I'm not sure, love,' Eleanor said at last. She could hear the infinite sorrow in her voice and wondered whether Brianna could tell. But was this the world's new reality, that people had to worry about being shot or mown down on *holiday*? And was there no respite for her family, anywhere, ever? Should they even be going on this trip?

Eleanor felt overwhelmed suddenly, as if there was no point even trying, when evil greater than anything she could comprehend seemed to be taking over the world, winning even . . . and then she reminded herself that that was no way to think, and that she had her children to consider, and that you could never submit to malevolence, as good would triumph in the end. She had to believe that as, otherwise, what hope was there for anyone?

Eleanor turned to her daughter, did her absolute best to brighten her tone. The truth would have to wait; they had a plane to catch. 'Come *on*, honey, we need to get a move on.'

75

Christie

Jake was due home any minute now, and Christie was part-dreading it, part-racked with an anticipation that was sending her nerves haywire. She wasn't even sure if he was going to show. Jake had never been known for his reliability, even before he'd become so detached from the family. But the truth was, he hardly ever came home any more, although it seemed he still saw Daisy sometimes – but Daisy was always rather circumspect about how her brother actually was, no matter how much Christie tried to find out.

And so today, the prospect of Jake not turning up was even worse for Christie than worrying about how she might find him. *What would be would be*, she thought. She just wanted to put her arms around her son and tell him she loved him. If he'd let her.

Christie went into the bathroom for the umpteenth time that morning, and her stomach felt unbalanced, as though it were awash with adrenaline. She checked her hair in the mirror, and despite her blonde highlights the grey down her parting was starting to become obvious now. She was in the sixth decade of her life, and it seemed that at last her body was beginning to show its age. She went back downstairs and checked on the casserole she'd made for Jake, and its smell was rich and meaty, and she hoped that he hadn't become vegetarian.

She went to the window, looked through the shutters down the street. Still he didn't come.

Christie sat down on the club chair she'd had covered for Paul's birthday in the softest champagne-coloured leather and opened her laptop to check her emails, the news, Twitter, in a bid to distract herself. There was an email from her accountant, which she immediately flagged for later, and then closed. After Paul had died she'd found the prospect of managing her finances one of the most overwhelming aspects of life without him, and she certainly wasn't in the right frame of mind to look at tax returns right now. She'd ask Piers when he came home from Bristol on Tuesday. She might have other misgivings about their marriage these days but at least she was grateful to him in that way. He'd really stepped in and helped relieve the pressure on her in sorting out the piles of paperwork that she barely understood anyway. Sometimes she thought about giving away the bulk of her money to the kids and just being done with it. And then she'd remember her concerns about Jake and quash the idea.

Christie felt a rancid, rotten sensation building in her gut as the minutes ticked by. There seemed to be such a fissure in her relationship with her son, and it was as if every second of his lateness was widening it, expanding it to the point of breaking. She didn't care any more if he thought she was harassing him, and she tried calling, and although it connected for once, the phone simply rang out. At least it was a British ringtone, she thought. At least he was definitely here in the UK, as he'd said he was. She went upstairs to her bedroom, looked out on to the quiet street again, but still no one came. The next-door neighbour's cat was lying out in the sun, its legs so stiff and perpendicular to its body that it appeared in the advanced stages of rigor mortis, although it always looked like that. There was an unknown car parked on the pavement opposite, and it was yellow, its lines soft and rounded, and from up here it reminded her of the paddling pool that Daisy and Jake used to have.

The trill of her mobile jolted her. *At last.* She pulled it out of her back jeans pocket, but it was her father rather than her son. She wasn't sure she could handle him just now. She found his confusion too upsetting. And then she thought of his own distress at being unable to reach her, and picked up.

'Hello, Dad,' she said. She tried to keep her voice bright and chirpy, hide the fact that she was close to tears.

'Jean. Is that you?'

Christie felt broken, as she did most times she spoke to her father now. Her voice was high and clear, like how you might talk to a nervous child.

'No, Dad, it's me, Christie. Your daughter.'

'Oh, Christie darling, how the devil are you? What are you ringing about? Your mother won't be home from the shops for another hour. Can you phone back?' And then she heard a few seconds' worth of clacking of plastic on plastic, and he was gone.

Christie studied her phone, wondered whether to try to call her father back. She just didn't know what to do any more. In one way she longed to bring him to Ware, close to her and Piers, so that she could look after him; but on the other she knew both men would hate it. And although Alice did her best, she and her husband lived too far away to offer their father much practical help. Christie was glad that at least she could afford a full-time carer for him. She decided to give the carer a call, just to make sure he was OK.

Maria's accent was thick, even thicker over the phone, but Christie was used to it now. And she was kind, which helped.

'Are you with Dad, Maria?' Christie said.

'Yes, she's here.'

'He sounded confused and upset. Has he taken his medication?'

'Yes, Chreestie. She's here right now. You want to speak to him?'

What is it about Maria, Christie thought, that her English is so good, but she just cannot get the hang of 'he' and 'she'? The doorbell rang. *At last.* Christie stood up, raked her hand through her hair, and headed out into the hallway.

'No, no, it's fine. I only wanted to make sure Dad was OK. I need to go now, Maria. Tell him I'll call him later.'

As Christie hung up and rushed to open the front door, she had no time to be nervous any more. She pulled it back, an eager smile on her face, and then, like the inevitable coming of nightfall, it faded.

76

Eleanor

'No,' Eleanor said. 'No. No. No.'

She was standing on their little terrace, her back to the Mediterranean, and all she could see was her husband illuminated against the patio doors, looking conflicted. The hotel room beyond him was freshly whitewashed, with tasteful dark-wood furniture and pretty blue and terracotta furnishings, and she should have been thrilled that it was so lovely, but none of that mattered any more. The sea was still sparkling in the sunshine, and yet it didn't feel like it should be when a few days previously a lorry had run over and killed scores of people just a few miles along the coast from them. The whole world felt bleak. Again, she thought that maybe this trip was fated. That perhaps they shouldn't have come at all.

'But Eleanor, I need to go back,' Alex was saying now. The desperation in his voice was pathetic.

'Alex, it's *not on*. We're meant to be on *vacation*, with our *children*. And, aside from that, I don't want to be stranded here after what's just happened. Surely they can manage without you for once.'

'Well, apparently not. They're calling everyone in, in case of copycat attacks in London.'

Eleanor thought of home, the old railway line, the eclectic café where she'd once met her ex-lover for a coffee. It didn't have to be like this. She didn't have to accept being put last the whole time by her husband. Something was pulling at her, making her crack, creating a chink for something else to creep into. What would it be? Rufus – or the route to oblivion? Why was the urge threatening to consume her all over again? Was it stress? Or was it him? But whenever Alex pissed her off, like now, she thought about both options afresh. Either way, it seemed she needed to know the truth about Rufus at last. She was bemused by him, and she had no idea whether to believe his claims that he'd never actually meant her to leave that bright spring day in Hampstead, that he'd just been confused by the fact that his old girlfriend had wanted him back – and that Eleanor had taken two plus two and made five hundred. But was it *really* true that he'd tried to track her down for months after she'd left? He'd failed though, of course, as no one had known where she was. Her vanishing trick had been slick, and entirely effective . . . and seemingly devastating for the young Rufus.

Eleanor felt dazed for a moment, and she leant against the balcony for support. Who knew exactly what had been the proverbial straw for her, but it seemed she'd had enough. She summoned all of her energy, marched across the terrace to her husband, took a hold of his polo shirt by the lapels, forced him to look straight at her. She almost felt sorry for him, at the anguish she saw in his eyes, the battle between family and duty. But not quite.

'Alex,' she said, and her voice was eerily calm, as if caught bang in the eye of the storm that was brewing inside of her. 'Let me be very clear. This wasn't what I signed up for. You were meant to have been *my* saviour – why d'you have to be the whole goddamn country's now? Why can't you just look out for your *family*, like other people's husbands do?'

'I have to, Eleanor,' Alex said. His voice had that wheedle to it, as though he were begging her.

'Alex,' she repeated. She took a step closer to him, twisted his shirt just that little bit tighter, almost enjoyed the pain it caused in her fingers. 'You are on holiday with your *family*. It's been booked for months.' She took a deep intake of air, and when she spoke she meant it with every last breath in her body. 'So, if you leave now, then that is *it*. Our marriage is over.'

77

Christie

'Alice!' Christie said, as she opened the front door to her sister, instead of to the son she'd been expecting. 'What on earth is the matter? Come on in.' She leaned forward and took Alice's arm, and drew her gently towards her, and then she ushered her through the hallway into the warmth of the kitchen, pulled out a seat and sat Alice down. Alice looked awful. Her hair was awry and she had mascara smudged under her eyes, as if she'd been crying.

'What's happened, Alice?' Christie said over her shoulder, as she put the kettle on. She crossed the kitchen and sat down next to her sister and took her hand. It felt solid and cold, corpselike. 'Is it Hugh?'

'No . . .' Alice took a long, dramatic breath. 'We're fine – or as fine as anyone who's been married for twenty-odd years can be. It's not that.'

'The girls?'

'No.'

'Well, what is it then?' As Alice continued to gape wordlessly at her, Christie was suddenly worried for her sister. Perhaps she was ill.

'It's something bad,' Alice said.

'Oh, love,' Christie said, instinctively. At that Alice started to cry, and even when they were children, Christie couldn't recall seeing Alice so utterly abject. It was discombobulating. Alice was the lucky one, the one whose stars were always aligned. Bad stuff wasn't meant to happen to Alice.

'*What*, Alice?'

'I've been to a medium.'

Oh, here we go, Christie thought.

'And?'

'But it's not just that, Christie. Honestly, I've thought it for a while, and I've spoken to Hugh, and he thinks so too.' Alice's shoulders started to shudder, and deep heaving sobs racked through her chest, until she was weeping so hard she could barely speak. Her words were almost impossible to decipher, but still they got through, shot a poison dart into the very centre of Christie's being. She found herself gazing out of the window, into the garden, watching the trees sway with the breeze – and the breeze would continue to blow, and the trees would continue to sway, long after any of this ever mattered to anyone.

'I think Piers is up to no good,' Alice said.

Time gets filled somehow. It gets filled with snatches of memory from when I was little, and my father was always disappointed in me. It's odd how much it still hurts. But maybe that's why I became who I am, and why I did what I did, and why I lost the person, aside from my children, who I loved the most in the world. Perhaps it was always inevitable that hate would prove more powerful than love. And so now here I am, a prisoner in body as well as in soul. Being in prison is like being nowhere, being nothing. Oh my.

Of course, one day I'll get out. But will I ever be free again? Will I look people up, ask their forgiveness? Is there any point? My children have disowned me, and in truth, although I deserve it, that's almost what hurts the most. I write them long letters, trying to explain it, but I know I'll never send them. I gaze at the scuffs and the marks in the walls, and the careless blobs and blots of my pen, and I think about how things used to be, when our children were little, so little, and we were a family still. I turn those gorgeous faces around in my head, longing to touch them, caress them, like I did when they were babies . . . and then reality hits once more, and I remember where I am, and how there is no escape in any meaningful sense from what I have done, and so I prefer to stay here, alone and ensnared – and where I'm shielded from the truth of it.

PART FOUR

The end

2016 to 2018

78

Christie

It was only after her father had died that Christie had first acknowledged that her sister might have been at least partly right about Piers. At the time she'd convinced herself that Alice really was turning into a crackpot, her obsession with what was written in the stars clouding her judgement of real life. Christie had known that Alice had meant well, but really! Turning up on her doorstep in a hysterical state and spouting all that poisonous rubbish about her husband. It hadn't been on.

But now things were different. Christie had come in to London specially today, and she was determined to find out the truth. Right now she was sitting in the window of a café, watching buses crash by, and pizza-delivery boys on rickshaws get up out of their saddles to make it up the hill, and Lycra-clad women rushing between gym classes and coffee dates. The café was crowded and Christie had been forced to share a table with a young girl who was concave-chested, with wrists and ankles the thickness of Mars bars, and the girl had had a smoothie sitting on the table between them for the past half an hour, and every now and again she would take the straw out of the blood-red liquid and suck it. Her eyes, over-large in her tight, shiny face, were sinkholes into hell.

Christie too felt uneasy, and it was as if she were waking up slowly, from a rainbow-coloured dream, to find the reality a shitstorm. She kept trying to work out when it was that she'd first had doubts about Piers, buried or not. Was it the morning after they'd got married, when she'd felt regretful rather than happy? Or when Piers had acted so weirdly after finding out about the terror attack in London, although to her knowledge no one close to him had even been involved? Or had her unease been due to the fact that Piers had been working away more than ever? Or even what Alice had said about him being up to no good, deranged as it may have sounded? Or was it that Piers seemed to be making her life a misery now, telling her what to do, who to see? Chipping away at her.

Or was it all of those things, plus the fact that he was spending her money?

Christie had first spotted it a while ago, perhaps even before Alice had said anything, but, as she realised now, she'd denied it to herself. It seemed it was far easier to pretend not to see things than have your reality come crashing down on you all over again. Maybe it had been weak, but it was all she'd felt able to do at the time. She'd married him, she'd told herself. She needed to give it a chance.

But now she'd changed her mind. The money was the least of it. Piers had crossed a line, and it was unforgiveable.

Christie felt wrathful tears forming, and she pretended to lean down and rummage in her handbag so the girl opposite wouldn't see. To give him his due, Piers had been all right with her father, had put up with being constantly called Paul, but he hadn't been there at key times during the old man's slow, painful decline. That was fair enough, she'd told herself at the time. Piers had had work commitments. But to have not come straight back from his conference when her father had *died*? How could Piers have let her down like that? It wasn't only how it had felt. It was how it had looked, which was disgraceful. There was no other word for it.

Christie took a nervy sip of her coffee. She was still wondering how to play it. Piers didn't know that she knew he'd taken £50,000 from one of her accounts, and the knowledge was sitting there, quietly. She was a fool.

Never trust never trust never trust.

Christie had worked so hard to reboot her brain after the early crises in her marriage to Paul. Failing to trust him had got them nowhere. In fact, she'd been so successful in wiping the gypsy woman's mantra from her brain that as the years had passed she'd pretty much forgotten all about it. Perhaps that was why she'd gone and fallen in love with a man who even now it appeared she didn't remotely know, and it seemed that what the old woman had said hadn't been rubbish after all. Christie could see it now – maybe *Piers* was the unknown husband Madame Magdalena had been warning her about all along. Perhaps Alice was right, and there was more to this fortune-telling lark after all.

And so now, regardless of the exact reason, Christie had made up her mind. She had to deal with this. Face it. She needed to find out what Piers was spending her money on. Or, more to the point, who. She was convinced now that her husband was having an affair. There was only one way to find out.

Christie paid her bill, downed the last of her coffee and stood up. She proffered a sympathetic smile goodbye to her table companion, whose bleak half-nod in return made Christie's eyes smart. She needed to get going. Her meeting with a private detective was in fifteen minutes.

79

Alex

For years Alex had been so used to the rhythm of his marriage to Eleanor being punctuated by shift patterns, or else long and frequent absences, or being taken up with their children, that it had been odd in a way, just hanging out for a week at home with her. But after the near-ruinous debacle of their trip to the South of France, Eleanor had insisted. He couldn't keep working under such strain for so long, she'd said. It was bad for his health, she'd said. In the end he'd had no choice but to capitulate. And yet his enforced time at home had worked out fine, had been more enjoyable than Alex had anticipated. He and Eleanor had pottered in the garden together, and gone out for walks and dinner and the cinema; had enjoyed long, lazy lie-ins. It almost felt as if they'd been new lovers, and he was surprised at how much he enjoyed being around her again. She looked better than she had in years too. Her latest fad diet seemed to have really paid off, and it almost reminded him of how she'd looked when they'd first met. Perhaps the old adage that absence makes the heart grow fonder was nothing but a big fat lie. With him and Eleanor, it had made strangers of them. Until now. The irony, he thought.

Alex was in the garden, sweeping up after having cut the hedge, and he knew he needed to come in soon. Eleanor had just gone inside to get ready, as they were walking into Crouch End for dinner, and he found he was looking forward to it. The evening was balmy, and the birds were boisterous, despite the lateness of the hour. The walk would be leisurely, the brutal hills precluding them from going too fast in the hazy, over-heated air. The tapas restaurant was excellent, and the meal would be delicious, and they'd share a bottle of wine, and he'd leave a handsome tip for the waiter, and he'd be the big man, treating his beautiful American wife.

Alex paused, blinked his eyes for a second. There was an empty feeling behind them, but he knew it was superficial, and that soon the familiar ache of his jaw clenching would invade, rearrange his pain sensors, send the headache he'd have, for the next twenty-four hours at least, booming in, permeating down into his neck and shoulders, freezing them into a type of mute bodily fury. The garden felt too small for him now, as if it were shrinking, folding in on him, and he had a sudden deep longing to bust out of the life he had made for himself and start all over again. Maybe he should jack it all in, change police force and move to the country, like Eleanor had suggested recently. It wasn't too late. He knew he'd have to be careful though, that he mustn't make any more mistakes. He couldn't risk losing her.

When Alex heard the doorbell he wondered who it might be. Instinctively he glanced at his reflection in the window, smoothed down his hair, checked how handsome he was still. He heard the bathroom window open. His wife's voice drifted down into the garden and it sounded soft and sultry, and he found in that moment that he loved her all over again. Loved her more than ever.

'Alex. Will you get that, honey?'

And then he heard another voice, calling him too, and the realisation was wretched, and surely too much to bear.

Worlds collide, and time stands still. And then it fast-forwards again, and the prospects are dim and dismal, and lives will be ripped apart, and it was all, every last bit of it, a fuck-up. *What should he do?*

He could cower here in the garden, or he could face it. Be a man for once. *Jesus Christ.* This wasn't what was meant to have happened. It was never meant to involve Eleanor.

The doorbell rang again, the finger pressed on the button, the dinging relentless, the voice increasingly shrill. It was no good. The game was up.

'Alex!' he heard Eleanor yell, and she didn't sound sultry any more. She sounded furious. '*Get the door!* I'm in the bathtub.'

Alex slammed himself back into the now, forced himself to think quickly. Maybe there was still a chance after all. He flung down the broom so hard it clattered against the paving stones, and then he raced through the house from the back to the front. When he opened the creaking front door he made sure to speak as quietly as he could.

'It's not what you think, Christie,' he said.

80

Eleanor

Eleanor was perched, wrapped in a towel, on the edge of the bath, in a state of shock. She had no idea what had just happened, and her face was clammy, and it felt like she was looking at one of those pictures where you thought the image was of a beautiful girl and then suddenly you realised it was an old crone. All was quiet downstairs, and it seemed the house was empty, and she had no idea where Alex had gone, but somehow she could tell that he wasn't coming back any time soon. She wanted to ask someone's advice, but whose? Perhaps it was better to work it out on her own for now, try to assess what was going on, before she involved anyone else. Her head felt like it was exploding and imploding at the same time, leaving it intact, but delicate, liable to shatter. It all seemed so obvious now – had she really been that much of an idiot? For Christ's sake, for the past few months she'd even known that Alex travelled on two passports, although she'd never dared let on. He'd come home from a training course one afternoon, but had gone back outside to take a call the minute he'd stepped through the door, and she'd been putting on a whites wash, and so she'd gone into his bag, and had accidentally found it, in a pouch at the bottom of his dirty clothes bag. At first she'd assumed it was someone else's passport, his lover's perhaps, and so she'd been relieved when she'd realised that it was an alias – and 'Piers Romaine' *had* sounded rather glamorous, had certainly had more of a ring to it than 'Alex Moffatt'. It had made her wonder just what he did in his job, what danger he faced. Secretly she'd even been impressed, her anger at not having known soon transmuting into a fierce swelling of pride in her husband, at what he did for a living. After all, she'd often joked that Alex was like James Bond.

And afterwards? Afterwards Eleanor had felt fearful, and all alone in the knowledge. She hadn't been able to tell him that she knew about the passport, but she hadn't been able to tell anyone else either. She and Alex had each been trapped in their own world of secrets – but it seemed that his secrets were even more outrageous than she could possibly have thought.

Eleanor's mouth filled with saliva. She got up from the bath, lifted the seat of the toilet, bent over and spat into the bowl, and her saliva was warm and stringy, hard to detach. As she stood up straight and wiped her face with the back of her hand, she was still trying to compute what everything meant. The woman had been yelling, 'Piers!' and that was the name on the passport, and Eleanor knew that the answer must be simple, so simple . . . and yet still it wouldn't come to her. All she knew was that she'd put down her own restlessness of late to Rufus's reappearance, and the kids having left, and Alex's job being so all-consuming, causing a space between them . . . And when at last she'd pulled rank, had insisted that Alex put his wife above his job for once, she'd thought things were better between them. Until this.

Eleanor's mind began to soften, lose its shape. She did her best to concentrate. It was so weird, that Rufus had been her very first love – and yet now she was unavailable, the more it seemed he wanted her. There must be a name for that kind of screwed-up mentality, Eleanor thought, of wanting what you cannot have. But what was the name for just *taking* what you cannot have, as it seemed Alex had done? Taking and taking and taking? Where did the lies start, and where on earth did they end?

Eleanor sat alone, her stomach alternately taut and heaving, waiting for something to happen – and yet all was silent. She'd spent so many years knowing nothing about her husband's job, believing that his allegiance was to Queen and country, crazy as it sounded for an American. She'd had no choice but to stay quiet, and respect that. And respect it she had. But now she remembered the dreadful day she'd thought he'd been killed, and yet the police had been unable to trace him. Did he even work in counter-terrorism? She had no idea any more. All she knew was that it seemed her husband was involved with someone else too, who called him Piers.

Eleanor threw back her head then, and started laughing, and laughing, and it echoed around the tiny white bathroom, until it seemed she couldn't stop . . . And now the laughter was turning to tears, and she went downstairs and double-locked the door, put the chain on. She wouldn't let him back into the house for now, maybe not ever again, not until she'd got her head straight. Who knew what might happen in the future, but the one thing Eleanor was certain of right now, in this particular minuscule moment in the history of the universe, was that there was so much she didn't know about her husband – and, perhaps most pertinently, just what he was capable of.

81

Christie

There was no fool like an old fool, Christie thought as she gazed at Piers in disbelief. He had come out of the little terraced house and escorted her away down the street, and now he was standing opposite her on the corner of the next road, looking utterly distraught. Her realisation was banal in its simplicity – the reason Piers had seemed too good to be true was because he *was* too good to be true. It seemed almost risible now, outside an unknown house somewhere in the labyrinthine streets of North London, that she had fallen for his charms. Maybe she'd simply been so bowled over by grief about Paul that she'd been an easy target for a handsome half-French man with substandard driving skills. She wondered now whether he really was a management consultant. Or whether his first wife had in fact died. It was a fucked-up macabre lie if it was one, and yet she didn't know what level of deceit Piers was capable of. Again, it made her wonder how much she knew him at all. Perhaps it would turn out to be like a house of cards, where as one truth tumbled others would follow in a flurry of facts disproved, lies rudely outed. The corniness of the narrative was almost funny. Rich widow. Handsome lover. And yet there had been something so winsome about Piers at first, about his puppy-dog eyes, his obvious need for adoration. He had seemed too naive to Christie to be a player. It was mind-numbing, how wrong this had gone. She remembered Alice's impassioned warning; how her children, and especially Jake, had always appeared to dislike Piers; how Piers had changed so much since they'd got married. It seemed her family had been right all along.

As Christie glared at her husband, her emotions were wavering between contempt and heartbreak. Piers was still speaking quietly, insisting that he could explain everything, but he was lying. Just a few minutes before she'd knocked, she'd *seen* the woman come out, in denim shorts and wellington boots, with a bagful of garden recycling. She'd been so pretty, had looked so happy. Was it possible that she didn't even know Piers was married, was as much of a mug as Christie was?

'Please, Christie,' Piers was saying now. 'You've got to believe me. I can explain everything.' And he seemed so convincing it was unnerving her, and she had a sudden crisis of confidence that maybe she had it all wrong, after all. And then she told herself that *of course* he was having an affair. The private detective had rung her earlier and told her he was at the exact address she'd just called at, although Piers had said he was still in Bristol. But Piers had been lying, and here was the absolute, irrefutable proof. For an instant Christie wanted to run at her husband and smash his faux-innocent face against the wall, and she swore she'd never had a violent inclination in her life before now. But it seemed so unfair, to lose Paul in that way, and now find out that Piers was nothing more than a thief and a liar and a cheat.

'Christie,' Piers said now, and he sounded almost frantic. He took her arm, and the firmness of his grip surprised her. She imagined it might be how it felt to be taken into custody. 'Please, love. Let's go home. I can explain everything.'

82

Eleanor

Alex still hadn't come back, and Eleanor could sense the danger, smouldering from afar. She could feel the heat of it. She knew there was something gravely wrong, and yet she couldn't work out what it was. All she had to go on was a name. *Piers Romaine*. Perhaps it was a matter for the police, she thought. And yet Alex *was* the police. Was it a legitimate part of his job to have that passport? Or was it a crime? Maybe he was one of those police infiltrators and had let an undercover relationship go too far. Eleanor didn't have a clue.

It was the morning after Alex had left and Eleanor was still in bed. She couldn't seem to stop shivering, even though she was under the covers and it was a warm day anyway. She had no idea where Alex had gone, or what was going on. All she knew was that Piers was Alex. Alex was Piers. But who was the woman? Eleanor could live with a simple betrayal, would have to deal with it. But if the situation was a part of his job somehow, where would that leave them both?

Eleanor tried to search through all the clues of her and Alex's life together. He was certainly away enough for something like this to be true. She couldn't get hold of him half the time, although she'd always put that down to his job. And yet he loved her, she was sure of it. Did people who loved their wives have affairs?

Eleanor raked through her thoughts, as if through sand, searching for lost treasure. There was something else about Alex, something he'd always kept private, that lately he'd been struggling to hide. What was it? Resentment? Jealousy? She knew he'd been jealous when they'd first met, but she'd worked hard over the years to convince him that there was no need to worry. She'd almost forgotten how insecure he'd seemed back then. But when she'd told him she'd seen Rufus again it seemed to have ignited some kind of pathology in him, which had been the opposite of what she'd intended. She'd wanted to be honest, of course, but also to shake Alex up, let him know that they needed to work on their marriage. She hadn't expected him to react the way he had.

Eleanor got out of bed, pulled on a pair of shorts and a T-shirt, walked barefoot along the landing, down and out through the kitchen, into the garden, and it looked nicer than it had in a long time. Newly installed wallflowers were nodding their glossy heads to the sunshine, starting to spread their leaves already, beginning to settle in. The hedge was trimmed neatly. They'd laughed when Alex had pretended to come at her with the electric cutter, but it didn't feel funny any more. Her whole life was in danger of being a sham, but that wasn't only what was concerning her. The air of menace felt physical too. *Think, Eleanor, think.*

Eleanor returned to the house and padded upstairs to their bedroom. She pulled out the drawers in Alex's bedside table. They were so neat, she almost wondered whether he had OCD. Hers were a mess, but she liked them that way. She never usually went through his stuff but, as suspected, there was nothing of any interest. She didn't even know what she was looking for.

As if on autopilot, Eleanor searched through the rest of Alex's drawers now. There were the T-shirts and jumpers and chinos that she'd last put away. In his underwear drawer she found odd socks, a broken watch, a card she'd given him last anniversary, his old epaulettes from when he used to be in uniform. She opened the wardrobe and felt in his jacket pockets, half-heartedly checked in his shoes. Her phone buzzed but she ignored it. She was concentrating, relying on her intuition. She went over to their bed, lifted up the mattress, searching for something. Searching for Piers Romaine. *Who on earth was Piers Romaine?*

Eventually Eleanor ran out of ideas. *She needed to know.* She went into Mason's room, with its skateboards and electric guitars hung on the inky grey walls, the edgy graffiti posters. It was far too tidy, the indisputable evidence that her teenage son was away at university too painful in this new version of her truth. Brianna's room was equally bereft of clues. She checked the cupboard on the landing. At the back, in the corner, was Alex's police bag. Surely there must be something in there. Alex tended to keep the bag at work, but he brought it home sometimes, usually when he was on leave, like now. It was padlocked, as always. One time he'd opened it up and shown her the pepper spray, but when she'd asked him if he had a gun in there too, he'd just smiled enigmatically and closed it, and she hadn't asked again. She tried her birthday, the children's birthdays, but it was hopeless attempting to guess the combination.

She needed to know.

Eleanor picked up the bag, and it was heavy. She took it downstairs and into the kitchen. It was a bit larger than a standard briefcase, made of thick black leather. The lock was solid metal. She opened the cutlery drawer and took out the largest carving knife she could find. She sized up the knife, and then she sized up the bag. She wondered what the charge was for destroying police property. And then she heard the voice, somewhere inside her own head, urging her on, and she knew she had no choice.

Eleanor lay the bag on its side on the floor, like a dead animal. She got down on her knees, the edges of the tiles digging against her bones. The knife was clutched between both her hands. She felt afraid and panicky, but she knew she had to do this.

Eleanor closed her eyes, said a quick prayer . . . and then she stretched her arms high above her head, leant forward, and brought down the glittering knife with all the force she could muster.

83

Christie

It seemed that Piers was planning on coming back to Ware with her, and Christie wasn't sure whether she even had a choice in the matter. He'd finally managed to persuade her to tell him where her Mini Cooper was parked, and he'd continued to hold her arm as they'd walked to the next street together. When she'd pressed the button to release the heavy, clunking locks, he'd proceeded to help her in and then had shut her door, dashed round to the passenger side and jumped straight in too. She'd still hesitated, though. Part of her had wanted to tell him to just fuck right off and leave her alone, but he was in her car now, and he'd promised to explain everything, so maybe she needed to at least give him a chance to tell his side of the story. She felt depressed and depleted after the confrontation she'd orchestrated, too tired to argue almost. Perhaps she'd hoped that her private detective had been wrong somehow, but the realisation that her marriage appeared to be nothing more than a sham was devastating.

'Christie, love,' Piers said now. 'Everything will be all right. I promise.'

Christie ignored him, put the car into reverse and squeezed the accelerator. She watched the live camera image of her car edging closer and closer to the one behind, heard the increasingly rapid beeps meld together to become one long blare, felt the peculiar satisfaction of the cars making contact. Metal on metal. Like how they'd met. It wasn't enough of a bump to cause damage, just one to show that she wasn't someone to be messed with.

'Christie!' Piers said. 'Careful!'

'Yeah, right,' Christie replied. '*I'm* the one who needs to be careful.' She turned and glared at her husband then, in his old shorts and shirt, the stripe of dried mud across his nose, the big blue eyes, the beseeching look. Emotions bubbled, threatened to reach the surface. She swung the Mini's stub nose out and roared off down the road like a teenager. When they hit the inevitably terrible traffic on the main road it was a relief in a way, at least helped make sure they got home in one piece.

The rest of the hour-long journey was uneventful. Piers didn't speak, and neither did she. But once Christie had turned the final corner into her street she had an abrupt vivid memory, of a sparkling Christmas tree, a fluffy owl in a wreath on the sage-green front door – the very last moment before her whole world had collapsed, the last time. She pulled into the driveway and cut the engine, dropped her head on to the steering wheel. She put her hands on her ears, pulled on the diamond studs Paul had given her, making the lobes stretch. She'd worn a new black silk shirt-dress, had made an effort with her make-up. Wronged wife or not, she'd wanted to look her best. Despair threatened to overwhelm her.

'It's OK, Christie,' Piers said. His voice was like treacle. 'Come on, sweetheart. Let's get you inside.'

84

Eleanor

It had taken a while, plus a variety of implements, but she'd done it. Eventually there had been enough of a hole in the bag for Eleanor to get her hand in, and she pulled out handcuffs, the pepper spray, an empty lunchbox, a jumper, two hats, various papers, an opened letter. But no gun. No poisoned umbrella tips. There was a wallet, though, one she'd never seen before, and a mobile phone, and when she opened the wallet, there were four £50 notes along with credit cards in the name of Piers Romaine, and a picture of an elegant-looking woman, smiling on a boat somewhere tropical, and a wedding band in the zipped-up section where the coins were. There was a driving licence too, with an address in somewhere called Ware.

Eleanor's mind was so scrambled, it was taking her ages to process what everything meant. The papers seemed to be mainly police stuff, but the letter was personal. The envelope was made from thick, creamy paper, the name and address neatly typed and official-looking. She remembered that envelope well. It had arrived a year or two ago, and when she'd picked it up off the doormat it had puzzled her, as the name was unknown to her. When she'd taken the letter into the kitchen and asked Alex whether it was for him, he'd virtually snatched it off her and left the room, and that had been the last she'd ever seen of it. When she'd asked him about it later he'd told her it had been junk mail, and she'd been busy making dinner at the time, so she'd not given it any further thought.

Now Eleanor studied the envelope with great concentration. The postmark was Holborn. The surname might be wrong, but the address was most definitely theirs, and the first name was Alexander. The letter inside was from a firm of solicitors. Was it the case that her husband actually had *three* identities? It was too confusing.

Eleanor took out her laptop. It was old and the keyboard was sticky with peanut butter and crumbs and the Internet was slow, but it would have to do. It was weird how she'd been married to a policeman for so many years and yet she had no idea how to trace someone. Maybe she could just text Alex and ask him outright. *No.* Somehow she knew she had to tread carefully.

Eleanor googled 'Piers Romaine', but nothing came up. Now she tried 'Alexander John Ingram', and again drew a blank. 'Paul Ingram' had far too many results. This Paul Ingram had died though. The letter said so. And so next she tried 'Paul Ingram death' – and this time she did find something.

'Local businessman falls from loft in tragic accident' was the headline in the *Hertfordshire Mercury*. The story was so sad. Apparently the poor man had been decorating the house for Christmas to surprise his wife, but she'd come home to find not only a beautifully decorated tree in the living room, but her husband upstairs with his neck snapped.

Eleanor's sorrow about the ghastly tragedy distracted her from being able to process the one relevant piece of information. She lay down on the floor for a moment and rested her cheek against the ransacked, ruined leather bag. She felt so tired, as if her brain was fully overloaded now. *Hungerford Way.* Her mind attempted to make sense of what she had read . . . It ambled through every last possible avenue . . .

Eleanor sat up, instantly alert again, scrabbled for the wallet. Her hands were trembling as she reopened it, stared at the address on the driving licence.

Piers Romaine, 18 Hungerford Way, Ware.

What the fuck was going on?

◆ ◆ ◆

It had taken her just over an hour to get there. It was a medium-sized red-bricked house, well kept, with tall Gothic-style windows, a bowling-green lawn. There was a black convertible Mini Cooper parked up in the U-shaped driveway. Eleanor didn't know what she should do. She had driven here with little more than a sense of extreme unease, as if maybe she should warn this other woman that there was something fucked up going on. But now she didn't know how to play it. She drove past and stopped fifty yards or so away, where the road curved, so that her car wasn't visible from the house.

It was a dreary day, the air inert and sagging with unshed rain. Eleanor jutted her jaw forward and blew upwards, so her fringe lifted off her forehead. She guessed that the situation might become volatile, but Alex owed both women an explanation, and she was goddamn sure he was going to give it to her.

The ding-dong of the doorbell was much deeper and richer than theirs. She could hear the sound linger through the house. When there was no answer she tried again. She pushed the heavy brass letterbox and peered through into a light-filled hall with a herringbone wood floor, a pale-grey rug runner. A lemon-yellow bunch of roses was on a table next to the stairs, and she couldn't help but notice how exquisite they were.

'Alex!' she yelled. 'Are you in there?'

85

Alex

Her voice was like a sliver of silver, tail flicking, arrowhead poisoned, coming at him through the letterbox, piercing his heart. How the fuck had she found him? It seemed impossible. He'd always been so careful to leave no clues. He longed to open the door and beg her forgiveness, but that wasn't an option now. Then again, if he didn't answer, maybe she'd call the police – and that would definitely be a whole lot worse.

Alex was pacing the kitchen, hyperventilating. His breath was sticking in his chest and he needed to man up, handle this. He had to think quickly, but the stress and panic were taking their toll. Maybe he could simply palm Eleanor off for now, give him enough time to sort everything out. Perhaps it would be possible. He went over to the radio, switched it on, turned the volume up. He forced himself to breathe air deep into the furthest reaches of his capillary network, count to ten. Everything was falling apart. He'd thought he was so clever, with all the tools he'd had at his disposal, and yet somehow Christie had rumbled him. And now so had Eleanor.

Alex wiped his eyes. He smoothed down his sideburns. Eleanor. The girl with the golden hair, who had dared him to dream. He had loved her so much once. He turned around and the whole world felt over-bright, brittle. His legs felt as if he'd been shot in both knees. As he made his way to answer the door he was still conflicted, utterly bewildered, uncertain which way he should play it. He would let his instincts decide for now. He had no other choice.

86

Eleanor

Alex had opened the door politely, invited her in and offered to make her a coffee, and she'd let him, in this other woman's house. In this other life. It had felt like the only thing for her to do in this weird parallel universe – and would at least give him a chance to explain himself.

So now Eleanor and Alex were sitting in someone else's smart, pin-neat kitchen with marble worktops and high-end appliances, and Alex was sitting between her and the door and somehow Eleanor knew she couldn't make any mistakes. She had never seen her husband like this before. She could smell the whisky breath from here, and yet she'd never known him to really drink spirits before. It was as if he were a different man, and perhaps he was.

'What's going on, Alex?' She said it gingerly, as if she were talking to Mason when he was three, after a bust-up with his big sister.

'It's part of my job,' Alex said evenly. 'I didn't want you to have to find out.'

'What's part of your job? Living with another woman?'

'Well, yes. Sort of.'

'I don't understand.'

'Look, I'm sorry, Eleanor,' he said, 'but I'm not allowed to tell you.'

'Oh, come on, Alex,' said Eleanor. Her eyes flashed dangerously. 'You might think I'm dumb, but I'm not that dumb.'

Alex's own eyes were veiled now, and again she felt as if she didn't even know him. She could feel his turmoil seething under the surface and it reminded her of the day on the Heath when she'd told him about Rufus. It had enraged him. Her husband never had liked surprises.

'Where is she?' she said.

'Where's who?'

'Who d'you think?'

Alex looked sucker-punched then, as if Eleanor had landed a blow. She was glad of it.

'It's not what you think,' he said.

'That's not what I asked.'

'She's gone out.'

'Well, maybe I can wait for her to come back, so we can all talk about this.'

'If you like,' Alex said. He folded his arms across his chest and sat back balefully, as if daring her. Just at that moment Eleanor heard the faintest of noises, and although she wasn't even sure what it was, she made sure not to acknowledge she'd heard it. Instead she leant forward and put her head in her arms on the table.

'It's just that this has all come as such a shock,' she said. And then she started to cry.

'I know, princess,' Alex said. 'I can explain everything, though.'

'OK,' she said. She lifted her head and gave him a wan little smile through her tears. As he smiled back, the relief on his face was almost endearing.

Eleanor wiped her nose, took a sip of her coffee and wondered what he would say, just how incredible the story would be. She listened intently, showed him she was prepared to give him a chance. And so, eventually, he opened up and told her about the special unit he was in, and how it was to do with some white British-born jihadist suspects, and how he would be sacked if anyone knew that she'd blown his cover, and so she really mustn't say anything to anyone. Eleanor nodded silently, until at last there was a pause and he waited expectantly, as if he wanted her to comment.

Eleanor opened her mouth to speak, still unsure what to say. His explanation was plausible at least. She had heard of police officers who'd gone undercover and formed relationships with women to gather intelligence. But wasn't that deeply unethical? And hadn't that practice been clamped down on years before? And besides, what the hell was that noise she'd heard from upstairs? There was more to this situation than Alex's bullshit story about police work, she was sure of it. A more dangerous truth.

Eleanor leant forward, clutched her stomach and stood up abruptly.

'Oh my God,' she said. 'Alex, I'm sorry, I don't feel too well.' There was extreme panic in her voice now. 'Where's the bathroom?'

87

ALEX

His feeling was one of dissociation, as if he were no longer Piers, and yet he wasn't Alex either. It was a strange, nausea-inducing sensation, as if he were neither here nor there, neither this nor that. As if he were stuck in the middle of nowhere, trapped in an elegant house in Hertfordshire, with one 'wife' upstairs and the other holed up in the downstairs toilet. While he waited for Eleanor, his thoughts were dragging him places he'd never wanted to go, asking questions it seemed there were no answers to. Where had this all started? What could he have done differently? How had his perfectly laid plans gone so awry? He stifled a groan. Maybe it was karma.

Eventually Alex's mind tracked back, to where he knew the truth lay, to when he'd been a frightened, bewildered little boy who constantly wondered what he'd done wrong, where the next attack was coming from. It had been his older brother who'd finally told him why their father was always angry with him, and to be fair it had been a hard burden for them both to bear. It had sounded so melodramatic, but even then Alex had known that what Paul had told him must be true. What man wouldn't secretly begrudge the child who'd killed the woman he loved through the very act of being born? Who wouldn't blame, if only self-consciously, the baby who'd got stuck, and had caused the mother to haemorrhage to death?

As Alex heard Eleanor retching on the other side of the door, he wondered what on earth was wrong with her. He was worried about her, in truth, about how she was coping with the shock of it all, but at least her sudden illness had given him a few minutes to try to get his head straight, calm himself down. Two bombshells in two days. Christie appearing at his house in London had been the true *Wizard of Oz* moment, the instant the curtain had first slipped, threatened to reveal the machinations behind the fantasy. But now Eleanor's arrival here was flooring him all over again. At least she'd seemed to believe his cover story, even if she was clearly far from happy about it. And yet that didn't really matter. The important thing was to keep her onside.

As Alex paced up and down his late brother's hallway, while Eleanor did God knows what in the toilet, his mind took another whirl around the dismal distant past. Bleached-out, jumpy scenes fitted and started, of him as little more than a toddler, being shouted at by a big scary man with rage in his heart. Alex whimpering and cowering, amplifying his father's vitriol to the point of explosion. His older brother looking on, mute, helpless. *Complicit.* But that was Paul through and through. He always had made sure he saved his own skin, had never tried to protect Alex. Christ, he'd even stood by and watched as his father had Alex taken away, had never once tried to contact him afterwards.

Alex glanced up the soft silver stairs and imagined his brother's body hanging from the loft hatch. At first he'd felt sorry for Paul when the solicitors had written to him and told him what had happened. But after the funeral he'd felt hatred, a hatred that had never gone away since. His desire for revenge had been immense. Grandiose. It had affected his mind.

All was quiet in the downstairs toilet now. What the hell was she doing in there? She couldn't be on her phone. He'd made sure he'd taken it from her as she'd rushed past him, telling her he was worried she'd drop it. Perhaps she'd passed out.

'Eleanor!' he called eventually. Fearfully even. 'Are you all right in there?'

88

Eleanor

Three fingers had been enough. Eleanor had stuck them so far down her throat the gagging was entirely genuine. As she coughed and spluttered the last of the vomit out, she could tell Alex was outside the door. She could feel his presence. She stood quietly for a long, long while, trying to sharpen her mind, prepare herself, but for quite what she still wasn't sure. Bad feelings danced inside her, twirled around possibilities too horrific to contemplate, returned to the banal, bopped back again. She was almost certain she'd heard a woman's stifled scream from upstairs, but maybe she was wrong after all. Common-or-garden cheat or psychopathic madman? Which was it?

'Eleanor,' she heard her husband say at last. 'Are you all right in there?'

'Not really, Al,' she said, through the door. 'Would you get me some water, please?'

'Sure,' he said. She heard his footsteps moving away across the wooden floor, towards the kitchen. She flushed the toilet, and then opened the door as quietly as she could. He didn't hear her, thank God, and at least Plan B had worked. She might not have been able to call the police, as she'd intended, but she still had a chance to rescue the situation. *Hopefully rescue the woman.*

Eleanor exited the downstairs toilet, silently closing the door behind her. She glanced anxiously around her, and then legged it soundlessly up the stairs.

89

Alex

Paul's ghost lived on in this fucking house and it seemed to be sending Alex insane. It had felt pretty good living in his brother's old home when he'd been able to be 'Piers'. But now he'd been outed as Alex, it was as if his brother were still here, ghoulishly hanging around, presiding over Alex's downfall. *Again*. Like how he had when Alex had been taken into care, as a delinquent and fractious twelve-year-old.

As Alex stuck a glass under the filtered-water dispenser, he thought of the father who'd abandoned him; the older brother who'd watched him being thrown to the dogs; the widow who'd known about his existence, and yet had sat and simpered at Paul's funeral as Alex's father had said that he might not have a son now, but that he would always have a daughter in Christie. As if he, Alex, had never even existed. Been airbrushed out of history. *Fucking hypocrites*. Alex had made the journey north to Paul's funeral with forgiveness in his heart (after all, Paul had left him something, a rather nice something in fact, in his will) but the slap had been too brutal. He'd expected it of his father, of course, but there was something about Christie's smug conspiratorial look at the funeral that had broken him. And then soon afterwards, when Eleanor had suddenly announced that she'd seen an ex-boyfriend he hadn't even known existed, it had just about sent him crazy with jealousy.

Alex took the glass and made his way back to the downstairs toilet, still brooding about how he hadn't meant it to be like this. He wasn't meant to ever have been discovered. He'd planned on it being a long, slow process of devastation. An undiscoverable one, but one that would have caused everyone involved sufficient compensatory pain – after all, Christie's misery would be his father's misery too. Yet surely there was a way still. There had to be. He knocked on the toilet door.

'Eleanor,' he said.

Silence.

'Eleanor!'

Still nothing. She was annoying him now. He tried the handle and the door swung mutely open.

Where the fuck had she gone?

90

Eleanor

She'd been right about the noises. Eleanor found the source of the stifled, anguished screams in the second bedroom she tried. The woman was a little older than her, with wavy fair hair, and she was wearing a black shirt-dress, which matched the tape on her wrists and ankles, although the tape on her mouth was red, like some kind of grotesque lipstick. Eleanor knew she had so little time. She ran over and pulled the tape off the woman's mouth, struggled to undo the tape on her ankles.

'It's OK,' Eleanor whispered. 'I'm here now.'

The woman stared at her, the look in her eyes one of extreme trauma.

'Who are you?'

'I'm Eleanor. What's your name, honey?'

'Christie.'

'It's OK, Christie, you'll be OK. You're safe now.'

The woman nodded mutely, but Eleanor was blagging. She knew neither of them was safe, yet she also knew she mustn't panic this woman. It would perhaps have been more prudent for Eleanor to have run away, knocked at a neighbour's door and begged for help, but it had been too risky for whoever else was in the house. Eleanor hadn't known how long it might take the police to get here, and she'd seen the madness in Alex's eyes, had been unsure of his ability to keep a lid on the situation. All sorts of unpalatable scenarios might have played out.

By the time Eleanor heard the inevitable pounding on the stairs, in sync with the heartbeat roar in her head, she'd just about managed to get the tape off Christie's ankles. She stood up, ready to face him. Only hours ago she'd thought her husband was a hero. And now . . . she had no idea who he was, or what he might yet do.

When Alex burst through the bedroom door the sight of him was even more appalling than Eleanor had imagined. His eyes were blue and brutish. A vein in his forehead was pulsing. It was as if his brain had shut off, was refusing to acknowledge what his body was doing. Bestial, Eleanor thought. It was the only word for it. And so when Christie shrieked, it was hideous and yet hardly surprising, and Eleanor even found herself wondering whether that was the same grotesque noise Christie had made when she'd found her husband, hanging from the loft. The knife Alex held in his hand was one of those kitchen cleavers with a wide rectangular blade, and even from here Eleanor could see that it was wickedly sharp, and he must have got it from Christie's smart designer kitchen. Eleanor imagined it being able to slice through skin, crunch through bones.

And so when Eleanor moved her body in front of Christie, it was a purely instinctive thing. There had been absolutely no desire to provoke him, but provoke him she clearly had. He leapt towards the two women, the knife glinting brightly.

'Get the fuck away from her, Eleanor,' he said.

91

Alex

He stood there, brandishing the cleaver, wondering how it had come to this. It was as if his bursting towards them had now rendered them all immobile. Eleanor had ignored his order to move out of the way, and Christie was cowering behind her, and his posture was villainous, like a comedy baddie. Christie's face was scarlet from where the tape had been ripped off and even though it made him feel a teeny bit sorry for her, she only had herself to blame. He'd managed to coax her back to the house easily enough, but she'd ended up making such a screeching fuss last night that he'd had no choice but to bind her arms and legs, tape up her mouth, just until he could work out what to do with her. He hadn't necessarily wanted to physically hurt her, but he'd needed to keep her from phoning someone, attracting attention from the neighbours, stop her blabbing. But now what could he do with her? He wasn't sure. Eleanor's unexpected arrival had scuppered everything.

'Alex,' Eleanor said. Her voice was silky, with that same cutesy lilt he'd always loved. 'Put the knife down, honey. We can fix this. We all just need to calm down.'

'No, Eleanor. You don't understand. Get out of the way.'

'No, honey.'

'This isn't what was meant to have happened.' He could hear that his voice was snivelly, as though his nose were filled with snot.

'I'm sure it wasn't,' Eleanor said. 'But it has, and we can fix it, Alex. Let's not make this situation impossible to get out of.'

'It's too late,' Alex said, sobbing now.

'It's OK, Alex. I love you. We can fix this together.'

Alex stared at Eleanor, contemplated putting the knife down at last, but then he saw the terror deep in her eyes and he knew that she was lying. She didn't love him. He'd lost her. She loved someone else. It was that last thought that finally unhinged him. He made a sudden move towards the bed, pushed Eleanor to the floor, grabbed Christie by the throat.

The screaming appeared to start a nanosecond too late, and it sounded like a pig on the way to the abattoir. He saw Eleanor lying, winded, on the carpet, blonde hair fanned out, legs sprawling, but the pictures and words were out of sync, like a badly dubbed movie, as if his eyes couldn't process what they were seeing in real time.

Just as he was holding the knife aloft, ready to plunge it downwards into Christie, into hard bone and soft yielding flesh, the bedroom door swung open and a big, heavy-bellied bald man entered the room.

'What the *fuck* is going on?' he said.

Time passes. Things change. And every now and again something happens that is so seismic in nature the whole world shifts, and nothing will ever be quite the same again. The sky will still be blue. The birds will still call out to each other. It's just that I won't see them. Does that make them not real? Or does that make me not real any more? It's a question that will go on to haunt me. Alex and Piers. Piers and Alex. Neither here nor there. Colliding into oblivion. Leaving wreckages of lives in their paths. Including mine. It is what it is.

And so. Being your mother's murderer and your father's nemesis might not be the best start to life, but I never wanted to complain. In fact, I came through, and for a while I was truly proud of myself. But after that it became too easy to manipulate the truth. Too easy to manufacture the world that I'd wanted. One that wanted me.

Yet now that world has crumbled and turned inside out, and it's all my fault. I became afflicted by madness, and passion, and love and jealousy, and greed, and white-hot hate, and every other last thing that makes us human . . . and although I'm aware it's no excuse, I guess some of us are weaker than others . . .

I regret it all now, of course I do. I've lost everything that was dear to me. I've ruined the lives of the people I loved. And so I'm sorry, truly, deeply sorry. For every last bit of it.

92

Alex

Although Alex wasn't being held at a police station he knew, it was the same grim set-up in Hertfordshire as in London, the same type of cell into which he'd thrown myriad burglars and robbers and rapists over the years. A single hard bunk with a plastic-covered mattress. A rimless toilet in the corner. A place fit for baddies and losers. Yet now it was him in here, and despite everything he'd done, until the last few days he'd never actually thought of himself as a criminal as such. But he certainly was one now. Fraud. Bigamy. False imprisonment. Attempted murder. It was a pretty damning rap sheet.

Alex looked up at the ceiling, imagined the sun in the sky that he wouldn't be seeing again for a very long time. He stayed completely and utterly still, ignoring the general cacophony around him, of shouts and wails and slamming steel doors. He'd tried so hard to make something of his life, and yet it had all gone to shit. Perhaps it had been inevitable.

Alex's brain was stewing. There was nothing to do, nowhere to go. His mind was turning tricks, trawling through the past, trying to identify the pivotal points in his story. He knew enough about the bad stuff. But there had been forces for good too, surely. His eventual foster parents who'd taken him in, given him their name, backed him, spotted his potential, had helped him apply to the police at eighteen. His pride at being accepted. The uniform. The feeling of power it had bestowed on him, of being important, for the first time ever . . .

And then there'd been Eleanor, of course. She'd been someone to save, someone to aim for . . . and it seemed his desire to be needed by her had superseded everything. It had made him bolder than he knew possible. Of course, he'd known it was wrong, to start sending her those vile packages, pretending they were from Gavin Hewitson – but if he was going to save her, he'd reckoned, she'd need to *be* saved. And Gavin Hewitson had never actually been convicted of anything, so Alex hadn't done anything that bad. Gavin had just been a weird kid who'd mistaken Eleanor's friendliness for more, and in the process had done Alex a massive favour.

The hatch on the door opened and a microwave meal got shoved through, which Alex took wordlessly, unwilling to engage with anyone. He knew they were all talking about him. A bent copper was always a good story, and his was rip-roaring.

And so. After that the lies had seemed too easy. He'd lied about his supposed promotions, when in fact he'd failed to get position after position, even after Manisha had put in a good word for him. Face-saving, he'd justified it as, especially as Eleanor had always been so proud of him. In the end he'd taken a job in police stores, which was where everyone going nowhere ended up – but on the plus side it had opened up a whole new world of possibilities. The stuff that had passed through his hands, mainly confiscated from criminals, had given him ideas. A fake passport and driving licence had been too easy to organise. Rolls of banknotes and other spoils that financed his plans were simply never logged in to police stores. It had been so simple to invent Piers Romaine, a glamorous-sounding half-Frenchman. Easier still to stake out Christie's house, watch her get into a taxi with a suitcase – and it had been a genius split-second idea for him to crash into the back of it. She'd been at her most vulnerable. He'd been at his most charming. It had been a walk in the park after that.

Alex lifted his arms in the air, alternately, like pistons. His muscles were tight, wound up, full of energy. There had been no need for them to get 'married', of course, but the fact that it was overseas had made it almost fool-proof, despite him having to wear factor 50 at all times to ensure he never got too suntanned. And yet that trip had almost been Alex's undoing anyway, thanks to an ill-timed terror attack while he'd been asleep on the other side of the world. When Christie had told him about it, he'd had to virtually shove her into the bathroom so he could dig out his other phone to text Eleanor, to let her know he was safe.

Alex knew he'd got too cocky after that. He'd burned through his brother's inheritance, and when that had run out it had seemed too easy to dip into Christie's funds to maintain Piers's supposed lifestyle. He knew she didn't have a clue about finances, so he was surprised that she'd sussed it. She might never have noticed if her father hadn't gone and died exactly when he was stuck in France with Eleanor, or if Christie's crackpot sister hadn't suspected him. He had to hand it to Christie, though, that she'd had the gumption to hire a private detective. When she'd turned up on his and Eleanor's doorstep it had totally thrown him. Made him do things he hadn't thought he was capable of.

And now, without warning, it was over. Just like that. In a way Alex was glad. He felt so tired. Of all the deceit and the lies. Stretched to breaking point. He imagined the news stories, and the anguish he had caused his kids. If only he could stop it, make it not happen, but it was too late.

As Alex let out an involuntary sob, he heard the jeers from the other cells. He ignored them. They could say what they liked, but at least he wasn't a murderer. He had the neighbours to thank for that – it seemed that Karen Sampford had heard the commotion and had sent her thug of a husband in to find out what was going on, while she called the police. Alex was grateful to the Sampfords though. He hadn't ever intended to kill Christie. He hadn't wanted that much revenge.

He'd only planned to fuck with her head – but he'd been backed into a corner.

Finally, inevitably, Alex's thoughts returned to Eleanor. His little Eleanor. He could still picture her face that first day she'd walked through the doors of Finsbury Park police station. There always had been something about her. Brave to the last. Lost to him. As he wondered whether she would go back to her ex-boyfriend, his heart hurt. His thoughts became scrambled. Finally, he turned to the wall and shut his eyes. It was too bad. He'd fucked everything up. It was over.

93

Christie

The one upside to Christie having married a bigamist and nearly becoming a murder victim was that her kids had come straight home. Both of them. She'd barely even recognised Jake at first – last time she'd seen him his appearance had worried her, but he'd cut his hair, shaved off his beard, and Christie had been so relieved to have her son back it had almost made the whole ordeal worth it. Daisy had seemed better too lately, and it was clear to Christie now how much both her children had detested Piers, but that she'd been too stupid, or love-struck, or bereft, to realise. Yet it seemed that that was partly why Jake had strung her along, implying he was up to no good in Turkey, when the truth was that his girlfriend had been a tour rep in Istanbul, and that they'd moved back to Manchester anyway. It had been a cheap trick, but an effective one. And although initially Christie had been cross at Daisy for not having told her, apparently Jake had insisted to his sister that if their mother thought so little of him that she believed he might be about to bloody well blow people up, well, then let her. Put like that, Christie had been relieved that Jake had forgiven her. He'd even introduced her to his girlfriend, and she was lovely, and she'd seemed to have tamed Jake, had made him a calmer, more settled person.

And so now that Christie's kids were on the way to being OK, and 'Piers' was in prison, Christie was trying to piece her own life back together. She had made some monumental mistakes, but slowly, over time, as the trauma subsided, she was learning that the only route back to happiness was to forgive herself. But how could she manage it? The longer that time went on, the more she missed Paul, found she longed to speak to him, even if only to have one last conversation, to say sorry. She felt sick about who 'Piers' really was, especially as she could see now how alike the two brothers were. And what would Paul have said about her relationship with Piers? It was too grim to contemplate.

But that wasn't the only source of Christie's grief. It seemed she'd never stopped blaming herself for Paul's death – and the inanity of his accident, the waste of his life, tortured her anew. Over and over again, she wished she'd thrown that stupid suitcase away. She'd kept it for nostalgic reasons only, but with its soft-porn contents, how could she possibly have shown Paul? She kept thinking of the photo the police had found next to Paul's body, and it was black and white, and arty, and Henry's face had been front of frame, and he and Paul had been so different, not just in looks, but in character too. Henry had shagged everything that moved, as it turned out, while Paul had been utterly faithful. Paul had brought Christie out of herself, had loved her, enabled her to trust again. She would always be grateful to him for that. And maybe that was why it had felt easy to believe Alice, when she swore recently that she'd had a message from Paul from the afterlife, that he hadn't died angry at Christie. That he'd died happy, safe in the knowledge he and Christie loved each other. Who knew? Christie would never know, and that was the thing she had to accept. Maybe the truths are simply those that you want to believe . . . and yet, thanks to her sister, that was Christie's truth now, and she found that it helped. She had her job, and her kids, and her memories of Paul, and an unexpected new person in her life, and that was enough for her.

94

Eleanor

In the immediate aftermath, Brianna and Mason had been Eleanor's first priorities, as witnessing their father go from hero to zero overnight had been a pretty shattering experience for them. Eleanor still berated herself for failing to protect them, for having been such an idiot. For not having realised. In fact, humiliation felt like a solid part of Eleanor now, one that would need to be melted away over time – even though she knew that it was his fault, not hers. It didn't help that she had no idea any more what the truth of her marriage was, whether she and Alex had ever been happy, seeing as even their getting together had turned out to be based on a big fat lie. Poor Gavin Hewitson. She was glad to hear via Lizzie, who was still in touch with his parents, that Alex's framing of him hadn't ruined Gavin's life.

The day was calm and silvery, the clouds high and heavenly, but Eleanor didn't notice. She was too deep in thought as she walked. She kept thinking about her husband, the despicable things he'd done, while trying to convince herself that at least he'd given her two wonderful children, so there must have been some good inside of him. He must have passed on some decent genes. And perhaps, she thought now, there was a finer line between good and evil than anyone can ever imagine.

When Eleanor arrived at the café, it was even more rammed than usual, and it flustered her, made her wish they'd arranged to meet somewhere else. And yet she'd grown to love it here, to fully embrace the kitsch, and at least the atmosphere was so buzzy no one would be able to overhear the extraordinary conversations they were surely destined to have.

Eleanor was early, but her companion was earlier, waiting for her in one of a pair of chintzy old armchairs. She'd grown her hair since the last time they'd met, and it suited her. She stood up and hugged Eleanor, and although physical contact was still a little awkward between the two women, it wasn't as bad as it used to be. They sat down, and all over again Eleanor reminded herself that they'd been legally married to brothers once, and that that made them bona fide sisters-in-law, and so it was fair enough that she and Christie had become such good friends. It was easier to think of it like that, rather than via their other, far more extraordinary, connection. And anyway, who cared? She and Christie were helping to heal each other, and that was the important thing. Alex of course would be horrified, but why should they even tell him? They owed him nothing.

Eleanor smiled at the waiter as he delivered her latte, and the sun was picking its way through the people now, and she felt a rare happiness at the fact that no matter how bad things might be, somewhere in the world there were people falling in love, or becoming friends, or getting together as a family, and that was enough for now. Maybe love would happen for her again one day and maybe not, and if Rufus wanted to wait for her, well, that was up to him. She couldn't promise, after what she'd been through, and besides, romantic relationships weren't everything. Rufus had been sanguine about it, saying that this was their test, and she was content with that. What would be would be. And in the meantime, she had her kids to look out for, and her friendship with Lizzie and the twins, all three of whom had been absolute saviours, and now with Christie too.

Eleanor took a sip of her coffee, and it was warm and had a sprinkling of chocolate on the top. As she looked at Christie, she felt an odd prickling of joy, that she was here, with this woman, that their lives had come to this precise juncture, and that the future was out there, for both of them. Everything would be OK, she was sure of it. They had each other's backs now. Eleanor swallowed down the sudden lump in her throat and smiled at Christie.

'So,' she said, 'how's things?'